High School Finals

Table of Contents

Chapter 1: The First Ride 1

Chapter 2 The Long Season Begins 15

Chapter 3: Finding His Rhythm 29

Chapter 4: Love and Loss 45

Chapter 5: Regional Finals 60

Chapter 6: State Finals 73

Chapter 7: United States Finals Bound 88

Chapter 8: The United States Finals...102

Chapter 9: The Results 115

Chapter 10: College Scholarships..130

Chapter 11: Life at College 145

Chapter 12: Epilogue..161

Acknowledgments...176

About the Author..177

High School Finals
by
Brett Shayler

AI tools like ProWritingAid, Grammarly, QuillBot, Canva, and Adobe Photoshop were used in this book for editing and cover design.

Dedication

This book is dedicated to the countless young rodeo athletes who pour their hearts and souls into their passion, enduring early mornings, blisters, broken bones, and the bittersweet sting of defeat. It's dedicated to the steady, familiar support of families who sacrifice their time, resources, and sleep, hauling horses across state lines, mending broken equipment, and offering unwavering encouragement, even when the dust settles on a less-than-perfect ride. It's for the quiet moments of connection between a rider and their horse—a silent understanding built on countless hours of trust and training.

This is for the smell of saddle leather, the roar of the crowd, the nervous energy before the gate opens, the adrenaline rush of the chase, and the quiet satisfaction of a well-executed run. This is for the grit, the grace, and the unwavering determination that defines the rodeo spirit.

It is dedicated to my own family, whose sacrifices and support fueled my rodeo dreams, who dusted me off after every fall, and who reminded me that even the toughest bronco can be tamed with patience, skill, and a whole lot of heart. To my uncle Richard Carl Clark, aka "Little Guy," a legend in the team roping world, whose mentorship and wisdom have shaped not only my roping skills but also my character. Your dedication, your skill, and the quiet strength you show have been an inspiration to me throughout my entire life. Thank you for teaching me the importance of finding that perfect harmony between ambition and family, between hard work and humility.

This is my fourth book in the equestrian series, which continues to explore the lives of young equestrians and the horses who help shape them. Each chapter highlights the highs and lows of competition, the strength of friendship, and the lessons learned through dedication and love.

To the parents, guardians, and mentors, your belief, guidance, and support lay the foundation for young hearts to grow and thrive. Thank you for showing up, cheering loudly, and believing endlessly.

Chapter 1: The First Ride

The smell of dust and sweat hung heavy in the air, a familiar perfume to fourteen-year-old Carl. The late afternoon sun beat down on the small, makeshift arena his uncle had carved out of their ranch land in rural Texas. Carl wasn't just practicing; he was living and breathing the sport of calf roping. Every muscle in his lean frame ached with the familiar, satisfying burn, a testament to hours spent honing his skills. His breath hitched in his chest, a rhythmic counterpoint to the steady thud of RJ's hooves on the packed earth. RJ, his horse — a magnificent gray with a spirit as fiery as its coat — stood patiently, his ears pricked, anticipating the following command.

Their bond went beyond rider and mount; it was a silent dialogue shaped by years spent side by side. A flick of the wrist, a subtle weight shift, a barely perceptible pressure on the reins — these were the nuances of their unspoken language, a ballet of skill and trust forged in the heat of countless practice sessions. RJ wasn't just a tool; he was an extension of Carl himself, a four-legged confidante who understood the rhythm of his heart, the tremor in his hand, and the fire in his soul.

Carl's dream wasn't just about winning buckles and ribbons; it was about something far more profound, something that pulsed in his blood like the relentless beat of a rodeo drummer. It was about earning a college rodeo scholarship, a ticket to a future where his passion could flourish, where the thrill of the chase, the adrenaline rush of the rope, and the satisfying thud of a perfectly executed throw wouldn't just be a weekend pastime but a pathway to a life lived on his terms.

He envisioned himself competing in the grand arenas of college rodeo, the roar of the crowd a symphony to his ears, the spotlight shining on his skill and determination. He dreamt of the prestige, the recognition, and the opportunity to refine his already formidable talent under the guidance of seasoned coaches and alongside equally driven competitors. But more than that, it was about silencing the whispers of doubt that sometimes crept into his mind, and about demonstrating the unwavering dedication and relentless pursuit of excellence that defined him.

The small ranch where he lived was his sanctuary, a place where the echoes of his dreams mingled with the comforting sounds of rural life. His mother, a woman whose resilience mirrored the strength of the Texas landscape, was his unwavering pillar of support. She never questioned his passion, never flinched at the early mornings, the dusty clothes, or the occasional injury. Her love was a quiet force, a constant presence that kept his resolve burning.

And then there was his uncle, Dale, a legend in the world of team roping —a multi-time world champion whose name evoked reverence among rodeo aficionados. Dale's influence on Carl was immeasurable. He wasn't just a blood relative; he was a mentor, a coach, a friend, a living embodiment of the very dreams Carl held dear. Dale's wisdom, gleaned from years spent at the peak of the sport, was a treasure trove of knowledge Carl eagerly absorbed, every lesson a step closer to achieving his goals.

The setting sun cast long shadows across the arena as Carl dismounted, RJ nuzzling his shoulder in a gesture of quiet companionship. The dust swirled around them, a visible testament to the hard work, the dedication, and the sheer grit that defined Carl's pursuit of excellence. He wasn't just a boy practicing; he was a future champion in the making, his heart set on conquering the challenging, exhilarating world of high school rodeo, one calf at a time. He knew the road ahead would be long and arduous, filled with challenges that would test his skills, his resolve, and his spirit. But Carl was prepared. He had his horse, his family, his uncle's guidance, and above all, the unwavering fire in his belly — a burning passion that propelled him forward, one determined step at a time.

He had started late compared to some of his peers. While many kids had been riding since they could walk, Carl's first real experience on a horse was at age ten. Before that, it was just fleeting encounters, helping his uncle with chores, sitting on a horse for a brief, thrilling moment. That first time, though, riding RJ's predecessor — a gentle old mare named Bess — had ignited the spark. Bess had a patient temperament that nurtured his initial nervousness. He remembers the way the wind whipped through his hair, the steady rhythm of

Bess's gait beneath him, a sense of freedom he'd never experienced before. It was a feeling of oneness, a connection that transcended the simple act of riding.

From that day on, Carl was hooked. He spent every spare moment learning, absorbing every piece of advice from his uncle, watching videos, and practicing endlessly. He cleaned stalls, mucked paddocks, and did anything to earn his time with the horses. He learned the art of horsemanship — not just how to ride, but how to communicate with the animal, to build a trust and understanding that is essential in the delicate dance of rodeo competition.

Calf roping is a demanding discipline that requires a rare combination of athleticism, timing, precision, and an intuitive partnership between horse and rider. It demanded hours of grueling practice, learning to read the subtle shifts in a calf's movements, anticipating its every twitch, reacting instinctively, and executing a flawless throw with the precision of a surgeon. It was a brutal test of physical endurance and mental acuity.

The pressure mounted as he neared his first high school rodeo. He'd spent weeks, months even, preparing. He knew the rules, he understood the strategy, he'd perfected his technique, but nerves still gnawed at him. He felt the weight of expectations, not just his own, but those of his family, his uncle, and his community. The dreams he held were not just his own; they were a shared legacy, carrying the weight of generations of cowboys and cowgirls.

He practiced his roping endlessly, his throws becoming more fluid and accurate, with impeccable timing. He worked on his horsemanship, teaching RJ to respond to the slightest cues, to anticipate his movements, to become a seamless extension of his own body. The connection between them deepened with every session, a growing bond that was both profound and exhilarating. He'd often find himself talking to RJ, sharing his hopes and fears, his dreams and anxieties. RJ would listen patiently, nuzzling his shoulder as if offering silent encouragement.

But amidst the physical preparation, it was the mental game that truly fascinated him. His uncle Dale stressed that mental toughness was as crucial as physical skill. He discussed controlling nerves, maintaining focus under pressure, visualizing success, and recovering from setbacks. Dale had imparted wisdom beyond the arena — the value of resilience, of perseverance, of maintaining a positive attitude even in the face of defeat. These weren't just lessons for rodeo; they were lessons for life.

The night before his first rodeo, Carl couldn't sleep. He tossed and turned, the anticipation and nerves a tangible entity in his bedroom. He imagined the bright lights of the arena, the cheers of the crowd, the smell of leather and hay, and the tension in the air — a potent cocktail of excitement and trepidation. He visualized each step, each move, each throw, rehearsing the sequence in his mind until it felt as natural as breathing. He knew that even with the best preparation, unforeseen challenges would arise. The unexpected movements of a calf, a sudden shift in the ground, an unpredictable reaction from RJ — these were the variables that could easily disrupt even the most meticulous plan.

But he was prepared not just physically, but mentally and emotionally as well. He had his horse, his family, his uncle's guidance, and an unshakable determination. He had trained tirelessly, planned strategically, and visualized every step toward success. His plan wasn't flawless, but he had a plan B, a plan C, and several more, ready for whatever challenges might arise. He would embrace the challenge, the pressure, the excitement — the whole incredible, nerve-wracking, exhilarating experience of his very first high school rodeo. He took a breath—ready, at last to ride.

The morning of tryouts dawned bright and crisp, a stark contrast to the nervous flutter in Carl's stomach. He'd spent the previous weeks perfecting his technique, his throws as smooth as polished river stones, his horsemanship honed to a razor's edge. But the high school rodeo team wasn't just about individual skill; it was about teamwork, camaraderie, and navigating the complex dynamics of a group of fiercely competitive teenagers.

He arrived at the dusty rodeo grounds, the air thick with the scent of hay, leather, and anticipation. The arena, usually bustling with activity, was relatively quiet, a temporary calm before the storm of tryouts. He spotted Coach Miller, a grizzled veteran with eyes that had seen countless rodeos, his weathered face etched with the wisdom of experience. Coach Miller gave him a nod, a silent acknowledgment of the young man's dedication.

The team was a motley crew, a microcosm of the diverse personalities that populated the rodeo world. There was Jake, a lanky kid with a mischievous grin and a talent for events like barrel racing that was both effortless and breathtaking. He was a natural, seemingly born with a horse whisper in his bones. He moved with the grace of a seasoned professional, his every action measured and precise, his horse responding instinctively to his slightest cues.

Jake's easy confidence was infectious, yet beneath the surface, Carl sensed a fierce competitive spirit.

Then there was Maria, a petite but powerful powerhouse in the goat-tying event. Her movements were a blur of controlled energy, her hands quick and deft, and her focus unwavering. Maria possessed an intense focus and determination that bordered on obsession. She kept to herself, mostly, a quiet observer who nonetheless commanded respect through her impressive skill. Carl admired her unwavering dedication, her relentless pursuit of perfection.

Next to Maria stood Travis, a bull rider with a reputation as wild as the animals he conquered. Built like an oak tree, Travis exuded a quiet confidence, a stoic calmness that belied the inherent danger of his chosen event. He was a force of nature, both intimidating and magnetic, his charisma attracting as much attention as his daring feats. But Travis, for all his bravado, possessed a surprising depth, a gentle side that emerged in moments of shared laughter and friendly banter.

And then there was Sarah, the team's sole breakaway roper. With her fiery red hair and an equally fiery spirit, Sarah was a captivating presence. She possessed a natural athleticism, her movements fluid and graceful, a stark contrast to the raw power displayed by Travis and Maria. Her skill was undeniable, her confidence unshakable, yet there was also a vulnerability in her eyes that hinted at the pressures of the competitive rodeo world.

Each member of the team represented a different facet of the rodeo lifestyle, a kaleidoscope of personalities, backgrounds, and skill levels. They shared a passion for the sport, a dedication to their craft, and an understanding of the hard work, sacrifices, and emotional rollercoaster that defined the world of high school rodeo.

The tryouts themselves were a blur of dust, sweat, and adrenaline. Carl executed his calf-roping runs flawlessly, his throws accurate and efficient, RJ responding perfectly to every cue. He'd never felt a better connection with his horse, their partnership finely tuned and seamless. He watched as others competed, learning from their successes, and observing their mistakes.

Once the tryouts were over, Coach Miller gathered the team around him to announce the final roster. Carl's name was among them, a wave of relief washing over him. A thrill of anticipation for the season ahead followed the relief. This was it, the beginning of his journey, the first step toward fulfilling his dream of earning a college rodeo scholarship.

Their first practice session was a mix of controlled chaos and structured learning. Coach Miller emphasized teamwork and collaboration, reminding them that individual success often depended on the support and encouragement of their teammates. They worked on drills, focusing on coordination and timing. They practiced techniques, refining their skills and developing strategies. They learned how to support each other, to cheer each other on, to be each other's biggest fans, and to be each other's fiercest competitors.

Carl found himself drawn to Jake and Maria, their dedication and passion mirroring his own. He discovered that Jake's outward confidence masked a competitive drive, just as Maria's quiet intensity veiled a heart that cared deeply for her fellow team members. He learned from their techniques, shared his insights, and discovered the power of collaboration.

Travis, initially intimidating, proved to be a surprisingly supportive teammate. His stories and laughter lightened the mood, relieving the pressure and forging unexpected friendships. Sarah's fiery spirit proved infectious, inspiring a fierce sense of camaraderie among the team members. They formed a bond, a mutual respect that transcended individual competition, a cohesive unit unified by a shared love for rodeo and a collective ambition.

The sun dipped below the horizon, painting the sky in shades of orange and purple as the practice session came to a close. Carl, his muscles aching and his mind buzzing with adrenaline, felt a sense of belonging he'd never experienced before. This wasn't just a team; it was a family, a brotherhood and sisterhood forged in the crucible of competition. He looked at his fellow teammates, each one a unique blend of skill, ambition, and personality. He knew the road ahead would be long and challenging, filled with both triumphs and setbacks. But he had a team, a support system, and a family who would share the journey with him, every exhilarating ride, every crushing defeat, every single moment of the high school rodeo season. He took a breath—ready, at last. He was part of something bigger than himself. He was prepared to ride. He took a breath—ready, at last to win.

The air crackled with a palpable nervous energy. It wasn't just the dust swirling in the late summer sun, kicked up by restless horses and hurried feet, but something more profound, a collective anxiety humming beneath the surface of the excited chatter. This was it. Carl's first high school rodeo. The culmination of months of grueling practice, the testing ground for all his hard work, and the beginning of a long, demanding season.

He stood backstage, RJ's warm flank pressed against his leg, a comforting weight against the tremor in his own. RJ, his trusty steed, remained calm, a seasoned veteran in this arena of nervous energy. But Carl? His stomach churned like a runaway washing machine. He'd visualized this moment a thousand times, replayed his runs in his mind until they felt ingrained in his muscle memory. Yet, the reality was more intense than anything he'd imagined.

The sounds of the rodeo were a cacophony — the rhythmic thud of hooves on packed earth, the excited shouts of the crowd, the sharp crack of a whip, and the low murmur of conversations blending into an almost hypnotic drone. The smell was a potent mix of hay, sweat, dust, and something indefinably "rodeo"—a" pungent blend of leather, liniment, and the raw animal energy that permeated the entire atmosphere. He could taste the dust on his tongue, a gritty reminder of the competition's intensity.

He watched other competitors, their movements blurring through a haze of his apprehension. A young girl flawlessly executed an event like a barrel racing run, her horse a blur of controlled motion. A boy, barely older than himself, wrestled a calf to the ground with impressive speed and precision. Their confidence and ease seemed to mock his internal turmoil. He wondered if they felt this same churning anxiety, this gnawing sense of self-doubt. Or were they truly as composed as they appeared?

His name was called. His heart leaped into his throat, a frantic bird trapped in a cage of ribs. He mounted RJ, feeling the familiar comfort of the saddle beneath him and the reassuring weight of the rope in his hand. The hushed murmur of the crowd faded, replaced by the pounding of his blood in his ears. As he rode into the arena, the bright lights seemed to intensify, blinding him momentarily. The cheering crowd became a hazy, indistinguishable mass. Only RJ remained, a constant, steady presence beside him.

The calf burst from the chute, a whirlwind of brown fur and frantic energy. For a moment, Carl froze, the carefully rehearsed movements seizing up, replaced by a stark terror that threatened to overwhelm him. He closed his eyes, taking a deep breath, trying to center himself, to reconnect with the rhythm he'd practiced countless times. He focused on RJ, feeling the horse's steady strength and its quiet confidence.

Then, he reacted. The next few seconds were a blur of controlled chaos — the sharp turn, the precise throw, the satisfying thud as the rope settled around the calf's legs. He dismounted, his hands moving swiftly, expertly tying the calf's legs. The final whistle blew, the silence a sharp contrast to the previous roar of the crowd.

He hadn't been as fast as he hoped and hadn't been as fluid as in his practice runs. The nervousness had cost him precious seconds, disrupted his rhythm, and introduced a hesitation into his usually seamless movements. He'd felt the pressure, the weight of expectation, and the crushing anxiety of his first rodeo. But he'd also felt the thrill, the exhilarating rush of adrenaline, and the fierce satisfaction of completing the run.

The judges' time was mixed. He'd secured a respectable, although not stellar, placing. The disappointment was tempered by the knowledge that he'd faced his fear, competed at a high level, and survived his first rodeo. It was a learning experience, a baptism by fire that would only serve to strengthen his resolve.

Later, as he and RJ cooled down, the initial disappointment gave way to a sense of accomplishment. He was now a high school rodeo competitor, a member of the team. He'd experienced the thrill of competition, felt the pressure, and learned from his mistakes. He'd also found something unexpectedly fulfilling: a sense of belonging and camaraderie among the team that transcended the competitive aspects of the sport.

He sat with his teammates, sharing stories and laughter. Jake, ever the charmer, regaled them with tales of his close calls and miraculous escapes from disaster. Maria, surprisingly chatty after her successful run, shared insights into her technique, her usual quiet demeanor replaced with a warmth that surprised even Carl. Travis, despite his apparent unconcern, offered words of encouragement, recognizing the struggle Carl had faced. Sarah, ever confident and fiery, gave him a wry smile, acknowledging the challenge but also hinting at the potential for future triumphs.

That evening, as he looked out at the setting sun, casting long shadows across the rodeo grounds, Carl reflected on his first rodeo. It had been a whirlwind of emotions — nerves, anxiety, excitement, disappointment, and ultimately, a profound sense of accomplishment. He realized that the journey would be long and arduous, filled with both victories and defeats. But he had a team, his horse, and a dream. And with every rodeo, with every ride, with every challenge faced, he would grow stronger, more confident, and more skilled. He was a rodeo competitor. He was in it to win it. His first rodeo was done, and the long road to the finals began. The next rodeo would be different. The next rodeo, he would be ready. He wouldn't just survive; he would thrive.

The next morning, the lingering scent of dust and sweat still clung to Carl's clothes, a tangible reminder of the previous day's adrenaline-fueled chaos. He found his Uncle Dale sitting on the porch swing, a steaming mug in his hand, the early morning sun illuminating the lines etched on his weathered face — lines earned through years of hard work, countless rodeos, and a lifetime spent under the relentless sun. Dale was a legend in the rodeo world, a multi-time world champion team roper whose name evoked respect and admiration among the rodeo community. To Carl, however, he was simply Uncle Dale, the man who held the key to unlocking his rodeo dreams.

"Morning, sleepyhead," Dale greeted, his voice rough but warm, the sound of years spent shouting over the roar of the crowd. He gestured to the space beside him on the swing. Carl gratefully settled onto the weathered wood, the familiar creak a comforting rhythm against the quiet hum of the morning.

"That was...intense," Carl admitted, running a hand through his sleep-mussed hair. The memory of his first run, the mixture of fear and exhilaration, still vibrated through him.

Dale chuckled, a low rumble in his chest. "Your first rodeo. They're all intense, kid. But you survived. And that's half the battle."

Carl shrugged. "I didn't exactly set the arena on fire." He recounted his run, the hesitation, the missed opportunities, and the gnawing disappointment of not performing to his full potential.

Dale listened patiently, his gaze steady and understanding. When Carl finished, Dale nodded slowly. "You let the pressure get to you. You let the nerves dictate your performance. That's something you'll have to learn to control. Rodeo isn't just about skill; it's about mental toughness, about staying calm under pressure."

"But how?" Carl asked, frustration creeping into his voice. "It's just so... overwhelming."

Dale took a sip of his coffee, his eyes twinkling. "It's about preparation, kid. Physical preparation, yes, but mental preparation is just as important, maybe even more so. You spend hours honing your skills, perfecting your technique. But you also have to train your mind and prepare yourself for the pressure cooker of competition."

He leaned forward, his voice dropping to a confidential whisper. "Remember that feeling you had before your run? The butterflies, the tight chest, the racing heart? That's your body preparing for battle. Don't fight it. Embrace it. Channel that energy. Use it to fuel your performance."

He paused, letting his words sink in. "It's like riding a bucking bronco. You don't fight the animal; you work with it, anticipating its movements, staying one step ahead. You become one with the Bronco, feeling its power, guiding its strength. It's the same with your nerves. Feel them, understand them, and then use that energy to your advantage."

Carl considered this, the analogy resonating with him. He'd spent countless hours practicing, perfecting his technique, but he hadn't focused on the psychological game of rodeo.

"What about RJ?" Carl asked, shifting the focus to his horse. "He seemed calm. How does he stay so calm in that environment?"

Dale smiled. "RJ's a seasoned veteran. He's been there, done that. But even the best horses can feel the pressure. It's about building trust, about establishing a bond, a connection that goes beyond just riding. It's about communication — not just through your reins and your legs, but through your whole being. You need to be in tune with each other, feeling each other's emotions, understanding each other's reactions."

He continued, "You need to spend time with him, not just riding him. Groom him, talk to him, and be with him. Build that connection. Learn to read his subtle cues. He'll tell you when he's nervous, when he's ready, and when he's confident. Trust him, and he'll trust you."

Their conversation stretched on for hours, spanning far beyond the technicalities of calf roping. Dale shared stories from his rodeo career, recounting both triumphant victories and crushing defeats. He spoke of the importance of perseverance, of learning from mistakes, and of the steady, familiar support of his family. He spoke of the value of integrity, respect, and sportsmanship, lessons that extended far beyond the rodeo arena and into life itself.

Dale's stories weren't just tales of daring feats and adrenaline rushes; they were narratives woven with honesty and vulnerability, illustrating the hard work, dedication, and sacrifice that paved the path to success. He spoke of times when his nerves had betrayed him, times when he'd faltered under pressure, and times when he'd doubted himself. He emphasized that these were not failures, but rather lessons and stepping stones on the road to mastery. He discussed the importance of maintaining a positive mental attitude, of visualizing success, and of focusing on the process rather than the outcome. He taught Carl techniques for managing his anxiety, strategies for calming his nerves, and methods for channeling his energy.

Carl listened intently, absorbing not only his uncle's rodeo wisdom but also the profound life lessons woven into his words. Dale's mentorship transcended the sport; it was about building character, resilience, and the importance of family. He instilled in Carl the understanding that the rodeo was not just a competition, but a journey of self-discovery and personal growth.

Dale's guidance extended beyond the technical aspects of calf roping. He emphasized the importance of teamwork, camaraderie among competitors, respect for opponents, and the significance of sportsmanship. He stressed the necessity of maintaining integrity both on and off the arena, a characteristic that Dale embodied flawlessly.

Throughout their conversations, Carl recognized the intricate interplay between family and his rodeo aspirations. Dale's words revealed a deep-seated familial bond, one built on a shared history of values that emphasized hard work, perseverance, and steady, familiar support. Their discussions painted a vivid picture of a family tightly knit together, their lives interwoven with the rhythms and traditions of rodeo culture.

Their bond transcended the typical uncle-nephew relationship. It was a partnership forged in shared passion, a mentorship built on trust and respect, and a connection deepened by the common language of rodeo. Carl left that day not only with invaluable rodeo tips but with a renewed sense of purpose, a strengthened resolve, and a deeper appreciation for the supportive family that stood beside him on this demanding journey. He felt better equipped to tackle the challenges ahead, his fear replaced by a calm determination fueled by his uncle's wisdom and unwavering belief in him. He knew the road ahead would be long and arduous, but he was no longer alone. He had the guidance of his uncle, the support of his family, and the steady presence of RJ. He took a breath—ready, at last to face the next rodeo, prepared to ride.

The rodeo grounds lay quiet now, the dust settling after the whirlwind of the first competition. Carl sat on the tailgate of his family's truck, the setting sun casting long shadows across the empty arena. He ran a hand through his hair, the familiar gritty texture a constant reminder of the day's events. It hadn't been a disaster, not precisely, but it certainly hadn't been the triumphant debut he'd envisioned. He'd finished mid-pack, a respectable showing for a first-timer, but far from the top of the leaderboard. The disappointment gnawed at him, a persistent ache beneath the surface of his exhaustion.

His uncle's words echoed in his mind: "Rodeo isn't just about skill; it's about mental toughness." He'd felt the pressure, the overwhelming weight of expectations, both his own and those unspoken but palpable expectations from his family, friends, and the community. He'd let it paralyze him, hindering his instincts, clouding his judgment. He'd stumbled, he'd hesitated, and he'd paid the price.

But amidst the disappointment, a flicker of self-awareness ignited. He had experienced the adrenaline, the fear, the exhilaration — the full spectrum of rodeo emotions. He had learned, firsthand, the brutal honesty of competition, the unforgiving nature of judging, and the importance of self-control under pressure. He'd also discovered the surprising resilience of his spirit, his ability to pick himself up after a fall, to dust himself off, and face the next challenge.

The following days were a blur of intense training. He rode RJ every morning before school, honing his roping skills and refining his technique. His uncle meticulously analyzed his runs from the first rodeo, pointing out areas for improvement and suggesting minor adjustments that would yield significant results. He focused on his timing, his positioning, and the precision of his throws. He practiced until his arms ached, his muscles screamed, and his fingers were raw. But it wasn't just physical training.

Dale insisted on mental conditioning. They spent hours discussing strategy, visualizing perfect runs, analyzing potential scenarios, and developing coping mechanisms for pressure situations. Dale taught him breathing exercises, meditation techniques, and visualization methods to calm his nerves and focus his mind. He emphasized the importance of positive self-talk, of replacing self-doubt with self-belief. He shared stories of his struggles and moments of doubt, stressing that even the most accomplished riders experience setbacks and that overcoming those obstacles is key to achieving mastery.

"It's about control, Carl," Dale would say, his voice low and steady. "Control of your horse, control of your technique, and most importantly, control of your mind. The rodeo is a mental game as much as it is a physical one." Dale introduced him to a sports psychologist, someone who helped him understand the psychological aspects of competition, teaching him techniques for managing anxiety and improving focus. He learned how to visualize success, creating a mental image of the perfect run that he played over and over in his mind until it felt real and became second nature.

Carl began keeping a journal, recording his training sessions, successes, and failures. He meticulously documented his progress, noting areas for improvement, analyzing his mistakes, and tracking his performance. It became a tool for self-reflection, and a way to track his growth over time.

He spent more time with RJ, building their bond beyond the confines of the arena. He groomed him patiently, speaking softly and stroking his coat. He learned to interpret RJ's subtle cues, understanding when he was restless, when he was confident, and when he needed reassurance. Their connection deepened, a silent understanding forming between boy and horse, a commitment to their shared goal.

Carl started to see a change in his approach. He wasn't just focusing on winning; he was focusing on the process, on the journey itself. He was learning to enjoy the challenge, to appreciate the thrill of competition, and to view setbacks not as failures, but as valuable learning experiences.

The next rodeo arrived sooner than he anticipated. He felt a familiar flutter in his stomach, the butterflies of nervousness, but this time, it was different. The fear was still there, but it was tempered by a newfound sense of calm, a quiet confidence that stemmed from his diligent preparation and the steady, familiar support of his uncle and RJ.

He executed his run with the precision and control he hadn't possessed before. His timing was flawless, his throws were accurate, and his partnership with RJ was seamless. The crowd roared its approval as he completed the run, a wave of exhilaration washing over him. He hadn't won, but his time was significantly improved. More importantly, he felt a sense of accomplishment, and a quiet pride in his performance.

The transformation wasn't merely physical; it was a profound shift in his mindset. He had learned to harness the power of his nerves, channel his anxiety into energy, and utilize it to fuel his performance. He had discovered the importance of mental toughness, of unwavering self-belief, and the invaluable support of family and friends. He had learned that rodeo was more than just a sport; it was a journey of self-discovery, a testament to the power of perseverance and the unwavering pursuit of one's goals.

He continued to compete throughout the season, facing challenges and experiencing setbacks, but always learning and growing. Each rodeo became a stepping stone on his journey, a chance to refine his skills, to test his mettle, and to further strengthen the bond he shared with RJ. He was still far from achieving his ultimate goal of a college scholarship, but the path ahead seemed less daunting; his steps were surer, and his confidence was more substantial. He knew that he'd had his first rodeo. Still, now he was ready to face the rest of the season, knowing that the most important victories were the ones he achieved over his self-doubt, and those that he won alongside the steady, familiar support of his family and RJ. The future rodeos wouldn't be simply about winning or losing. These opportunities would provide avenues for continuous growth and self-improvement.

Chapter 2 The Long Season Begins

The August sun beat down mercilessly on the dusty rodeo grounds, turning the air thick and heavy. It was the kind of heat that clung to you, a suffocating blanket that stole your breath with each inhale. This was it — the official start of the long season, twenty-two rodeos stretching to the state finals in May. Carl wiped the sweat from his brow, the salty residue stinging his eyes. He adjusted his hat, the worn leather offering little respite from the relentless sun. The first rodeo had been a learning experience, a baptism by fire that had humbled him and kept his resolve burning. Now, the real test began.

The next three weeks blurred into a dizzying montage of travel, competition, and relentless heat. Each rodeo was a grueling test of endurance, a relentless cycle of preparation, performance, and recovery. The days were long, filled with the tension of competition, the adrenaline of the runs, and the exhausting routine of caring for RJ. The nights were a little better, the air thick with the smell of dust and sweat, sleep a fleeting luxury snatched between the clatter of trucks and the hushed whispers of tired competitors. Evenings were spent at motels or camping, depending on the location and budget. Sometimes, his family managed to cook dinner at the campsite, under a sky bursting with stars —a welcome contrast to the sweat-soaked days.

One particular rodeo stands out in memory — the one held in a small, forgotten town on the edge of the desert. The heat there was something else entirely, an unrelenting furnace that seemed intent on melting the very ground beneath their feet. Carl's throat felt perpetually parched; his lips cracked, and he found himself constantly reaching for his water bottle, his tongue thick and heavy in his mouth. The air shimmered with heat waves, distorting the already hazy landscape.

During this event, he watched other competitors struggling in the heat. He saw seasoned veterans, their faces drawn and weary, their movements sluggish and labored. He noticed younger competitors, their eyes glazed with exhaustion, their usual energy replaced with a kind of listless defeat. Even RJ seemed affected; his usually bright coat was slightly dull, and his movements were less energetic than usual.

Between events, Carl sought out the shade of whatever he could find — the skeletal frame of a nearby building, the meager cover of a weathered truck, even the small patch of shadow cast by a lone mesquite tree. He meticulously applied sunscreen, a thick, white paste that offered little protection from the relentless glare. He drank gallons of water, trying to replenish the fluids lost through sweat, his body working overtime to stay alive.

But even the most careful preparation couldn't fully compensate for the extreme conditions. During one of his runs, the heat haze distorted his vision, making it hard to judge the distance to the calf. His usually sharp focus wavered, his timing slightly off. He still managed a decent run, but it wasn't his best, a stark reminder of the challenges posed by the relentless August heat.

His uncle, Dale, noticed his exhaustion and urged him to slow down, to prioritize his well-being over the competition. "It's a marathon, not a sprint, Carl," Dale had said, his voice a calm counterpoint to the frenetic energy of the rodeo. "The season is long. We need to pace ourselves."

Dale's words echoed in his ears as he carefully monitored his performance and his body's response to the intense heat. It was challenging for him to adjust his mindset from striving for perfection to prioritizing long-term success. He began to incorporate more rest days into his training schedule, ensuring his body had sufficient time to recover between events. He also paid closer attention to his diet, ensuring he consumed an adequate amount of electrolytes and nutrients to replenish those lost through sweat.

He experimented with various hydration strategies, including trying electrolyte drinks and incorporating more fruits and vegetables into his diet. His mom's homemade electrolyte drinks became a staple in his life. He learned the signs of dehydration early on — the headache, the dizziness, the muscle cramps. He learned to recognize them and take action before they became debilitating. And most importantly, he learned to listen to his body, to respect its limits, and to rest when it needed it.

The small victories—finishing a run despite the heat, managing to keep RJ calm and hydrated, seeing a slight improvement in his time despite the exhausting conditions—were all fuel for his motivation. The challenges shifted from competing with others to overcoming the elements, proving that his tenacity and willpower could withstand the most extreme conditions. He learned the importance of planning, strategic scheduling, and most importantly, paying attention to his own physical and mental wellness throughout the long rodeo season. It was a harsh lesson, but one that would serve him well in the years to come.

The relentless schedule continued, a blur of dusty arenas, roaring crowds, and the ever-present August heat. But Carl persevered, driven by his dream and fueled by the steady, familiar support of his family, his uncle, and RJ. He wasn't just competing; he was learning, adapting, and growing stronger with each passing rodeo. He discovered that success wasn't just about speed and skill; it was about endurance, resilience, and the ability to adapt to any situation, even the scorching August heat. The long season was testing him, pushing him to his limits, but he was ready to face what the coming months would bring. He was toughening up, both physically and mentally. The heat was unforgiving, but so was he. Each rodeo was a battle, and he was determined to win, not just against his competitors, but against the elements themselves, one grueling event at a time. The journey was long, but he persevered through it to the end. His spirit, like the desert landscape, was proving to be both resilient and unforgiving. He'd endure. He'd win. He just had to keep going.

The relentless rhythm of the rodeo circuit continued, each weekend a whirlwind of travel, competition, and the ever-present dust. But amidst the grueling schedule, something unexpected began to bloom: genuine friendships. It wasn't just the shared passion for rodeo that bound them; it was the crucible of shared hardship, the camaraderie forged in the face of adversity. These were bonds built on mutual respect, unwavering loyalty, and a deep understanding of the sacrifices required to chase a dream.

At first, it was the small things that caught my attention. The shared glances of understanding during a particularly tough run, the silent nod of encouragement before a crucial performance, the casual banter between events—a way to relieve the tension. They shared stories, jokes, and anxieties. These small exchanges gradually built a tapestry of mutual trust and respect, cementing their bond.

There was Jake, a wiry kid from a small town whose family worked tirelessly to make it to each competition. Jake's specialty was bareback bronc riding, a dangerous event that demanded incredible strength and courage. He was quiet and reserved, but when he spoke, it was with a depth that belied his years. He often shared stories of his family's struggles and triumphs, revealing a resilience that mirrored Carl's own. They'd spend hours discussing riding techniques, exchanging tips and advice, the bond between them deepening with each shared secret and whispered confidence. Carl respected Jake's courage, and he came to see the quiet determination that propelled him forward.

Then there was Maria, a fiercely independent girl who dominated the events like a champion on a barrel racing circuit. Maria was a whirlwind of energy and enthusiasm, her laughter echoing through the rodeo grounds. She was quick with a joke and even quicker with a helping hand. Maria had no time for drama or pettiness; her focus was laser-sharp, and her determination was unyielding. She'd always make sure Carl had the right tools to maintain his equipment or offer to help with RJ's care if he were too busy preparing for his next run. Carl, in turn, would often help her repair her trailer or assist with the upkeep of her horses. Her positive attitude, contagious laugh, and selfless acts of support always seemed to lift his spirits.

And there was Miguel, a skilled steer wrestler who possessed a calm demeanor that often contrasted with the frenetic energy of the rodeo. Miguel was Carl's rock. He offered sage advice and words of encouragement, always present, always supportive. He was the voice of reason. He helped Carl strategize about his runs, discussing his technique and finding ways to improve his timing. He understood the pressure Carl was under and always knew just the right things to say to calm his nerves or bolster his confidence before a big performance.

Their friendship wasn't just about their shared love for rodeo. It was about the shared struggles, disappointments, and triumphs. It was about the long hours spent in dusty arenas, the sleepless nights on the road, and the camaraderie that blossomed in the face of adversity. They learned to trust each other implicitly, to rely on one another for support, and to celebrate each other's successes as their own.

During one particularly grueling three-day rodeo in a remote town, the weather turned sour. A sudden downpour turned the arena into a muddy swamp, making the runs even more challenging. The conditions were treacherous, but they supported one another. Jake, despite a nasty fall that left him bruised and battered, helped Carl check RJ's hooves for injuries after each run. Maria, with her years of experience in these events, adjusted Carl's rope to better adapt to the mud. And Miguel, ever the calm presence, kept them organized, making sure they had everything they needed.

The mud and rain tested their resolve, but it also reinforced their bonds. They huddled together during the storms, sharing stories and laughter, their spirits lifted by the shared experience of overcoming the challenge. Carl realized that the success in rodeo, as in life, was as much about the people you had alongside you as it was about the individual performance.

It wasn't always easy. Competitions brought out anxieties and tensions. There were moments of frustration, disagreements about strategy, and the usual rivalries that inevitably arise amongst competitors. But these moments were easily resolved with a shared laugh or a simple gesture of support. The friendships were deep enough to withstand the rough patches, proving that their bonds were stronger than any competitive edge could break.

The camaraderie extended beyond the immediate group. They found themselves forming bonds with other competitors, exchanging stories, and sharing the joys and frustrations of the rodeo life. The moments lived shoulder-to-shoulder transcended any rivalries; there was a unique understanding and empathy that only those who lived the grueling rodeo lifestyle could truly appreciate.

There were late-night talks in motel rooms, shared meals on the road, and countless hours spent sharing experiences, stories, and dreams. They learned about each other's families, hopes, fears, and aspirations. Carl discovered that their paths, though seemingly disparate, shared an underlying similarity: the relentless pursuit of a dream, the unwavering commitment to their passion, and the quiet strength it took to balance the demands of competition with the realities of life.

As the season progressed, Carl watched his friends grow, both as competitors and as people. He saw their strengths and their weaknesses, their triumphs and their failures. He learned from their experiences, was inspired by their resilience, and found comfort in their support. The long season was not just about winning or losing rodeos; it was about the bonds he formed, the friendships he forged, and the community he discovered within the high school rodeo circuit. These friendships, forged in the heat and dust of the arenas, would prove to be as invaluable as any trophy he could win. They were his support system, his family away from home, and the cornerstone of his journey toward his dreams.

He knew that these bonds, tested and strengthened through the long and challenging rodeo season, would last long after the last rodeo ribbon had been awarded. They were the lasting legacy of a season that tested him, changed him, and ultimately made him stronger, not just as a calf roper but as a person. The friendships forged in the heat and dust of the rodeo arena were a prize that far outweighed any trophy he could win. They were the real treasures of the season.

The second rodeo of the season in Saginaw was a brutal lesson in humility. Carl had been riding high after a strong showing in the opening rodeo. He felt confident, RJ was responsive, and the rhythm of his roping felt almost effortless. He'd even managed to impress his Uncle Jesse, a feat that usually felt as elusive as winning the world championship. But Saginaw had other plans.

His first run was disastrous. He missed his catch entirely, the calf darting away, leaving him with a time of zero. The crowd's murmurs, usually a comforting hum of anticipation, felt like a chorus of criticism. His second run was slightly better, but a clumsy dismount cost him precious seconds, leaving him with a disappointing time. He'd finished near the bottom of the pack, a stark contrast to his previous victory. The sting of defeat was sharp, a bitter taste he hadn't anticipated. A crushing disappointment replaced the usual excitement that thrummed through him.

The drive home was quiet. Even RJ seemed to sense his rider's dejection. The usually boisterous atmosphere in the truck, filled with the excited chatter after a rodeo, was replaced by a heavy silence. Carl's mother, generally quick with words of comfort and encouragement, placed a hand on his shoulder, her touch conveying more than words ever could. Uncle Jesse, a man of few words but immense experience, offered a simple, "It happens, kid." His tone wasn't dismissive but rather an acknowledgment of the inherent unpredictability of rodeo.

That night, Carl barely touched his dinner. He replayed his runs in his head, dissecting every movement, searching for the elusive flaw that had led to his failure. He focused on the missed catch, the hesitant dismount, and the slight hesitation in his swing. He replayed each moment, scrutinizing his actions, searching for the answers he knew were buried within his performance.

The next few days were a blur of self-criticism. He felt a gnawing sense of inadequacy, questioning his skills, his dedication, and even his passion for the sport. Doubt, a shadow he'd rarely acknowledged, began to creep into his thoughts. He'd always prided himself on his resilience, his ability to bounce back from setbacks. But this loss felt different; it felt personal, almost a betrayal of his potential.

Uncle Jesse, sensing his nephew's struggle, took him aside for a quiet talk. He didn't offer platitudes or empty assurances. Instead, he shared his own stories of devastating losses, of championships lost by fractions of a second, of near misses that had left him wondering what could have been. He described the agony of defeat, the crushing weight of expectation, and the seemingly insurmountable challenge of picking oneself up after a fall.

"Rodeo ain't about never losing, Carl," Uncle Jesse said, his voice gravelly but firm. "It's about how you get back on that horse. It's about learning from your mistakes, not letting them define you. Every loss is a lesson if you're willing to learn it."

Uncle Jesse's words resonated deeply. He showed Carl videos of his past competitions, pointing out minor details and subtle technique errors that had cost him crucial points. He emphasized the importance of self-analysis, of not shying away from the mistakes, but dissecting them, understanding their root causes, and developing strategies to prevent their recurrence. He emphasized the importance of meticulous preparation, focusing on details and the fine-tuning that distinguishes the good from the great.

He pushed Carl to reassess his training regimen, focusing on specific areas where he'd shown weakness. They spent hours in the arena, working on his dismounts, refining his technique, building muscle memory, and strengthening his connection with RJ. They worked on his rope, ensuring it was conditioned correctly and the knots were securely tied. They worked on Carl's mental game, developing strategies to manage anxiety and to maintain focus under pressure. Uncle Jesse emphasized the importance of visualization, mentally rehearsing each run, anticipating potential problems, and formulating strategies to overcome them.

The following weeks were a period of intense focus and deliberate practice. Carl immersed himself in his training, pushing himself more than ever before. He was determined to learn from his mistakes, to transform his failures into fuel for his future successes. He paid close attention to the advice of his mentor and friends. Jake suggested a slight adjustment to his saddle position. Maria, ever observant, pointed out a tendency to tense up during the crucial moments of the run. Miguel analyzed Carl's breathing patterns, suggesting ways to regulate his nerves before each run.

At the next rodeo in Saginaw, the results were immediately noticeable. His runs were smoother and more controlled, his timing sharper, and his approach more confident. He didn't win, but his times had significantly improved. He was no longer at the bottom of the pack; he was a contender. More importantly, he learned to cope with the pressure, to manage his anxiety, to handle the weight of his ambition.

The season continued, with its mix of wins and losses. There were more disappointing performances, more setbacks, more moments where doubt threatened to creep back in. But each time, Carl drew strength from the lessons he'd learned in Saginaw. Each loss became an opportunity for growth, for refinement, and for a deeper understanding of himself and his craft. He realized that resilience wasn't about avoiding failure; it was about getting up after each fall, dusting himself off, and continuing the journey, stronger and more determined than before.

He also learned the value of sportsmanship. He witnessed competitors handle defeat with grace, offering congratulations to their rivals, exhibiting humility in victory, and demonstrating a mutual respect that extended beyond the competition. He saw firsthand the importance of empathy, the understanding that every competitor faced challenges and setbacks, and that shared experience created a bond stronger than any individual victory.

By the time the state finals rolled around, Carl wasn't just a skilled calf roper; he was a seasoned competitor, battle-tested, mentally tough, and brimming with newfound confidence. He still felt the sting of defeat, but a quiet determination replaced the fear of failure. He understood that success was not merely the absence of failure but the result of continuous learning, adaptation, and a relentless pursuit of excellence. He took a breath—ready, at last to give it his all, not just for the prize but for the journey, the friendships, and the lessons learned along the way. The losses hadn't broken him; they had forged him into something stronger, more resilient, and more determined. The long season, with its highs and lows, had taught him more than any textbook ever could, molding him into the rodeo competitor he was always meant to be. He knew this was only the beginning of his journey, and he was ready for the challenges ahead.

The relentless Texas sun beat down on Carl and RJ during their afternoon practice sessions. The air hung heavy with the scent of dust and sweat, a familiar aroma that Carl had come to associate with the long, grueling rodeo season. Saginaw had been a harsh awakening, a brutal reminder that even with talent and hard work, success wasn't guaranteed. The sting of defeat lingered, but Uncle Jesse's words — about getting back on the horse — echoed in his mind. He knew he had to rebuild their relationship in Saginaw, not just as rider and horse, but as partners.

RJ, usually a picture of eager energy, seemed subdued. The typically bright gleam in his eyes was dulled, a reflection of Carl's despondency. He sensed a hesitancy in RJ's movements, a lack of the usual sharp responsiveness. It wasn't just the physical connection that was faltering; there was a subtle tension that hung between them. Carl realized he hadn't taken the time to understand RJ's perspective, to acknowledge his role in their shared disappointment. He'd been so focused on his self-criticism, he'd neglected the horse that was just as much a part of their partnership as he was.

He began by spending more time with RJ outside the arena. He'd groomed him meticulously, whispering words of encouragement and apology, acknowledging RJ's contribution, both to the victories and the losses. He'd noticed subtle changes in RJ's behavior, little things only a keen observer would pick up on. A slight stiffness in his gait, a reluctance to respond immediately to some of Carl's cues. He realized that RJ, like him, needed time to process the Saginaw debacle. They weren't just a team; they were a family, and family supported each other through thick and thin.

Their bond deepened through these quieter moments. He'd lead RJ on long, gentle rides, allowing the horse to set the pace. He'd let RJ graze in the lush pastures, allowing him to be a horse, not a competitor. He'd spend hours just sitting with him, brushing his coat, whispering, sharing his anxieties and hopes. It was during these intimate moments that Carl began to understand RJ on a deeper level, beyond the mechanics of roping and riding.

One evening, as the sun dipped below the horizon, painting the sky in hues of fiery orange and deep purple, Carl felt a shift in their dynamic. As he brushed RJ's coat, he felt the horse lean into his touch, a subtle sign of trust and affection. RJ's eyes, usually expressive and intelligent, now held a newfound warmth, a quiet acknowledgment of their shared journey.

Their renewed connection showed in every training session. RJ moved with newfound energy, shedding the hesitation that had slowed him. Carl felt a surge of confidence, not just in his skills but in the unbreakable bond with his horse, built on understanding and mutual respect.

The next rodeo in Saginaw was a test of their renewed partnership. Carl felt a calm confidence he hadn't experienced since the first rodeo. The anxiety was still there, a familiar tremor in his hands, but it was manageable, replaced by a determined focus. He visualized each run, felt the rhythm of RJ's movements, and anticipated every move of the calf. He rode with a sense of unity with RJ, trusting their shared instinct, their deep connection.

The runs were clean and precise, each maneuver executed with a newfound grace and timing. He didn't win, but he came in second place, a marked improvement. More importantly, he felt a sense of accomplishment that went beyond the competition itself. He'd overcome a setback, not only in his performance but also in his relationship with RJ. He'd learned that true partnership wasn't just about shared success; it was about weathering the storms together.

The long season continued, with its share of triumphs and disappointments. There were times when doubt crept in, times when fatigue weighed heavily on both horse and rider. But through it all, their bond remained strong, a steady anchor in the turbulent waters of competition. They faced further challenges, some involving injuries to both Carl and RJ, requiring extended periods of rest and rehabilitation. There were days when Carl questioned his abilities, doubted his determination, and wondered if his dream was worth the relentless grind. RJ's quiet patience and his unwavering trust served as a constant source of encouragement.

The meticulous care Carl gave RJ extended to his diet and well-being. He learned about the intricacies of equine nutrition, ensuring RJ's diet was balanced and tailored to his training schedule. He learned to interpret RJ's subtle cues, recognizing when he was tired, stressed, or in need of rest. He became acutely aware of the symbiotic relationship between their well-being and their success in the arena.

Carl's dedication to RJ wasn't just about physical health, but also about emotional well-being. He realized that a horse's temperament is significantly affected by the rider's attitude. Carl's anxiety had, at times, subtly been transmitted to RJ, causing him to react poorly. Through patience, self-awareness, and calm encouragement, Carl learned to manage his anxieties, ensuring that RJ remained calm and responsive. He began to recognize the intricate dance between the emotions of a horse and its rider.

As the state finals drew near, Carl felt not only the pressure of the competition but the weight of his responsibility towards RJ. He knew that their performance was a reflection of their shared commitment, their deep-seated bond in Saginaw, their unwavering connection. He understood that he wasn't just competing; he was representing a partnership forged in the heart of the rodeo, a partnership built on mutual respect, understanding, and trust. The final rodeo held no guarantees, but whatever the outcome, Carl knew he and RJ had overcome more than just the challenges of the competition; they had overcome a testing period in their relationship, emerging stronger and more united than ever before.

The Saginaw rodeo, though not a victory, had served as a crucial turning point. The second-place finish wasn't just about the points; it was a testament to the rekindled bond between Carl and RJ. Uncle Jesse, ever the astute observer, saw this too. He'd watched Carl's runs with a critical eye, his weathered face betraying nothing until the final calf was roped. Then, a slow, approving nod.

"That was better, boy," he said, his voice gruff but laced with pride. "Much better. But we can still refine it."

That evening, under the vast Texas sky, filled with the twinkling brilliance of a million stars, Carl and his uncle sat on the tailgate of their truck, the aroma of campfire smoke mingling with the night air. Between them lay a worn, leather-bound notebook filled with meticulous notes on Carl's previous runs, as well as detailed analyses of his strengths and weaknesses. It was a testament to Uncle Jesse's dedication, his unwavering commitment to his nephew's success.

"Saginaw exposed some flaws," Uncle Jesse began, pointing to specific entries in the notebook. "Your dally was inconsistent. Sometimes too tight, sometimes too loose. And your positioning as you approach the calf... needs work. You're rushing the process."

Carl listened intently, his gaze fixed on his uncle's weathered hands, hands that had won countless world championships, hands that held the wisdom of decades spent on the rodeo circuit. He'd learned early on that Uncle Jesse's critiques weren't personal; they were born out of a deep-seated desire to help him succeed.

Uncle Jesse went on to explain the importance of a consistent daily routine, as well as the subtle art of balancing control and speed. He drew diagrams in the dirt, showing Carl the optimal angle of approach, the precise moment to execute each maneuver. He emphasized the need for patience and a calm, measured approach to avoid the anticipatory rush that had plagued his performance in Saginaw.

"It's not just about brute strength, Carl," Uncle Jesse explained. "It's about finesse, about strategy. It's about knowing when to pull, when to hold back, when to trust your instincts, and when to override them. Calf roping is a dance, a subtle interplay between you, RJ, and the calf. You have to anticipate the calf's movements, yes, but not rush to meet them. You have to be one step ahead, but not overreact."

They spent hours that night discussing strategies, analyzing previous runs frame by frame, and dissecting every detail. Uncle Jesse pointed out how Carl's body position affected RJ's movements, the subtle weight shifts that could throw off their balance, and the importance of maintaining a harmonious rhythm between horse and rider. It wasn't just about roping; it was about the symbiotic relationship between rider, horse, and the unpredictable nature of the calf.

Their new strategy involved a three-pronged approach. First, perfecting the dally — refining his technique, practicing until the motion became second nature. This required countless hours in the arena, working with RJ, refining the synchronization of their movements, until the dally became a seamless extension of their partnership. Carl focused on the feeling of the rope in his hands, the precise moment of application, and the delicate balance between strength and control.

Secondly, they focused on improving Carl's approach to the calf. This meant mastering the art of anticipation without the rush. This was where the partnership between Carl and RJ was truly put to the test. Carl needed to communicate effectively with his horse, guiding him subtly, utilizing a blend of visual cues and physical prompts to ensure seamless movement, setting the stage for a perfect roping. Uncle Jesse emphasized the importance of patience, of waiting for the opportune moment rather than forcing the issue.

The third element focused on analyzing each opponent's strengths and weaknesses. Uncle Jesse taught Carl the art of competitive observation, emphasizing the importance of assessing each calf's unique movements and tailoring his strategy accordingly. He also taught Carl to analyze his opponents' techniques, identifying their strengths and weaknesses, and using this knowledge to strategize accordingly.

The next few weeks were a whirlwind of practice. Carl spent hours perfecting his dally, honing his approach, refining his technique until it flowed effortlessly. He and RJ ran countless practice runs, each run meticulously observed by Uncle Jesse, who offered constant feedback, making minute adjustments to Carl's position, the angle of his approach, and the timing of his movements. It was a process of continuous refinement, a relentless pursuit of perfection.

They incorporated video analysis into their training, reviewing each run, dissecting every detail, and analyzing their performance with the cold, critical eye of a seasoned professional. Uncle Jesse taught Carl to interpret his body language, to recognize the subtle cues that betrayed his tension or uncertainty, and to correct them before they impacted his performance.

The change was noticeable. Carl's roping became more precise, more controlled, more confident. His runs were smoother and more fluid; his dally was consistent; his approach was measured. He learned to read the calf's movements, anticipating its every turn and shift, adapting his strategy with an almost instinctive grace.

The next rodeo in Saginaw was a clear demonstration of their new strategy. Carl's performance was transformed. He roped with a newfound precision and control, his runs clean and efficient, the result of weeks of dedicated practice and constant refinement. He didn't win, but his improved performance was evident, showcasing the effectiveness of their new approach. It wasn't just about winning; it was about consistent improvement, about the steady refinement of skills, and the development of a comprehensive strategy. The long season stretched before them, full of challenges, but Carl felt ready.

He carried a plan, not perfect, but his, a strategy, and most importantly, a renewed partnership with RJ, a partnership forged in the crucible of competition and strengthened by their shared dedication and mutual trust. The journey was far from over, but for the first time, Carl felt truly prepared to face whatever lay ahead. The next rodeo was another stepping stone on his journey to the state finals, a journey filled with both challenges and triumphs, but one he now faced with newfound confidence, fueled by strategic planning and the steady, familiar support of his uncle and his loyal horse, RJ.

Chapter 3: Finding His Rhythm

The Saginaw rodeo, while not a win, was a significant victory in itself. It was a tangible demonstration of the progress he'd made since Saginaw, a testament to the power of consistent practice and the steady, familiar support of his uncle. The refined technique, improved synchronization with RJ, and a calculated approach to each run—all came together, revealing a new level of performance. Uncle Jesse's quiet pride was palpable as he watched Carl dismount after each run, a subtle nod or a barely perceptible tightening of his jaw the only outward expressions of his approval.

The next few rodeos followed a similar pattern: focused practice, meticulous analysis, and steady improvement. Each competition became a learning experience, providing an opportunity to identify weaknesses and refine strategies. Carl began keeping a detailed logbook, mirroring his uncle's, to record his times, analyze his mistakes, and document his progress. He started to notice patterns, recognizing the subtle nuances in his performance that contributed to success or failure. He learned to identify his "tells" — the unconscious tightening of his grip, the slight hesitation in his approach, the barely perceptible shift in his weight that could throw off his balance.

The discipline required to maintain this level of focus was immense. It wasn't simply about showing up for practice; it was about the relentless pursuit of perfection, the unwavering dedication to refining every aspect of his technique. He spent countless hours in the arena, practicing his dally until his arm ached, his rope felt like an extension of his body, and the motion flowed effortlessly. He worked on his approach, honing his ability to read the calf's movements and anticipate its every shift and turn, adjusting his strategy accordingly. He visualized each run, picturing the perfect roping, the flawless execution, the triumphant dismount.

His relationship with RJ deepened during this period. The horse, sensitive and intuitive, seemed to respond to Carl's heightened focus and determination. Their partnership transcended the purely physical; it was a connection forged through shared effort, mutual trust, and a common goal. Carl treated RJ with the respect and care he deserved, ensuring the horse was well-fed, well-rested, and properly cared for. He spent time simply grooming RJ, talking to him, and building a bond that extended beyond the demands of competition. He'd learned from his uncle that a successful partnership was based on mutual understanding, respect, and unwavering dedication.

Uncle Jesse remained Carl's constant guide and mentor, offering steady, familiar support and insightful critiques. He was more than just a coach; he was a confidante, a source of inspiration, and a reminder of the hard work and dedication required to succeed in this demanding sport. Their conversations extended beyond the technical aspects of calf roping; they discussed strategy, mindset, and the mental fortitude needed to perform under pressure. Uncle Jesse emphasized the importance of maintaining a positive attitude, of focusing on his strengths, and learning from his mistakes. He stressed the importance of self-belief, of knowing that even on days when everything seemed to go wrong, he could overcome adversity and persevere.

The winter months presented a unique set of challenges. The cold weather often made training uncomfortable, and the limited daylight hours reduced the time available for practice. But Carl persevered, adapting his training regimen to the changing conditions. He found creative ways to maintain his fitness, incorporating weight training into his routine to focus on building strength and stamina, and ensuring he was in peak physical condition when the rodeo season resumed. He used the downtime to study films of top calf ropers, analyzing their techniques, observing their body mechanics, and identifying elements he could incorporate into his style.

The spring rodeos brought with them a new level of intensity. The competition intensified as the state finals drew nearer. The pressure mounted, the stakes grew higher, and the challenges became more complex. But Carl approached each competition with a newfound calm and confidence. He had developed a solid foundation of skill and strategy, honed through months of dedicated training and unwavering perseverance. His approach was measured and deliberate, his techniques refined and consistent, and his partnership with RJ seamless and intuitive.

He still had setbacks. There were runs where he missed his mark, where the calf bucked unexpectedly, where the timing was off, and his dally went awry. But even in defeat, Carl learned to adapt his strategy, refine his techniques, and work to correct his mistakes. He didn't dwell on his failures; instead, he analyzed them, identifying areas where he could improve, and focused on the process of learning and growth. His resilience, his ability to bounce back from adversity, became as much a hallmark of his performance as his technical skills.

The final rodeo before the state finals was in Fort Worth. The atmosphere was electric, the competition fierce. Carl felt the pressure, the weight of expectation bearing down on him. But he focused on his breathing, visualized his run, trusted his training, and relied on the steady, familiar support of his uncle and his trusty horse. He executed his runs with precision, his dally was consistent, his approach deliberate, and his partnership with RJ seamless. The result wasn't simply a win; it was a triumphant statement of his dedication, perseverance, and the power of consistent practice.

The victory in San Angelo wasn't just about the points or the prize money; it was a testament to his hard work, his unwavering commitment, and the power of relentless improvement. He'd proven to himself that he could perform under pressure, that he had the mental fortitude to overcome adversity, and that his hard work had yielded tangible results. The journey to the state finals wasn't over, but he felt ready. He felt prepared to face any challenge, confident in his skills, his strategy, and his partnership with RJ. The confidence he carried wasn't arrogance, but a quiet certainty born of countless hours of practice, relentless dedication, and unwavering self-belief. He took a breath—ready, at last to showcase the result of his consistent practice at the state finals, where the actual test of his skill and determination awaited.

The state finals loomed as a daunting prospect, but one he embraced with a sense of calm determination. He knew the competition would be fierce, the pressure immense, but he also knew that he was better prepared than he'd ever been. The long hours of practice, the countless runs with RJ, the meticulous analysis with Uncle Jesse — it all culminated in this moment. He took a breath—ready, at last not just to compete, but to win. He'd faced setbacks, overcome challenges, and learned from his mistakes. He'd developed a strong foundation of skills, forged a robust partnership with RJ, and discovered a resilience that would serve him well in the face of any obstacle. He had found his rhythm, his flow, his groove. And he was ready to show the world what he had learned. The culmination of years of work, dedication, and the steady, familiar support of his family and his horse would be on display at the state finals. He took a breath—ready, at last. He was prepared. He was ready to ride.

The string of victories began subtly, a quiet ripple in the otherwise turbulent waters of the rodeo circuit. It started with a second-place finish in Abilene, a significant improvement over his previous performances. A surprising surge of satisfaction replaced the familiar sting of near-miss; he'd been so close, and the feeling was intoxicating. He'd pushed himself harder than ever before, and the result, though not a win, was a validation of his dedication. The tangible reward—a check and the climbing points tally—were secondary to the intangible boost to his confidence. He felt a subtle shift, a realignment of his inner compass, guiding him toward a more assertive and confident approach.

The next rodeo in Stephenville was different. This time, it was a win. The roar of the crowd, the exhilaration of a perfect run, the triumphant wave of relief washing over him as he dismounted—it was a sensory overload, a powerful rush of adrenaline that left him breathless. The feeling was completely unexpected, a raw, unfiltered joy that transcended the competitive aspect of the sport. This wasn't just about skill; it was about the intoxicating blend of risk, reward, and the sheer, unadulterated thrill of the ride. It was a victory not just over his opponents, but over his self-doubt.

The victory in Stephenville unleashed something within Carl. It was more than just the points; it was a breakthrough, a shift in his perception of his capabilities. The self-doubt that had lingered like a shadow began to dissipate, replaced by a growing confidence that radiated from him, influencing every aspect of his training and competition. He found himself approaching practice with a new focus, a newfound intensity born of his recent success. He was pushing harder, striving for greater precision, demanding more of himself and RJ.

The wins kept coming. Brownwood, Coleman, and then a stunning victory in San Antonio. Each win fueled the next, creating a positive feedback loop that propelled him forward. The pressure that had once paralyzed him now seemed to energize him. The weight of expectation, previously a burden, became a source of motivation. He thrived on it. The nervous energy that once manifested as mistakes was now channeled into focused intensity —a honed precision that allowed him to execute his runs with near-perfect grace and efficiency.

The thrill of the competition was no longer just about the outcome. It was about the process. He relished the anticipation, the tension in the air before each run, the roar of the crowd, the pounding of his own heart, the rhythmic beat of RJ's hooves on the packed earth. He appreciated the intense concentration demanded by each run, the absolute focus required to execute the precise movements, and the delicate interplay between himself and his horse. He found himself relishing the challenge, pushing his boundaries, and testing his limits.

Uncle Jesse watched with a mixture of pride and cautious observation. He understood the delicate balance between confidence and overconfidence, the potential for success to breed complacency. He continued to offer his guidance, his critiques remaining sharp and insightful, but his tone had shifted subtly. There was a newfound respect in his voice, a recognition of the transformation that had taken place within Carl. They still spent countless hours analyzing videos, poring over details, refining techniques, but the sessions now had a different feel. There was a shared sense of accomplishment, a recognition of their progress, and a quiet confidence that permeated their conversations.

Carl's relationship with RJ had deepened, too. The horse seemed to sense the shift in Carl's demeanor, responding with a newfound intensity and focus. Their partnership transcended the purely athletic; it had become a deep, intuitive connection forged through moments lived shoulder-to-shoulder, mutual trust, and unwavering commitment. RJ sensed Carl's growing confidence and mirrored it, responding with heightened agility and precision. Their runs flowed seamlessly, a harmonious blend of skill, timing, and instinct. There were still moments of uncertainty, moments when the calf would buck unexpectedly or when the rope wouldn't fall exactly as planned, but even in those moments, their partnership remained strong, their connection unbreakable.

The media started to take notice. Local newspapers featured Carl's name and pictures, highlighting his remarkable winning streak. He began receiving calls from sponsors, and the offers, once hesitant and few, now flowed in. He managed his attention with the same quiet focus he applied to his roping, staying grounded and aware that success was fleeting and could disappear as quickly as it had arrived. He remained polite, respectful, and focused, a quiet dignity radiating from him. The victory in San Angelo was a culmination of this consistent success. He wasn't just winning; he was dominating. He was transforming from a promising talent into a force to be reckoned with.

The pressure intensified as the state finals approached. The media attention mounted, the expectations grew, and the weight of his winning streak loomed over him. The previous setbacks, the near misses, the moments of doubt — they faded into the background, replaced by a powerful self-assurance, a belief in his ability to perform under pressure.

But even with the newfound confidence, the pressure was palpable. He knew the competition would be fierce, the talent extraordinary, and the risk of defeat very real. He spent extra hours practicing, pushing himself and RJ to their limits. Each run was a refinement, a honing of his skills, a sharpening of his focus. He analyzed every detail, meticulously examining his technique, seeking out areas for improvement, and constantly striving for perfection.

Yet, amid this intense preparation, he maintained a sense of calm. He understood that his success wasn't just about physical skill; it was also about mental strength, the ability to control his nerves, focus on the task at hand, and maintain a clear, confident mindset. He employed visualization techniques, picturing himself executing his runs flawlessly, envisioning the success he sought.

This wasn't just a winning streak; it was a metamorphosis. Carl was a competitor, a champion in the making, and he was ready to face the ultimate challenge: the state finals. The journey had been long and arduous, filled with triumphs and setbacks, but he'd emerged stronger, more resilient, and more confident than ever before. He took a breath—ready, at last to prove himself. He was prepared to ride. The roar of the crowd, the anticipation, the pressure—he welcomed it all. This was his moment.

The tension in the air at the Mineral Wells rodeo was thick enough to cut with a knife. The scent of dust and sweat hung heavy, mingling with the nervous energy radiating from the competitors. Carl, perched atop RJ, felt the familiar pre-competition jitters, but this time, it was different. A healthy respect for the competition tempered the quiet confidence he'd cultivated over the past few months. This wasn't just another rodeo; this was where he'd face the heavy hitters, the guys who'd been on his radar since the beginning of the season.

First up was Trey Miller, a lanky kid from Saginaw with a reputation for lightning-fast roping skills. Trey possessed an almost supernatural ability to anticipate the calf's movements, his rope a blur of motion as he effortlessly secured the catch. He was a master of finesse, relying on precision and speed rather than brute force, a stark contrast to Carl's more powerful and aggressive style. Watching Trey in the practice arena was a masterclass in efficiency, with each movement economical, deliberate, and flawlessly executed. He was a quiet competitor, letting his roping do the talking, a cool customer who seemed immune to the pressure of the competition.

Then there was Cade "The Hammer" Henderson from Saginaw. Cade was everything Trey wasn't, all raw power and aggressive determination. His roping style was a whirlwind of muscle and momentum, a display of pure athleticism. Cade didn't rely on finesse; he overpowered the calves, his throws forceful and decisive. He was a showman, a boisterous presence in the arena, relishing the roar of the crowd and the thrill of the competition. He wasn't just good; he was a spectacle, a force of nature that left a trail of dust and defeated calves in his wake. His mere presence seemed to amplify the energy in the arena, a palpable wave of intensity that was both intimidating and exhilarating.

The third rival, and perhaps the most formidable, was Wyatt "Wild Bill" Jones from Fort Worth. Wyatt was a veteran of the high school rodeo circuit, possessing a combination of speed, power, and an almost uncanny intuition for the game. He possessed a quiet intensity, his calm demeanor masking a deep-seated competitiveness. He was a student of the game, analyzing every aspect of his performance and constantly seeking ways to refine his technique. He was the complete package, combining the raw power of Cade with the precision of Trey. He was a strategist and a tactician who would exploit any weakness in his opponents' game. His roping was a masterpiece of controlled aggression, a flawless blend of technique and instinct.

Carl's first run against Trey was a nail-biter. Trey's speed was breathtaking. Carl held his breath, watching as Trey's rope flew through the air in a perfect arc that perfectly captured the calf. The time flashed on the timeboard: a blistering 7.2 seconds. Carl knew he had to be perfect to beat that. He took a deep breath, focused on RJ, and executed his run with unwavering precision. He felt the surge of adrenaline, the familiar pounding of his heart, and the rhythmic beat of RJ's hooves beneath him. His throw was accurate, fast, and efficient. The time displayed on the screen was 7.1. The crowd erupted. He'd beaten Trey, but he knew the challenge wasn't over.

Facing Cade was a different beast entirely. Cade's raw power was something to behold. The calf was a bucking bronco, but Cade wrestled it to the ground with astonishing strength and speed. His throw was a testament to his physical dominance, a blur of motion that brought the crowd to its feet. Cade's time was 7.8 seconds, a respectable time considering the calf's resistance. Carl found himself needing to dig deep to find an answer to Cade's brute force. He focused on maintaining his form, controlling his movements, and letting his technique do the work. He managed a time of 7.6 seconds, enough for second place but not a win.

Wyatt was the ultimate test. The calm exterior belied a burning competitiveness. Wyatt seemed to read Carl's every move, anticipating his strategy and adapting accordingly. His roping style was fluid and adaptable, a testament to his years of experience. He was a chameleon, seamlessly shifting his technique to match the challenges presented by each calf. His throw was a thing of beauty—precise, powerful, and flawlessly executed. He completed the run in an astonishing 6.9 seconds, a time that stunned everyone in the arena. Carl, despite a strong run and a near-perfect technique, found himself trailing, achieving a time of 7.3 seconds.

The competition highlighted not just the individual skills of these ropers but also the unpredictable nature of the sport. Calves, like human athletes, had good days and bad days. A seemingly docile calf could suddenly turn into a bucking bronco, and a single slip-up could undo a champion. Carl, despite the losses, found the experience invigorating. He learned more from these defeats than he did from his victories. He observed their techniques, analyzed their strategies, and adjusted his approach accordingly. He watched videos of their performances, identifying their strengths and weaknesses.

He spent countless hours practicing, honing his skills, and refining his technique. He focused on his footwork, his timing, his dally, every single element of his roping. He pushed himself and RJ to the limit, striving for perfection in every aspect of their performance. He also concentrated on his mental game, developing strategies to manage his nerves and maintain focus under pressure. He practiced visualization techniques, picturing himself executing his runs flawlessly, envisioning the success he desired.

The rodeo circuit was a brutal proving ground, a test of skill, stamina, and resilience. But Carl welcomed the challenge, relishing the competition and the opportunity to learn and grow. He realized that his rivals, far from being just opponents, were teachers. Each contest, each victory, and defeat was a valuable lesson, a stepping stone on his journey to becoming a champion. The camaraderie among the competitors, despite the fierce competition, was a surprising aspect of the rodeo world. These rivalries were intense, yet they were ultimately respectful, a testament to the shared passion and dedication that united them.

The highs and lows of the competition became lessons in perseverance, resilience, and sportsmanship, lessons that extended far beyond the arena and into the fabric of Carl's life. He found himself forming an unlikely bond with Cade and Trey, bonding over their moments lived shoulder-to-shoulder and mutual respect for the sport. They learned from each other, even sharing tips and strategies outside of the competitions. The respect was mutual; they were competitors, yes, but they were also fellow athletes, united by their shared passion for the sport. Carl emerged from each rodeo a stronger, more experienced calf roper, determined to chase his dream of winning a college scholarship. The path was arduous, filled with setbacks, but he was ready to face the challenges ahead. His rivals were fierce, but he was prepared to ride.

The roar of the crowd faded as Carl rode RJ back to the stables, the adrenaline slowly ebbing away. The Mineral Wells rodeo, while exhilarating, had been a stark reminder of the relentless pace of the high school rodeo circuit. Twenty-two rodeos, plus finals — a schedule that seemed designed to test the limits of human endurance. And that didn't even take into account high school.

The reality of balancing his burgeoning rodeo career with the demands of academics hit him with the force of a runaway calf. High school wasn't some side gig; it was a critical part of his future. His parents, ever supportive, emphasized the importance of education, a college scholarship being the ultimate goal that fueled his rodeo aspirations. But how could he possibly juggle grueling practices, long road trips to rodeos across Texas, and the ever-present pressure of maintaining good grades?

The first few weeks were a chaotic blur. He'd cram for tests on the bus between rodeos, snatching moments of sleep between events. His backpack overflowed with textbooks and rope bags, his calendar a bewildering mix of rodeo schedules, school assignments, and practice sessions. He felt like he was constantly running on empty, teetering on the edge of exhaustion. His grades, which had once been consistently strong, began to slip. The pressure was immense, a constant weight on his shoulders.

His uncle, a multi-world champion team roper, recognized the strain immediately. "Carl," he said one evening, his voice a low rumble, "you're spread too thin. You gotta find your rhythm, boy. This ain't just about roping; it's about balance."

His uncle's advice proved invaluable. He helped Carl develop a meticulous schedule, a detailed plan that meticulously allocated time for schoolwork, rodeo practice, and even some much-needed downtime. Carl learned to prioritize tasks, focusing on the most pressing assignments first, then tackling the rodeo preparations. He divided his study time into smaller, more manageable chunks, incorporating these study periods into the downtime between rodeos and practice.

The key, his uncle stressed, was efficiency. Carl had to learn to maximize every minute, minimizing wasted time. He started studying during long car rides, using audiobooks and online learning platforms. He even found himself studying during some of the more extended waiting periods at rodeos, using the downtime productively. He learned to say no to some social engagements, prioritizing his studies and rodeo. This wasn't about sacrificing his social life completely; it was about being selective and mindful of his time.

His mother played a crucial role in this balancing act. She helped manage his schedule, ensuring he completed his schoolwork, had his meals prepared, and organized his travel arrangements. She became his logistics manager, taking the burden of administrative tasks off his shoulders, allowing him to focus on his studies and his rodeo performances. This support system helped him tackle the increasingly complex demands.

There were still days when Carl felt overwhelmed, when the pressure seemed unbearable. He learned to identify his stress triggers and develop coping mechanisms. Regular exercise became a crucial part of his routine, a way to release tension and clear his head. He discovered the therapeutic benefits of spending time with RJ, finding solace in the quiet companionship of his horse. The bond with RJ was more than just a partnership; it was a source of comfort and support amidst the chaos.

He also learned to communicate his needs, asking for help when he needed it. Whether it was seeking clarification on an assignment from a teacher or asking his friends for support, he realized that it was okay to ask for help; it didn't diminish his abilities. This was a critical part of his journey, as he recognized his limitations and sought support from his support network.

He started using a digital planner, meticulously scheduling every minute of his day, and setting reminders for upcoming assignments and rodeos. This helped him stay organized, ensuring he didn't miss any deadlines or commitments. His use of the planner was meticulous, every entry carefully logged and reviewed daily.

The school administration also stepped in, offering flexibility in scheduling and providing academic support. They recognized the unique challenges faced by student-athletes, offering extended deadlines and alternative assignments whenever possible. The school's understanding of his particular circumstances allowed him to succeed in both academic and athletic spheres.

Throughout the year, Carl's journey wasn't a constant triumph, but a series of incremental successes. Some weeks, he excelled in academics while struggling in the rodeo. At other times, it was the opposite. He discovered that consistent effort and adaptability were essential. He didn't aim for perfection, but for consistent progress. This approach led to a much more sustainable lifestyle.

The highlight of the year arrived at the state finals. The competition was fierce, the pressure immense. But Carl was prepared. He had meticulously managed his time, balancing his schoolwork with his rodeo training. He approached the competition with a calm confidence, the result of months of diligent effort and careful planning. He rode well, roped flawlessly, and secured a top-five finish. It wasn't the win he had dreamt of, but it was a testament to his ability to balance two seemingly incompatible worlds.

The victory was not just about the rodeo; it was about his ability to manage the chaos of his life, to create a rhythm that allowed him to excel in both academics and athletics. It was a lesson in perseverance, time management, and the importance of a strong support system. He had found his rhythm, not just in the arena, but in life.

The following year brought new challenges. Increased academic rigor, the added pressure of college applications, and the ever-increasing demands of the rodeo circuit made the balancing act even more difficult. He faced a significant academic challenge in his junior year when a demanding Advanced Placement course threatened to overwhelm his already busy schedule. He addressed this challenge by forming a study group with his classmates, sharing resources and supporting each other's learning. The collaborative approach proved effective, and he successfully achieved a good grade while balancing his rodeo commitments.

He learned to prioritize sleep, realizing the negative impact of exhaustion on his performance. His schedule was now meticulously designed to include adequate rest, understanding the importance of recovery in maintaining both academic and physical peak performance.

By his senior year, Carl had become a master of multitasking, able to study while traveling, practice while waiting for his next event, and socialize without sacrificing his commitments. He had become incredibly efficient, maximizing his time and minimizing distractions.

The college application process added another layer of complexity. He had to manage his academic workload, his rodeo training, and the demands of writing essays, requesting letters of recommendation, and attending college visits. He utilized his planner more rigorously than ever.

The culmination of his hard work and dedication was the receipt of multiple college rodeo scholarship offers. His consistent academic performance, combined with his impressive rodeo record, made him an attractive candidate. He chose to attend a university with a renowned rodeo program and a strong academic reputation, representing the perfect blend of his passions.

Carl's story was one of triumph, but it also served as a testament to the importance of hard work, resilience, and a well-structured life. The path he followed wasn't easy, but he never lost sight of his dreams. He learned that success in one area of life didn't require sacrifice in others. It was about finding the rhythm, the balance, the harmony between school and rodeo, between the classroom and the arena. His success served as an inspiration to other student-athletes, demonstrating that with dedication and effective management, it is possible to excel in both academic and athletic pursuits. The actual test of character wasn't just in winning, but in the ability to persevere and overcome the obstacles that stood in the way of achieving one's goals. He had finally found his rhythm, not just as a calf roper, but as a student, a son, and a friend.

The state finals had been a whirlwind, a blur of adrenaline, dust, and the satisfying thud of a perfectly executed roping. The top-five finish hadn't secured him a college scholarship, not yet, but it had given him the confidence to keep pushing, to keep striving. The following season loomed, bigger and more demanding than ever. The financial strain of the rodeo circuit was becoming increasingly apparent. Travel, entry fees, horse upkeep—it all added up to a significant sum, a sum that was far beyond what his family could comfortably manage. He knew he needed more than just their steady, familiar support; he needed a sponsor.

The search for a sponsor began almost immediately after the state finals. He started by reaching out to local businesses, many of which he knew personally from his community involvement. He crafted a compelling presentation, highlighting his achievements, his dedication, and his plans for the future. He included photos from his rodeos, emphasizing his consistent performance and his strong connection with RJ. He even created a simple website showcasing his rodeo career. Many initially expressed interest, but the commitments were hesitant, the sponsorships rarely covering more than a small fraction of his expenses. The reality of securing meaningful sponsorship was proving to be far more challenging than he'd anticipated.

Discouragement gnawed at him. He felt the weight of expectation from his family, the pressure of maintaining his grades, and now the added burden of financing his rodeo career. Doubt crept into his mind, whispering insidious suggestions about his abilities, questioning whether he was good enough, dedicated enough to warrant a significant sponsorship. He confided in his uncle, who, with his usual laconic wisdom, offered encouragement.

"Son," his uncle said, "finding the right sponsor ain't about luck; it's about persistence. You have to sell yourself; show them what you bring to the table. It's a business, just like roping."

His uncle's words ignited a new fire in him. He revamped his presentation, making it more professional, more focused on the value he could offer a sponsor. He researched potential sponsors more thoroughly, focusing on businesses that aligned with his values and his image. He understood that securing a sponsor was not just about obtaining financial support; it was about establishing a mutually beneficial partnership.

He broadened his search, extending it beyond local businesses to include companies with a national presence. He spent countless hours researching potential sponsors, tailoring his pitch to each business, emphasizing the unique opportunities for branding and marketing that his high-profile rodeo career offered. He knew that sponsors weren't just giving money; they were investing in his talent, his future, and the potential for return on their investment.

Then, a breakthrough came. A regional agricultural supply company, "Texas Best Feeds," expressed serious interest. Their representative, a friendly, grizzled man named Earl, had seen Carl compete at several rodeos and had been impressed by his skill and his dedication. Earl saw beyond the winning and losing, recognizing the value of a young, talented athlete with a growing fan base, especially within the tight-knit rodeo community. He saw the potential for cross-promotion, a chance to reach a specific and dedicated market.

After a series of meetings and negotiations, Carl signed a sponsorship agreement with Texas Best Feeds. The terms were generous, covering a significant portion of his competition expenses. The sponsorship was a vote of confidence in his potential.

The impact of the sponsorship was immediate and profound. The financial burden lifted, allowing Carl to focus entirely on his training and studies. He could afford to enter more rodeos, gaining valuable experience and exposure. He could purchase better equipment, improving his performance and reducing the risk of injury. The sponsorship opened doors that he never thought possible. The improved equipment, the ability to travel to more rodeos, the reduction in the financial burden on his family—these were all tangible effects of the partnership.

Moreover, the partnership gave Carl a sense of legitimacy, a validation of his hard work and dedication. He felt a sense of pride wearing the Texas Best Feeds logo on his shirt and his horse's saddle pad.

The sponsorship extended beyond financial support. Texas Best Feeds provided Carl with opportunities for public appearances, allowing him to interact with fans and connect with the community. He participated in promotional events, showcasing his skills and representing the company. He made appearances at local schools and community gatherings, inspiring young people to pursue their dreams. It was a rewarding experience that extended his reach and elevated his profile.

Earl, his new sponsor, became a mentor, sharing his wisdom and experience, offering advice not only on rodeo but also on life. Earl understood the pressures of competition, the sacrifices required to succeed, and the importance of maintaining balance. His guidance proved invaluable, enriching his rodeo career while providing him with a role model and a source of inspiration.

The sponsorship gave Carl a sense of stability, a reassurance of his path. It wasn't just about the money, although that was crucial; it was about the belief, the confidence, and the partnership. He found that rodeo wasn't solely an individual sport; it required teamwork, support, and collaboration. This partnership with Texas Best Feeds taught him the importance of networking, building relationships, and understanding the business side of athletic competition.

But the sponsorship also came with responsibilities. Carl understood that he was now representing not just himself, but Texas Best Feeds. He was acutely aware of the importance of maintaining a professional image, both on and off the rodeo grounds. He understood that his actions, his words, and his performance reflected not only on himself but also on his sponsor. He had to be a role model, an ambassador for the company, carrying himself with integrity and professionalism at all times. He kept up with his school work, maintained a positive attitude, and adhered to a strict ethical code of conduct, mirroring the values of the company that had taken a chance on him. He understood that a sponsorship was a two-way street, a symbiotic relationship requiring mutual respect and commitment.

As the rodeo season progressed, Carl's performance improved, fueled by the confidence and support of Texas Best Feeds. He knew he had to deliver results to justify the investment. And he did. He won several rodeos, consistently placing in the top three, and he qualified for the United States Finals. He began to focus on his college applications, understanding that he needed to maintain a strong academic performance to balance his athletic success.

The sponsorship with Texas Best Feeds wasn't just a financial lifeline; it was a turning point in his career, a testament to the power of partnerships and the importance of building strong relationships within the rodeo community. It was a crucial step in his journey toward achieving his dreams, a step that transformed his future. The support and mentorship of Earl provided him with invaluable guidance, extending beyond the arena, and helped him navigate the complex world of professional rodeo, as well as the business aspects of his burgeoning career. His success became a compelling narrative, a showcase of the value of dedication, resilience, and the strength of collaboration in competitive sports.

Chapter 4: Love and Loss

The United States Finals were a whirlwind, a culmination of years of hard work, dedication, and steady, familiar support. The roar of the crowd, the smell of dust and leather, the electric energy of the competition—it was everything Carl had ever dreamed of and more. He performed exceptionally well, placing high enough to attract the attention of several college rodeo programs. The scholarship offers started rolling in almost immediately after the finals concluded. The relief was palpable, a weight lifted from his shoulders, a validation of his years of hard work and dedication. He'd done it. He'd secured his future, his path to a college education paved with the dust of the rodeo arena.

But amidst the celebrations, amidst the whirlwind of college visits and scholarship negotiations, something else began to blossom—a romance. Her name was Sarah, and she was everything he wasn't. Where Carl was quiet and reserved, she was outgoing and vibrant, her laughter ringing out like a clear bell in the crowded rodeo arenas. They met at a regional competition, their eyes meeting across the crowded stables. He noticed her immediately, her fiery red hair a stark contrast to the muted tones of the dusty arena, her enthusiasm infectious. She was a barrel racer, her skill as precise and breathtaking as his calf roping.

Their initial conversations were tentative, punctuated by the nervous energy of the competition. They discussed their horses, training routines, and future aspirations. He learned about her dedication to her horse, a spirited palomino mare named Sunny, her devotion mirroring his unwavering commitment to RJ. She was aware of his profound love for the sport. They found common ground in their shared passion, a language spoken not in words but in the shared understanding of dedication, discipline, and the thrill of competition.

Their relationship bloomed slowly, nurtured by the moments lived shoulder-to-shoulder of the rodeo circuit. They spent hours together at rodeos, watching each other compete, offering encouragement and support. They would discuss strategies, analyze performances, and dissect every run, every barrel, every roped calf. Their shared language of rodeo, their mutual understanding of the demands and sacrifices of the sport, forged a bond that was unique, intimate, and deeply fulfilling. Their conversations extended beyond the arena, evolving into late-night talks under the starlit sky, where they shared dreams, fears, and aspirations. They found solace in each other's company, a refuge from the pressures of competition and the demands of their hectic lives.

He learned to appreciate her boundless energy, her infectious enthusiasm, her capacity for joy. She learned to appreciate his quiet strength, his unwavering determination, his quiet intensity. Their differences complemented each other, their personalities intertwining like the intricate patterns of a braided rope. He learned to step outside his comfort zone, encouraged by her vibrant spirit; she learned to embrace the quiet moments, her frenetic pace slowing under his calming influence. The rodeo circuit, often perceived as a lonely and solitary pursuit, became a shared adventure —a journey they undertook together.

Their relationship wasn't always easy. The demanding schedule of the rodeo season often kept them apart, their time together precious and fleeting. They navigated the challenges of long distances, missed events, and the ever-present pressure of competition. They learned to communicate effectively, support one another through setbacks, and celebrate each other's victories. They understood that their relationship, like their rodeo careers, required dedication, compromise, and unwavering commitment.

One particularly challenging rodeo, the state finals, tested their relationship. Carl suffered a minor injury, a pulled muscle that threatened to derail his season. Sarah was his steady, familiar support, her presence a constant source of strength and encouragement. She assisted him with his physical therapy, offering both emotional support and practical assistance. She reassured him, reminding him of his skills, dedication, and resilience. He, in turn, offered his support when she experienced a setback in her competition. They learned the importance of mutual support, understanding that their relationship was a partnership, built on mutual respect and shared sacrifice.

Their relationship wasn't just a romantic connection; it was a partnership built on mutual respect and shared goals. They were both driven and ambitious individuals, each with their dreams and aspirations. They supported each other's ambitions, celebrating each other's successes and offering solace during setbacks. Their connection was a testament to the power of shared passions, a bond forged in the heart of the rodeo arena, a love story woven into the fabric of dust and leather, of horses and dreams.

Carl's college applications were equally successful. He received several full-ride scholarship offers from prestigious rodeo programs across the country. Choosing where to go wasn't just a matter of selecting the best athletic program; it involved a significant decision regarding where he and Sarah would continue their relationship. Sarah was also receiving considerable attention from several excellent events, such as barrel racing programs. The prospect of potentially being geographically separated added another layer of complexity to their already complicated lives.

After countless conversations, emails, and late-night calls filled with nervous laughter and anxious silences, they reached a decision. They chose universities that, while not geographically close, were within reasonable driving distance, allowing them to maintain their relationship without compromising their academic and athletic goals. Their love story wasn't just about romantic gestures; it was about making difficult choices, showing up for each other through challenges, and demonstrating the strength and resilience of a partnership built on shared dreams and mutual respect. The romance was a constant, a comforting presence amidst the chaotic world of competitive rodeo and the pressures of higher education. It was a reminder that even in the face of adversity, the steady, familiar support of a loved one could make all the difference. Their relationship, born in the heart of the rodeo arena, became a testament to the power of shared passions, the strength of mutual support, and the enduring beauty of a love story forged in the dust and sweat of competitive sport. It was a love story for the ages, a narrative as thrilling and unpredictable as the rodeo itself. A love story that was beginning.

The regional finals loomed, a behemoth of expectation casting a long shadow over Carl's usually sunny disposition. The carefree joy that had accompanied his earlier successes was replaced by a low-level hum of anxiety, a constant thrumming beneath the surface of his daily routine. The pressure wasn't just external; it was internal, a relentless self-critique that gnawed at his confidence. He'd secured scholarships, yes, but the regional finals were different; this was a stepping stone, a proving ground for the national stage. Failing here meant not just a missed opportunity, but a potential shattering of his carefully constructed future.

He found himself meticulously examining every aspect of his performance, replaying past runs in his mind, dissecting each movement, each twist of the reins, each subtle shift in RJ's gait. He'd always been a perfectionist in the arena, but now the self-criticism was overwhelming, a relentless tide threatening to pull him under. He spent hours in the practice arena, pushing himself and RJ beyond their limits, striving for that elusive perfection that felt increasingly out of reach. The usual rhythm of his training, the comfortable routine that had served him so well, felt chaotic and unsettling.

Sleep became elusive, his nights filled with restless tossing and turning, visions of missed catches and clumsy dismounts playing on repeat in his mind. He'd wake up with a start, his heart pounding, his muscles tense with the phantom strain of a non-existent run. The pressure was affecting him physically, manifesting as tension headaches, stomach aches, and an almost constant state of fatigue. Even RJ seemed to sense the shift in Carl's energy; his usually placid demeanor was replaced with restless fidgeting. The bond between them, once unshakeable, felt strained, almost brittle.

Sarah, ever perceptive, noticed the change. She saw the shadows lurking beneath his carefully constructed facade of calm confidence, the weariness etched into the lines of his face, the tremor in his hands. She didn't pry, didn't push, but offered her quiet support, her presence a comforting anchor in the storm of his anxiety. She listened patiently as he poured out his fears, his worries, his doubts. She reminded him of his strengths, his past successes, and his unwavering dedication. She brought him back to the simple joy of riding, reminding him why he'd started this journey in the first place—not for the scholarships, not for the accolades, but for the love of the sport.

She encouraged him to take breaks, to step away from the arena, to find moments of peace and calm amidst the chaos. They spent evenings simply talking, sharing stories, and laughing; the familiar comfort of their connection was a balm to his frayed nerves. She helped him to focus on the things he could control, reminding him that he couldn't control the outcome, only his preparation and his performance. He learned to trust her instincts, to lean on her strength, and to find solace in her unwavering belief in him.

His uncle, a seasoned rodeo veteran, recognized the signs of his nephew's mounting pressure. He knew the demands of the sport, the relentless pressure it placed on competitors, the mental toll it could exact. He pulled Carl aside one evening, his voice calm and reassuring. "Son," he said, "the pressure's real, but it ain't gonna win this one. You've put in the work, you've trained hard, you've got the skill. You're stronger than this pressure."

His uncle's words were a lifeline, a reminder of his resilience and ability to overcome adversity. He shared stories from his rodeo career, recounting moments of intense pressure, near misses, and unexpected setbacks. He emphasized the importance of mental fortitude, the ability to stay calm and focused under pressure, and the power of positive self-talk. He taught Carl breathing exercises to manage his anxiety, techniques to center himself before a run, and strategies to quiet the relentless chatter of his self-doubt.

The training shifted, becoming less about physical exertion and more about mental preparation. They spent less time in the arena and more time talking, strategizing, and practicing mental exercises. Carl learned to visualize success, replaying perfect runs in his mind, and build his confidence through positive affirmations. He learned to trust his instincts, let go of self-criticism, and embrace the uncertainty of competition.

The day of the regional finals arrived, a day that had once filled him with dread, now infused with a newfound calm. He still felt the pressure, the weight of expectation, but it no longer threatened to overwhelm him. He approached the arena with quiet confidence, his breathing steady and his mind clear. He had done everything he could to prepare, both physically and mentally. The rest, he knew, was out of his hands.

RJ, sensing his rider's newfound composure, was calm and responsive. The run itself was a blur, a seamless blend of skill, precision, and instinct. He executed each move with precision and grace, the years of training culminating in a performance that was both powerful and effortless. The roar of the crowd was a distant hum, a background noise, as he focused on the task at hand, his mind clear, his body relaxed, his heart filled with a quiet sense of confidence.

He didn't win the regional finals, but his performance was exceptional. He placed high enough to secure his spot at the United States Finals, a testament to his skill, his dedication, and his ability to overcome the relentless pressure of competition. The relief was immense, a wave of exhaustion and exhilaration washing over him as he dismounted RJ, the weight of weeks of anxiety finally lifted.

The experience had changed him, though. He'd learned the importance of self-compassion, the value of support, and the power of mental resilience. He'd discovered a new strength within himself, a strength forged not just in the dust of the arena but in the crucible of pressure and anxiety. He now understood that the journey wasn't just about winning; it was about growth, learning, and pushing his limits, both physically and mentally. He'd come to understand that the toughest competitions weren't always against other riders, but sometimes, against the inner demons that tried to derail him. He'd won that battle, too. The pressure had been immense, but it had not broken him. It had made him stronger. And that, he knew, was a victory in itself.

His relationship with Sarah, his uncle's guidance, and his unwavering dedication to his craft had been his greatest assets. He took a breath—ready, at last for Nationals, not just with skill and talent, but with a renewed understanding of his resilience.

The crisp autumn air, usually a welcome change after the scorching summer rodeos, held a chilling edge for Carl. The United States Finals were just weeks away, the culmination of years of hard work, sweat, and unwavering dedication. But a shadow hung over his preparations, darker and more menacing than any pre-competition anxiety. RJ, his steadfast partner, his four-legged confidante, was injured.

It happened during a seemingly innocuous practice run. A misstep, a sudden twist, a jarring sound that sliced through the quiet concentration of the arena. At first, Carl hadn't registered the severity. RJ, usually stoic and resilient, flinched, his powerful muscles tense with pain. A sharp cry escaped the horse, a sound Carl had never heard before. It was a sound that burrowed into his gut, a primal scream of pain and fear that echoed the panic rising within him.

The veterinarian's diagnosis was brutal: a strained ligament in RJ's hind leg. It wasn't a career-ending injury, the vet stressed, but it was severe enough to jeopardize his participation in the nationals. The next few weeks were a blur of treatments, therapies, and agonizing uncertainty. Carl spent countless hours by RJ's side, applying liniments, massaging his leg, whispering reassurances.

He watched, helpless, as his partner, usually a picture of robust health and athleticism, struggled with discomfort and restricted movement.

The familiar rhythm of their training, the unspoken communication that had defined their partnership for years, was shattered. The arena, once a sanctuary of shared effort and mutual understanding, now felt like a cruel reminder of their current predicament. The silence, broken only by the rhythmic ticking of the clock, amplified Carl's anxiety, each tick a relentless countdown to a deadline he might not meet.

The emotional toll was immense. The bond between horse and rider is a unique entity, a partnership forged through trust, respect, and countless hours of shared experience. It's a silent language, a mutual understanding that transcends words. Now, that bond was fractured, threatened by the unpredictable nature of RJ's injury. The thought of competing without RJ was inconceivable, a betrayal of their years of mutual commitment and dedication. It felt as though a part of him, a vital piece of his identity, was wounded alongside his horse.

His uncle, sensing his nephew's despair, tried to offer words of comfort, but even his wisdom seemed inadequate in the face of this unforeseen adversity. He spoke of the unpredictable nature of rodeo, of the countless setbacks faced by even the most experienced competitors. He reminded Carl of his resilience, his ability to adapt and overcome challenges. But Carl struggled to find solace in these words. This was different; this was a threat to his partnership, the very core of his success.

Sarah, his steadfast girlfriend, was his rock, offering a much-needed respite from his overwhelming anxiety. She didn't try to diminish his feelings, didn't offer empty platitudes. Instead, she listened patiently and empathetically, allowing him to express his frustration, his fear, his helplessness. She helped him channel his energy into positive actions, encouraging him to focus on the aspects of RJ's recovery he could influence.

She researched alternative therapies, contacting equine specialists nationwide to seek new treatments and innovative approaches. She became his research assistant, his cheerleader, his constant source of support. She reminded him, constantly, that their journey was about more than just winning; it was about the strength of their partnership, the enduring bond between horse and rider. And that bond, she insisted, remained unbroken.

The days stretched into weeks, each morning bringing a renewed assessment of RJ's progress. Some days were better than others. Some days, a flicker of hope emerged, marked by a subtle improvement in RJ's gait and a lessening of his stiffness. Other days, the frustration was almost unbearable, as setbacks threatened to undo the slow, painstaking progress.

Carl's training regimen shifted, focusing less on physical practice and more on mental preparation. He spent hours visualizing himself and RJ in the arena, executing perfect runs, their partnership seamless and strong. He meditated, practicing mindfulness techniques to manage his stress and anxiety. He spent long hours reading about equine rehabilitation, devouring information on injury management and recovery strategies.

He learned about the delicate balance of rest and exercise, as well as the careful management of RJ's recovery. He understood the importance of patience, the need to trust the process, even as doubts gnawed at his confidence. He began to view RJ's recovery as a test of his resilience, not just as a rider, but as a partner, a testament to the strength of their shared journey.

The approach of the United States Finals loomed large, but the weight of expectation now felt different. It was a mix of hope and fear, a blend of ambition and apprehension. The question wasn't whether Carl would compete, but whether RJ could compete as well.

The day finally arrived when the vet gave the verdict: RJ was cleared to compete. It wasn't a full recovery, the vet stressed, but he was fit enough to participate, albeit with careful monitoring and adjustments to his usual routine. The relief was overwhelming, a tidal wave of emotion that washed over Carl. Tears streamed down his face as he embraced RJ, his voice choked with emotion. He knew this was a testament to their enduring bond, to the strength of their partnership, their mutual commitment, and their resilience in the face of adversity.

The competition itself was a blur. Carl wasn't at his peak performance, he knew. RJ, too, showed signs of his recent injury, needing more support and guidance than usual. But the run was a success. They rode as one, defying the expectations of many and proving that even in adversity, the strength of their bond could overcome any obstacle.

The outcome of the nationals was ultimately secondary. Carl had already won. He'd won the battle against doubt, the fight against despair, and the challenge of an unforeseen injury. He had learned the importance of patience, resilience, and the unwavering power of a shared commitment between horse and rider. The experience had deepened his understanding of his craft and his relationship with RJ, solidifying a bond that went beyond the arena and into the heart of a true partnership forged in the crucible of adversity and sustained by love and unwavering commitment. He rode out of the arena, not just as a competitor, but as a testament to the enduring strength found in overcoming setbacks and the power of love, loyalty, and an unbreakable partnership.

The news of RJ's injury had spread through the close-knit rodeo community like wildfire. Phone calls and texts poured in, a wave of support washing over Carl and his family. His mother, a woman whose quiet strength belied her gentle nature, was his anchor. She didn't offer platitudes or empty reassurances. Instead, she provided practical help, managing the farm chores, ensuring his meals were prepared, and leaving him free to focus on RJ's recovery and his mental well-being. Her presence was a constant comfort, a silent affirmation of her unwavering faith in him and his ability to overcome this obstacle.

His mother spent hours with Carl, listening to his anxieties, validating his fears, and reminding him of his past successes. She would recount stories of his early years, of his stubborn determination to ride a horse before he could even walk, of his innate talent that even as a toddler captivated the seasoned rodeo hands. These were stories not of wins and losses, but of grit, resilience, and the unwavering pursuit of a dream. She reminded him that this setback, while significant, was just one chapter in the broader narrative of his life —a narrative filled with passion, dedication, and the enduring power of family support.

His uncle, a legendary team roper with a string of world championships to his name, became Carl's mentor and confidant. His experience provided a unique perspective, drawing on a wealth of knowledge gained from years spent navigating the unpredictable world of professional rodeo. He didn't sugarcoat the situation, acknowledging the gravity of RJ's injury and the uncertainties that lay ahead. Yet, he never wavered in his belief in Carl's capabilities. He shared stories of his setbacks, including times when he faced crippling injuries, devastating losses, and crushing defeats. Each story was a testament to his resilience, a reminder that setbacks are not the end, but rather an opportunity for growth, adaptation, and renewed determination.

Uncle Joe's coaching transcended the physical aspects of rodeo. He taught Carl the importance of mental fortitude and the need to cultivate an unwavering self-confidence, even in the face of adversity. He emphasized the importance of self-care, the need for adequate rest and proper nutrition, and the benefits of mindfulness practices in managing stress and anxiety. He encouraged Carl to visualize success, mentally rehearse perfect runs, and build confidence, thereby strengthening his resolve. He insisted on regular family dinners, creating a space for shared meals, laughter, and the reassuring presence of family support.

His younger sister, Maria, initially struggled to understand the depth of Carl's despair. Used to seeing her older brother as invincible, she found his vulnerability unsettling. But she, too, found ways to contribute, offering small gestures of support that held immeasurable value. She'd bring RJ apples and carrots, carefully brushing his coat, murmuring words of encouragement in a soft voice. She would spend hours searching for alternative healing methods, finding articles on equine therapy, and new treatments for ligament injuries. Her unwavering devotion, though initially unspoken, ultimately became a source of strength for Carl, a reminder that even small acts of love and support could have a profound impact.

Even his grandfather, a man of few words but immense wisdom, played a vital role. He wasn't involved in the day-to-day aspects of Carl's rodeo life, but his presence was a quiet force of strength. He'd sit with Carl in the barn, sharing stories of his youth, of a time when family support was the only safety net in a challenging life. His stories spoke of resilience, of overcoming hardship through hard work and unwavering determination. He didn't offer advice or solutions, but his simple presence and steady gaze conveyed a profound message: that he believed in Carl, in his abilities, and in his strength to overcome this challenge. He embodied the enduring spirit of family support, a silent but powerful force that anchored Carl during this turbulent period.

The extended family, too, rallied around Carl. Aunts, uncles, and cousins came to help out on the ranch, offering their time and skills to alleviate the burden on his mother. Friends from the rodeo community offered their support, sharing their experiences, offering words of encouragement, and providing a network of friendship that bolstered his spirit. This collective support formed a protective shield, a buffer against the anxieties and uncertainties he faced.

The collective support went beyond just physical and emotional assistance. His family also became his financial safety net. The expenses associated with RJ's veterinary care were considerable, exceeding their immediate budget. However, without hesitation, his extended family pitched in, pooling their resources to ensure that RJ received the best possible care. This wasn't just about money; it was about family commitment, a testament to their shared belief in Carl's dreams and their steady, familiar support for his pursuits.

This unwavering financial backing wasn't just a matter of practical assistance; it was symbolic of their deep-seated faith in Carl's potential and his dedication to his craft. It underlined the idea that success in rodeo isn't solely defined by individual talent, but is profoundly influenced by the strength of the support system that surrounds a competitor.

One evening, during a quiet moment amidst the ranch's bustling activity, Carl sat with his mother, the scent of hay and leather filling the air. He confessed his doubts, his fears of failure, and his anxieties about the upcoming nationals. His mother's response wasn't a lecture on perseverance or a pep talk on overcoming adversity. She reached out, taking his hand in hers, and said, "Carl, remember who you are. Remember where you come from. You've got the heart of a champion, the grit of a pioneer, and the steady, familiar support of a family who believes in you more than you believe in yourself." Her words, simple yet profound, resonated deeply, reinforcing the belief that the support of his family wasn't just a safety net but the very foundation upon which his dreams were built.

The family's support didn't just encompass the immediate crisis; it extended to the long-term implications of RJ's injury. They discussed alternative strategies, explored possibilities of leasing another horse for future competitions, and considered ways to manage the financial consequences of prolonged rehabilitation. They weren't just concerned with winning the United States Finals; they were concerned with Carl's well-being, his future, and the sustainability of his passion. Their support was holistic, encompassing all aspects of his life, and highlighted the crucial role of family in shaping not just an athlete but a person.

Throughout the arduous journey of RJ's recovery, Carl's family remained his unwavering rock, providing him with the emotional resilience, practical support, and unshakeable belief he needed to navigate the challenges and triumph over adversity. Their support was a testament to the enduring power of family bonds. This force transcended the boundaries of a competitive sport and extended into the heart of a young man's journey of self-discovery and personal growth. This family unit, bound by love, loyalty, and a shared passion, became the cornerstone of Carl's resilience, reminding him that even in the face of setbacks, he wasn't alone. Their collective strength was his strength, their unwavering faith his unwavering belief. He was not just a rodeo competitor; he was a son, a brother, a nephew, and a grandson, surrounded by a tapestry of unwavering love and steadfast family support, a tapestry as strong and enduring as the bond between him and RJ.

The rhythmic thud of RJ's hooves on the packed earth, once a familiar comfort, was now a distant memory. Weeks bled into months, each day a slow, agonizing crawl towards recovery. The barn, usually alive with the energy of training and the anticipation of competition, felt eerily quiet, the absence of RJ's presence a palpable void. Carl spent countless hours by his horse's stall, brushing his coat, whispering, sharing his anxieties and hopes. He felt the familiar ache of loss, not just the loss of his partner, but the loss of the routine, the rhythm, the very essence of his life.

The veterinarian, Dr. Evans, a seasoned professional with decades of experience, had been cautiously optimistic from the start. He'd explained the extent of the ligament damage, the delicate nature of the recovery process, and the uncertainties that lay ahead. But he'd also praised RJ's resilience, his inherent strength, and Carl's unwavering dedication to his care. He'd described the painstaking process of physiotherapy, the slow, incremental progress, and the inevitable setbacks. Carl learned to read the subtle shifts in RJ's demeanor — the slight flinch of muscle, the hesitant lift of a leg, and the soft sigh of relief when an excruciating exercise was over. These small, almost imperceptible changes became milestones, indicators of gradual improvement, fuel for his unwavering hope.

Maria, his younger sister, remained an unwavering source of support. Her initial uncertainty had transformed into a dedicated commitment to RJ's well-being. She devoured veterinary textbooks, online forums, and research papers, becoming an unexpected expert on equine rehabilitation. She'd bring RJ special treats, carefully selected based on their purported healing properties — apples for their vitamins, carrots for their sweetness, chamomile tea for its calming effect. Her quiet diligence and tireless efforts became a source of strength for Carl, a reminder that even in the face of adversity, there was always something to be done and something to hope for.

Carl couldn't ride, and he couldn't practice his calf-roping technique in the usual way. But he didn't let this inactivity derail his determination. He adapted, focusing on physical conditioning, honing his strength and stamina through rigorous workouts. He'd run cross-country, his feet pounding the dusty trails, mimicking the bursts of energy required in a calf roping run. He'd spend hours in the gym, building muscle, improving flexibility, ensuring his body was ready to perform at its peak when the time came. He practiced his roping technique using dummies, perfecting his throws, refining his timing, building muscle memory, all the while visualizing himself executing flawless runs, the dust swirling around him, the cheers of the crowd ringing in his ears.

His uncle Joe, the legendary team roper, remained a constant source of guidance and encouragement. He introduced Carl to mindfulness techniques, teaching him to focus on his breathing, to quiet the clamor of his anxious thoughts. He shared stories of his battles with injury, emphasizing not just the physical recovery but the mental resilience it required. He discussed the importance of visualization, the power of positive self-talk, and the necessity of cultivating an unshakeable belief in one's abilities, even when the odds seemed stacked against them.

The weeks turned into months, and the months into a year. Slowly, painstakingly, RJ began to regain his strength and mobility. The limp in his gait became less pronounced, the hesitation in his movements less frequent. There were setbacks, days when the progress seemed negligible, when despair threatened to overwhelm Carl. But he persevered, drawing strength from his family, his friends, and the unbreakable bond he shared with RJ. He remained steadfast in his commitment to their shared goal and dream.

Finally, the day arrived when Dr. Evans declared RJ fit enough to begin light training. It was a moment of immense relief, a bittersweet victory that underscored the challenges they had overcome. The first tentative rides were cautious, slow, and carefully monitored. But each ride built confidence; each movement was a testament to their resilience and unwavering dedication. Slowly, gradually, RJ's power and agility returned. The rhythmic thud of his hooves on the earth, once a faint memory, now filled the barn with a sense of hope, a promise of a future reclaimed.

The return to competition was gradual, a careful re-entry into the demanding world of high school rodeo. Carl began with local events, using them as opportunities to rebuild his confidence, reestablish his rhythm, and regain his competitive edge. Each rodeo was a step forward, a measure of their progress, a validation of their combined strength. The victories were sweet, hard-earned, and infused with the bittersweet tang of a near-loss. The minor setbacks were viewed as learning opportunities, as chances to fine-tune their skills and to solidify their bond further.

The nationals approached like a distant storm, looming on the horizon. The pressure was immense, the stakes higher than ever. Carl felt the familiar flutter of anxiety, but this time, it wasn't the crippling fear of failure. It was the excitement of competition, the thrill of the challenge, and the anticipation of putting their months of hard work and dedication to the test. The steady, familiar support of his family, the quiet strength of his friends, and the steadfast bond he shared with RJ kept his resolve burning.

On the day of the finals, Carl rode into the arena with unwavering confidence. He wasn't just competing against other riders; he was competing against the adversity, against the odds, against the possibility of defeat. He was a testament to the unwavering power of family support, the value of perseverance, and the gratifying feeling of overcoming challenges. As he executed a flawless run, the crowd erupted in cheers, and he knew, in that moment of triumph, that the journey, the struggles, the setbacks, had all been worth it. The victory was not just his; it was RJ's, his family's, and the collective triumph of a community that had rallied around him during his darkest hours.

It was the testament to the unbreakable bond between a boy and his horse, a bond forged in the heart of rodeo country. The story of their comeback resonated deeply within the hearts of those present, a testament to the power of resilience, of hope, and the unwavering belief in the strength of the human-animal bond. It was a narrative woven into the very fabric of the rodeo's rich heritage; a story of love, loss, and ultimate triumph that will be etched in the annals of rodeo history. The echoes of their success would reverberate through the community, inspiring countless others to pursue their dreams with the same unwavering determination. And as Carl celebrated his win, he knew that the lessons learned during their journey of overcoming the odds were far more valuable than any championship trophy could be.

They had conquered adversity, not only securing a place in the rodeo's history but also in their hearts, forever bonded by the shared experience of resilience, faith, and triumph over seemingly insurmountable odds. The story of their comeback would become more than just a tale of rodeo success; it would be a symbol of hope and perseverance for years to come.

Chapter 5: Regional Finals

The air crackled with anticipation, a palpable tension hanging heavier than the dust kicked up by restless horses. The regional finals weren't just another rodeo; they were a crucible, a brutal test of skill, endurance, and nerve. Carl felt the pressure tightening around him, a vise squeezing the air from his lungs. He'd spent months rebuilding, painstakingly coaxing RJ back to full health, and now, the culmination of all that effort hung precariously in the balance. The arena felt like a pressure cooker, with each bleacher seat a potential judge and each spectator's gaze a critical assessment.

The other competitors were a blur of motion, a whirlwind of focused energy. He saw the steely determination in their eyes, the practiced ease of their movements, the almost imperceptible tension in their shoulders. He knew their strengths and weaknesses, their riding styles, and their competitive fire. Some he considered friends, while others he considered rivals. This was a clash of wills and skill that would determine who would have the chance to chase their dreams on a bigger stage.

He watched as a young woman, her face a mask of concentration, expertly guided her horse through flawless events, such as barrel racing runs. The precision of her movements, the symbiotic connection between horse and rider, was breathtaking. He admired her skill, acknowledging her as a formidable opponent. Then came the steer wrestling, a brutal display of strength and agility, where human power wrestled against the raw strength of a steer. The intensity was palpable, the crowd roaring with each near-miss, each successful takedown. Carl felt the pressure building, a knot tightening in his stomach.

He found his uncle Joe, his calm presence a small island of stability in the turbulent sea of competition. Joe, with his years of experience and countless victories, offered a quiet nod of encouragement, his eyes understanding the weight of expectation bearing down on his nephew. Joe didn't need words; his mere presence was enough to offer Carl a sense of calm amidst the storm.

The calf roping events began, and the tension ratcheted up even further. Each competitor executed their runs, the skill levels varied, but each rider displayed their dedication and grit. Some runs were flawless, while others were clumsy; near-misses and frustrating mistakes marked some. Carl watched intently, studying the techniques, identifying the small nuances that made the difference between a winning performance and a disqualified run.

He felt the familiar butterflies in his stomach, the tightening of his chest, the quickening of his pulse. This was it, the moment he had worked so hard for. Months of grueling physical therapy, hours of solitary practice, the steady, familiar support of his family—all of it culminated in these few crucial minutes. He felt RJ's warm breath against his leg, the familiar weight of his saddle, the steady rhythm of his heartbeat beneath him. RJ seemed to sense the intensity, his muscles tense, his focus unwavering. Their bond, forged in sweat and shared struggle, was palpable.

The announcer's voice boomed over the loudspeaker, calling Carl's name. He took a deep breath, letting out a long, slow exhale. He focused on the present moment, blocking out the roar of the crowd, the pressure of expectations, and the weight of his aspirations. He closed his eyes for a moment, visualizing the perfect run, the precise movements, the seamless coordination between himself and RJ. He saw the rope flying, the calf tumbling, the smooth dismount, the judges' times.

Then, he opened his eyes, his gaze fixed on the gate. He felt the familiar surge of adrenaline, the mixture of excitement and fear. He spurred RJ forward, the horse launching into action with a surge of power and precision. The calf burst from the chute, a blur of brown fur and thrashing hooves. Carl felt the familiar thrill of the chase, the adrenaline coursing through his veins. Time seemed to slow down, stretching out; each movement was deliberate and precise. He roped the calf with a fluid grace, the loop settling perfectly around its legs.

The ground trembled beneath RJ's powerful strides as he effortlessly turned the calf, the roped animal struggling in vain. Carl's hands worked swiftly, dismounting with a practiced ease and speed. The dust swirled around them, the crowd holding their breath. It was a masterful performance, a testament to years of dedication and countless hours of training. The seconds stretched into an eternity before the final time was announced. The announcer's voice, clear and precise, filled the stadium, relaying the results with precision.

The time was perfect, or nearly so. The relief that washed over him was immense, but a single point shy of perfect felt like a heavy rock on his shoulders. It was good, but not good enough. The pressure of the competition hadn't lessened; it had simply shifted. He'd done well, but the possibility of victory still hung in the balance, dependent on the performances of his rivals.

The subsequent few runs were a blur of motion, a rollercoaster of emotions. He watched competitors, some performing flawlessly, others faltering under the pressure. The standings shifted with each run, the tension mounting with every passing moment. Each competitor presented a new challenge, a new test of his skills, and he had to maintain his focus despite the mounting uncertainty.

The final results were announced, each name called with a building suspense that threatened to burst. Finally, his name was called. A wave of relief and euphoria washed over him, almost overwhelming. He had done it. He had qualified for the next stage of the competition, his dream of a rodeo scholarship still alive, still within reach. But there was no time to bask in the glory of the achievement. The regional finals were over, but the greater challenge-the ultimate test—still lay ahead. The road to nationals was long, arduous, and fraught with peril; yet, he was ready to face it. His spirit unbowed, his determination unwavering. The pressure had been immense, the struggle had been real, and yet they had prevailed. The journey had been a trial by fire, forging Carl and RJ into an indomitable force. And as he looked to the future, he knew that the road ahead would be equally challenging, but with the experience of this hard-fought victory behind them, they were prepared to face whatever came their way. Their eyes were set firmly on the horizon; the nationals beckoned.

The tension in the arena was a palpable entity that vibrated in the air, thick and heavy with the scent of dust and sweat. Carl felt it pressing down on him, a physical weight that made it hard to breathe. He'd seen the other competitors earlier, their faces grim with determination, their bodies coiled tight with nervous energy. Now, watching them perform, he saw the culmination of months, maybe years, of dedication poured into those few seconds of adrenaline-fueled action.

First came the events like barrel racing. A lithe young woman named Kayla, known for her aggressive riding style and uncanny connection with her palomino mare, blazed through the course. The crowd roared its approval as the mare, a blur of golden muscle, navigated the turns with breathtaking precision, Kayla barely seeming to touch the reins. Carl admired her skill; Kayla was a serious contender, a force to be reckoned with. He'd seen her at several rodeos throughout the season, and she always delivered a performance that was both beautiful and brutally efficient. This was no exception.

Then came the steer wrestling, a brutal ballet of strength and agility. This year's regional finals featured some serious contenders in steer wrestling; several competitors were known for their aggressive style and lightning-fast takedowns. Each wrestler seemed to possess superhuman strength, their bodies a whirlwind of motion as they wrestled the massive steers to the ground. The ground shook with the impact of each takedown, the air filled with the sounds of grunting muscles, and the crowd erupted in thunderous applause. Carl watched, his heart pounding in his chest, learning from each performance, analyzing their techniques, searching for any subtle flaw he might exploit in his run.

The anticipation for the calf roping was almost unbearable. The air thrummed with a collective held breath. Carl watched as competitor after competitor entered the arena, their faces set in expressions of grim determination. He saw the familiar faces of his friends and rivals. There was Jake, a quiet but fiercely competitive kid from a neighboring town, renowned for his lightning-fast roping skills. Then came Marcus, a lanky kid with nerves of steel, whose calm demeanor belied a remarkable talent for keeping a cool head under pressure. He also knew the more seasoned competitors, some of whom had participated in the regional finals for years. These older competitors were seasoned veterans of the rodeo, with years of experience under their belts.

Each run was a microcosm of the competition itself—a tense dance between man and animal, skill and instinct, preparation and chance. Some runs were picture perfect, flawlessly executed from start to finish. Others were marred by clumsy mistakes, near misses, and frustrating errors. Carl saw a competitor struggle to get his rope around the calf's legs; the calf bucked, danced, and finally escaped, leaving the competitor dejected and frustrated. He felt a pang of sympathy mixed with a grim determination. This competition was not for the faint of heart.

The pressure was immense. Each competitor carried the weight of months of preparation, endless hours of practice, and the hopes and dreams of their families and communities on their shoulders.

Then, it was Carl's turn. The announcer's voice boomed over the loudspeakers, calling his name. He felt the familiar butterflies in his stomach, a cocktail of nerves and excitement. He took a deep breath, trying to calm the frantic rhythm of his heart. He glanced over at his uncle Joe, who offered a reassuring smile and a subtle nod. That simple act was enough to soothe the rising anxiety.

He mounted RJ, feeling the familiar comfort of the saddle beneath him, the steady rhythm of his horse's breath against his leg. RJ, as if sensing the intensity of the moment, stood perfectly still, his muscles tense but relaxed. Their connection was a silent language, a bond forged in shared sweat and countless hours of practice. They were one, a single entity ready to face the challenge ahead.

The gate swung open, releasing the calf. It burst forth, a brown blur against the dusty arena floor. Carl's hand shot out, his movements fluid and precise. The rope flew, a perfect arc against the sky. It settled around the calf's legs with the practiced ease of a seasoned professional. The thrilling chase began; it was a dance of controlled chaos, a test of skill and timing.

RJ responded with power and grace, smoothly turning the calf. Carl dismounted with a speed and efficiency honed over years of practice, the dust swirling around him. He wrestled the calf down to the ground, his movements quick and precise. The crowd roared its approval, the sound a wave that crashed over him, momentarily overwhelming. He'd done it; he'd executed the run perfectly. A wave of relief washed over him, almost knocking him off his feet.

The tension remained; however. The times were still to come. He felt a tightening in his chest as he oversaw the judges assess his performance, their faces impassive masks that gave nothing away. The judge's times were called out—a near-perfect run, yet not quite a perfect time. He held his breath, still not sure of his standing against the other competitors. Each succeeding run felt like an eternity, each competitor's time a hammer blow, either lifting his spirits or sinking them.

The announcement of the final times felt like a lifetime, a slow and agonizingly torturous process that left him breathless. When his name was finally called, a wave of relief washed over him, overwhelming and profound. He had done it. He had qualified for the United States Finals. But even as the euphoria swelled, he knew the hard work wasn't over. The victory was sweet, but the road ahead was still long and challenging. The next leg of the journey to the national competition was just around the corner, and Carl was ready. The nationals awaited.

The regional finals weren't just about flawless execution; they were a crucible, forging competitors in the fires of unexpected adversity. Carl's seemingly perfect run, while earning him a high time, wasn't without its near-misses. The calf, a particularly spirited animal with a surprising burst of speed, had almost slipped his grasp just as he was about to make his final throw. For a heart-stopping moment, the rope hung loose, the calf threatening to bolt. It was a fraction of a second, a blink of an eye, but in that instant, Carl's years of training kicked in. His instincts, honed by countless hours spent practicing in the dusty arena, took over. With a lightning-fast adjustment, he'd regained control, his rope snaking around the calf's legs with a precision that defied the chaos of the moment. The crowd held its breath, the collective gasp audible even above the usual roar. Then, the wave of relief that followed his successful catch was immense.

The next competitor, a seasoned veteran named Boone, faced a distinct challenge. Boone, known for his calm and methodical approach, had an unexpected mishap at the start. His horse, a magnificent paint stallion, stumbled just as the gate swung open, throwing Boone off balance. The stallion quickly recovered, but the delay was enough to disrupt Boone's rhythm. He managed to rope the calf, but the initial setback cost him valuable seconds, ultimately affecting his final time. It was a stark reminder that even the most experienced cowboys are not immune to unexpected obstacles. The crowd felt for Boone, knowing he had thrown a nearly perfect run, apart from the unfortunate stumble.

Later, during the tie-down roping, a sudden squall swept across the arena, whipping dust and sand into a swirling vortex. Visibility was drastically reduced, turning the already challenging event into a near-blind gamble. The wind buffeted the contestants and their horses, creating a chaotic environment of unpredictable conditions. Several competitors struggled, their horses spooked by the sudden change in conditions. One competitor's horse bolted, throwing the rider to the ground. Thankfully, the rider wasn't seriously hurt, but the incident highlighted the unforgiving nature of rodeo. The rodeo officials, however, decided to continue the competition. The event proceeded, with the competitors adapting to the severe and sudden weather change.

Carl, facing the same blinding sandstorm, had to rely on his instincts and RJ's exceptional responsiveness. He couldn't see the calf clearly, but he could feel RJ's tension, sensing the horse's anticipation. Trusting his horse implicitly, Carl followed RJ's lead, the horse instinctively navigating the wind-whipped arena with surprising grace. It was a testament to the deep bond they shared, a connection forged through years of working together. He roped the calf successfully despite the near-zero visibility, proving his adaptability and the powerful partnership with his horse. This exceptional run even caught the attention of the judges, who later complimented his skill and composure.

The challenges extended beyond the immediate arena. A critical piece of equipment malfunctioned during the competition, causing the schedule to be thrown into disarray. A timing gate failed, requiring a complex and time-consuming repair. The delay heightened the tension, compounding the pressure on the waiting competitors. The atmosphere grew thick with anxious anticipation, the murmurs of the crowd a palpable undercurrent to the storm raging outside. Carl used the break to clear his head, focusing on his breathing and maintaining his mental fortitude. He knew that allowing stress to consume him would only hinder his performance, so he remained calm, using the extra time to practice visualization techniques and to reassure RJ.

The unexpected delays also created a ripple effect, changing the flow of the competition and impacting the overall schedule. The longer wait increased the intensity and pressure on all the competitors, testing their mental and physical stamina. Some competitors visibly grew restless under the pressure, their body language betraying the mounting tension. Carl, however, remained calm and collected, focusing on his breathing and visualizing his next run. The additional time allowed him to reinforce his confidence further and improve his connection with RJ.

Beyond the technical challenges and weather setbacks, Carl also faced subtle psychological pressures. The fierce competition, the constant weight of expectations, and the relentless pursuit of excellence all took their toll. He found himself questioning his abilities, battling doubts that gnawed at his confidence. This was particularly true in the calf roping event, the one he was most passionate about. He felt the mounting pressure of the times and the expectations surrounding his performance. There were moments when he felt the weight of the expectations crushing him. The pressure to perform flawlessly, to live up to his high standards, and to meet the expectations of his family and friends was immense.

He found solace in unexpected places. A casual conversation with a veteran competitor, a quiet moment spent grooming RJ, and a supportive word from his uncle all helped to recenter him. These small moments reminded him of his passion for the sport, his love for his horse, and the steady, familiar support of his family. His uncle, a legendary team roper, reminded him that rodeo wasn't just about winning but about perseverance, learning from mistakes, and enjoying the ride. This simple pep talk reinvigorated Carl. It made him focus on his love for the sport and not let the stress get the better of him.

Throughout the regional finals, Carl discovered a resilience he hadn't known he possessed. He learned that success in rodeo wasn't just about skill and talent, but about adaptability, mental toughness, and the ability to overcome unexpected obstacles. He'd learned to handle setbacks with grace, to adjust his strategies in the face of adversity, and to draw strength from the steady, familiar support of his loved ones. The experience cemented his understanding that rodeo wasn't just a competition, but a journey of personal growth, a testament to the power of perseverance and the importance of embracing challenges as opportunities for learning. The pressure, the setbacks, the unexpected twists—all of it shaped him, making him a stronger, more resilient cowboy. His experience at the regional finals wasn't just about qualifying for nationals; it was a defining moment, a pivotal experience that would shape his future approach to life and competition. He stood ready, not only for the national competition, but also for whatever other unexpected challenges lay ahead. The journey continued. The nationals were within his grasp.

The arena lights glinted off the sweat beading on Carl's brow. The hush before his final run was almost palpable, the expectant silence broken only by the rhythmic thump of his own heart. He'd watched the other competitors in the calf roping final, their performances a rollercoaster of near misses and stunning successes. Boone's stumble had been a sobering reminder of how quickly fortune could shift, while others had demonstrated breathtaking skill and precision. The pressure was immense, a physical weight pressing down on his chest, making each breath a conscious effort.

He glanced at RJ, his trusty horse. The paint stallion stood motionless, his muscles coiled tight, mirroring Carl's internal tension. RJ's breath plumed faintly in the crisp evening air, a silent testament to their shared anticipation. Their connection transcended words; years of moments lived shoulder-to-shoulder had woven an unspoken language between them, a quiet conversation understood only by the two of them. He ran a hand over RJ's smooth coat, feeling the strength beneath the sleek hide. It was a ritual, a grounding moment that calmed his racing thoughts.

The announcer's voice boomed over the loudspeaker, jolting Carl back to the present. His name was called. This was it, the moment of truth. He took a deep, steadying breath, trying to center himself and focus on the task at hand. The crowd's murmur swelled, a rising tide of anticipation, a collective holding of breath that amplified the pressure. He felt the weight of expectation not only from the judges but also from his family, friends, and even himself.

As he mounted RJ, the familiar weight of the saddle grounded him. It was a comfort, a familiar presence that helped him to focus. The gate swung open, and they were off. The calf, a particularly robust specimen, exploded from its chute, a blur of brown and white against the dusty arena. RJ responded instantly, his powerful muscles propelling them into a smooth, controlled pursuit. Carl's focus was absolute, his senses sharpened, honed by years of training. He saw nothing but the calf, his mind a void except for the execution of the task.

The chase was a ballet of controlled chaos. RJ tracked the calf with uncanny precision, every movement a seamless collaboration between horse and rider. Carl leaned into the turn, his body flowing with the horse's movements, a testament to their practiced harmony. The feeling was exhilarating, a blend of adrenaline and concentration so intense it pushed away all doubts and fears. He felt like an extension of RJ, their bodies and minds working in perfect synchronicity.

The throw was everything. It had to be precise, swift, and accurate. Any hesitation, any miscalculation, could mean the difference between victory and defeat. He felt the rope leave his hands, the familiar weight and feel guiding his aim. The loop sailed through the air, an elegant arc against the twilight sky, a testament to years of unwavering dedication and practice.

Time seemed to stretch, slow down, and almost come to a standstill. The loop landed, perfectly encircling the calf's legs. The animal bucked, the rope taut, but it held. The successful catch triggered a wave of relief so profound it washed over him, leaving him almost breathless. He dismounted, his heart still pounding in his chest, his hands slightly trembling, but his face reflected a quiet pride and satisfaction.

The judges scrutinized his performance, their faces impassive, betraying nothing of their evaluation. The silence stretched, every tick of the clock echoing in the hushed arena. It felt like an eternity, a time frozen in suspense. The tension was almost unbearable, a physical weight pressing down on him, his body rigid with anticipation.

Then, the announcement came. A roar erupted from the crowd, a thunderous wave of sound that washed over him, drowning out all other thoughts and feelings. He had done it. His time was high enough; he had won. The journey to this moment had been long and arduous, a testament to his perseverance and resilience. All the early mornings, the grueling practices, the setbacks, the sacrifices — they all culminated in this one glorious victory.

The relief was immediate, a cathartic release that shook him to his core. He allowed himself a small smile, a rare expression that only appeared in such extreme moments of overwhelming victory. Tears welled in his eyes, a mixture of joy, relief, and the exhaustion of months of intense training and competition. He looked up towards the stands, catching sight of his mother's beaming face, her eyes filled with pride and happiness. His uncle, a legendary team roper himself, gave him a small, yet knowing nod —a silent gesture of mutual understanding, a connection shared only by those who understood the grueling demands and the rewarding feeling of rodeo life. The moment captured a lifetime of effort, hard work, and the incredible relationship he had with his horse, RJ.

The victory wasn't just about the win itself; it was a symbol of his growth, his resilience, and the steady, familiar support of his family and friends. He'd faced adversity and emerged victorious, a testament to his steadfast determination and his ability to overcome challenges. He had proven to himself, and to the world, that he could succeed under immense pressure.

The euphoria of winning didn't last long; the reality of the United States Finals was already looming large. He knew that the regional finals were merely a stepping stone, a necessary hurdle on his path to a college scholarship. The upcoming competition would be even more challenging, with competitors from across the country, each equally skilled and determined. The work ahead of him would be even greater. But for now, he basked in the glow of victory, allowing himself a moment of well-deserved celebration before focusing on the next challenge. He had conquered the regional finals, but his journey was far from over. His eyes were on the United States Finals, a pinnacle he was determined to reach and destroy. The regional victory was a testament to his perseverance and fueled his ambitions for the future.

The roar of the crowd was deafening, a wave of sound that crashed over Carl, washing away the tension and anxiety that had clung to him like a second skin for the past few hours. Confetti rained down, a kaleidoscope of color swirling in the arena lights, a celebratory blizzard marking his triumph. He sat atop RJ, the paint stallion still quivering slightly from the adrenaline of the run, but now seemingly as content as Carl felt. The weight of the saddle, usually a comforting presence, felt almost insignificant now, replaced by the lightness of victory.

His uncle, a living legend in the rodeo world, rode over, his weathered face splitting into a grin that showcased a lifetime of triumphs and tribulations. He dismounted, his movements as fluid and precise as Carl had ever seen, a testament to years spent honing his craft. A hearty clap on Carl's shoulder shook him from his stunned silence. "Well, kiddo," his uncle boomed, his voice thick with emotion, "you did it. You really, truly did it."

The words were simple, yet they carried the weight of years of shared understanding —a silent conversation between a seasoned champion and his rising protégé. They didn't need flowery language; the unspoken understanding, the bond forged through sweat, shared anxieties, and countless hours of practice, spoke volumes. His uncle's nod of approval was more valuable than any trophy.

His mother rushed into the arena, her face radiant with pride, her eyes brimming with unshed tears. She embraced him tightly, a hug that squeezed the breath from his lungs, but felt wonderfully comforting. Her scent, a familiar mix of lavender and sweat, was a reassuring anchor in the whirlwind of emotions that threatened to overwhelm him. He mumbled incoherently, a mixture of joy and exhaustion escaping his lips, but her embrace held all the understanding he needed.

The next few moments were a blur of congratulations, handshakes, and back pats. Friends, competitors, even strangers, came to offer their praise and admiration. The euphoria was intoxicating, a heady mix of relief, joy, and the sheer disbelief of having accomplished such a monumental feat. He felt a surge of pride, not just for his accomplishment, but for all the hard work, dedication, and steady, familiar support that had led him to this moment.

The scent of sawdust and leather filled the air, mingling with the sweet perfume of victory. The rhythmic pounding of a country song played faintly in the background, the celebratory music a vibrant backdrop to the joyous chaos. He allowed himself to bask in the glow of accomplishment. It was a moment he had dreamed of, visualized countless times during those grueling hours of practice, when the only sounds were the rhythmic thud of his heartbeat and the soft whinny of RJ.

The presentation of the trophy was an anticlimactic yet satisfying event. The weight of the trophy itself was surprisingly heavy, a tangible representation of the years of effort, sacrifice, and perseverance that had gone into it.

He gave a small, almost hesitant, speech, his voice trembling slightly as he thanked his family, his uncle, his friends, his sponsor, and especially RJ. The crowd roared its approval, a thunderous applause that shook the very ground beneath his feet. He felt a profound sense of gratitude, and a deep appreciation for the people who had been instrumental in his journey. His success wasn't solely his own; it was a collective effort, a testament to the power of teamwork, support, and shared ambition.

Backstage, amidst the celebratory chaos, the reality of his victory began to sink in. The regional championship was a huge milestone, but it wasn't the end goal. The United States Finals loomed large, a challenge even greater than the one he had just overcome. The competition would be stiffer, the pressure more intense, and the stakes even higher. He knew he needed to maintain his focus, continue training, refine his skills, and prepare for the ultimate test of his abilities.

His uncle pulled him aside, his tone shifting from celebratory to focused and strategic. He pointed out areas where Carl could improve, offering subtle suggestions and critiques that only a seasoned champion could provide. He spoke of maintaining his focus, reminding Carl of the importance of discipline, consistency, and unwavering dedication. The brief conversation shifted the momentum; the afterglow of celebration was replaced by the familiar buzz of anticipation and the quiet hum of preparation for the next challenge.

The next few weeks were a blur of practice, fine-tuning his technique, and strengthening the bond with RJ. They spent hours in the arena, refining their maneuvers, honing their precision. The collaboration between man and horse was undeniable, a testament to years of shared training and unwavering trust. Carl's dedication was unwavering, fueled by the adrenaline of victory and the determination to push himself even further.

He also focused on strengthening his mental game. He worked with a sports psychologist, learning techniques to manage pressure, build focus, and maintain composure in high-pressure situations. He discovered that mental preparation was just as crucial as physical training, a critical aspect of the rodeo lifestyle often overlooked. He found that the calm confidence he developed allowed him to manage pressure and remain focused on his technique rather than his anxieties. This was a crucial element of his future success.

The celebration of his regional championship was a welcome respite from the relentless pressure of the season, a moment to savor the rewards of his dedication and hard work. However, it was also a reminder that his journey was far from over. The United States Finals awaited, a challenge that would test the limits of his skill, his determination, and his unwavering partnership with RJ. As the weeks flew by, he knew the celebration was a fuel to power him forward, a source of energy to propel him towards the ultimate goal: national champion.

Chapter 6: State Finals

The state finals weren't just another rodeo; it was a different beast entirely. The regional championship had been a hard-fought battle, but this? This was the culmination of a year's worth of sweat, sacrifice, and relentless pursuit of excellence. The air crackled with a different kind of energy, a palpable tension that hung heavy in the air, thicker than the dust kicked up by countless horses. Carl could feel it in the bone-jarring vibrations that pulsed from the ground as the other competitors practiced, their horses restless under the pressure, their riders equally tense. This wasn't the familiar comfort of his regional rivals; these were the best of the best, honed to a razor's edge.

He ran a hand through his hair, feeling the familiar prickle of anxiety. RJ, sensing his rider's unease, nuzzled against him, a comforting weight against his leg. The paint stallion, usually a picture of controlled energy, was a little more skittish than usual. Even RJ could sense the difference in the atmosphere, the heightened stakes of this competition.

The first day of competition was a blur of adrenaline-fueled runs and nail-biting finishes. Carl watched other competitors, his eyes scanning their techniques, analyzing their strategies, and mentally noting their strengths and weaknesses. He saw seasoned veterans with decades of experience, their movements fluid and precise, a testament to years of dedication and relentless pursuit of perfection. He noticed the young guns, fearless and aggressive, their raw talent matched only by their youthful exuberance. Some seemed to be almost instinctively connected with their horses, a symbiotic dance of skill and trust that left Carl awestruck. He saw the tension etched on their faces as they approached the gate, the fear of failure and the desire to succeed locked in a desperate embrace. He knew that even a momentary lapse in concentration could cost him the competition.

His runs were a mix of brilliant successes and frustrating near misses. There were moments of sheer exhilaration, where everything clicked — the perfect dismount, the flawless roping, the horse's responsive movement, all working together in flawless harmony. In those runs, time seemed to slow down, his every muscle working in perfect concert with RJ's, the result a picture of graceful power and precision. But then there were other runs; runs where his rope slipped, where RJ stumbled, where the slightest hesitation cost him precious seconds. Those runs, plagued by self-doubt, were excruciating, a bitter reminder of the unforgiving nature of competition. Each mistake served as a harsh lesson, a reminder of the need for continuous improvement and unwavering focus. He found himself pushing himself beyond his perceived limits, tapping into a reservoir of mental and physical reserves that he hadn't known he possessed.

His uncle, ever observant, provided invaluable feedback between runs. His critiques were sharp and concise, devoid of sentimentality, but always laced with a bedrock of support. He didn't sugarcoat his observations; he called out Carl's mistakes with brutal honesty, pointing out areas where he needed to refine his technique, his posture, even the subtle nuances of his communication with RJ. His uncle emphasized that even the most minor details could be the difference between victory and defeat at this level of competition. He stresses the importance of mental fortitude, maintaining a calm and focused demeanor despite immense pressure, and harnessing his nerves into productive energy.

The nights were long, filled with a restless energy. Sleep was elusive, the constant replay of successful and unsuccessful runs playing on an endless loop in his mind. He'd review his runs in his head, analyzing each movement, each decision, searching for ways to improve. His uncle's words echoed in his ears: "It's not just about the roping, Carl. It's about control, precision, and partnership. It's about you and RJ becoming one."

The mental game proved to be as demanding as the physical one. The sheer number of competitors, each one striving for the same coveted spot, created a pressure cooker of intense competition. The weight of expectation, both his own and his family's, added to the pressure. But he was learning. The sports psychologist he'd started working with had helped him develop strategies for managing his anxiety, techniques for quieting the internal chatter that threatened to overwhelm him. He discovered the importance of visualization, the power of picturing himself performing perfectly, of running the entire event in his mind before he even set foot in the arena. He practiced mindfulness techniques, learning to focus on his breath, to center himself, to bring himself back to the present moment.

The competition was fierce, and Carl felt the pressure mounting. He watched friends stumble, their runs cut short, their dreams unraveling. The camaraderie that had united them at regionals was fading, replaced by a ruthless determination. The stakes had never been higher.

In the final round, Carl faced the current state champion, a seasoned veteran named Jake. Jake was legendary, known for his lightning-fast roping skills and his uncanny ability to remain calm under immense pressure. The crowd buzzed with anticipation, a palpable excitement hanging in the air. Carl knew this was it; this was his biggest challenge yet.

He focused on his breathing, clearing his mind, and tuning out the roar of the crowd. He looked at RJ, and the horse responded with a reassuring calmness. The connection between them was unwavering, a silent promise of shared effort and mutual trust. As the gate swung open, Carl felt a surge of adrenaline, a mixture of fear and excitement. This was his moment; this was the challenge he'd been working towards all year. He felt the energy surge through him, channeling his nerves into pure, focused energy. The run was a blur of motion—the perfect start, the precise timing, the smooth dismount—a ballet of man and horse, working together in perfect harmony. The crowd erupted as he completed his run, a thunderous roar that shook the ground beneath his feet. His heart pounded in his chest, and he looked at his uncle, who gave a curt nod, a silent acknowledgement of the effort. The tense silence that followed was almost as ominous as the previous roar had been.

As the times came in, Carl held his breath. The tension was almost unbearable. He knew he had given it his all; there was nothing left to give. The announcer's voice was clear and distinct, announcing his name as the state champion. The sense of relief that washed over him was absolute. He embraced his uncle and his mother, their joy mirroring his own.

The moment was overwhelming, filled with a joyous relief that eclipsed even the previous victory. The celebration was underway, but he knew, even in that moment, that this was only the beginning of another journey and that the United States Finals, a new and even greater challenge, lay ahead. The road to national champion was far from over, but he was ready. The state championship was just another step in the long journey ahead. The victory felt bittersweet, a moment of celebration, reflection, and preparation for what lay ahead. He knew that his journey would continue, a challenging but exhilarating path toward his ultimate dream.

The adrenaline rush of the first day had faded, giving way to a quiet intensity. The state finals weren't just about physical skill; they were a grueling test of mental endurance. Carl knew this intellectually, but the reality was a completely different beast. The pressure was a tangible thing, a weight pressing down on his chest, making each breath feel labored. He saw it in the drawn faces of other competitors, in the tense muscles of their horses, in the hushed whispers and anxious glances exchanged between families in the stands.

He sought refuge in the steady rhythm of routine. His pre-competition ritual, a deliberate sequence meant to center him, felt more vital than ever. It began with grooming RJ, a meditative practice that deepened their bond. The feel of the horse's coat beneath his hands, the measured strokes of the brush, and the careful cleaning of hooves grounded him, anchoring him in the present and quieting the anxieties that threatened to overwhelm him.

After grooming, came the visualization. He closed his eyes, picturing himself flawlessly executing his run. He saw himself smoothly guiding RJ into the arena, the horse responding effortlessly to his every cue. He visualized the perfect loop of his rope, the calf's quick and decisive fall, the swift dismount, the clock stopping with a time that would secure his place in the championship round. He repeated this mental rehearsal several times, each time strengthening the neural pathways associated with successful performance. He didn't just visualize success; he felt it, the exhilaration coursing through his veins, the taste of victory sweet on his tongue.

His sports psychologist, Dr. Ramirez, had introduced him to mindfulness techniques, teaching him to focus on his breath, to anchor himself in the present moment. This was harder than it sounded. The constant barrage of internal chatter — the self-doubt, the fear of failure, the pressure to perform — made it a continuous battle to quiet the noise in his head. Dr. Ramirez had emphasized the importance of recognizing these thoughts without judgment, allowing them to pass like clouds across the sky. It wasn't about eliminating negative thoughts, but rather about not allowing them to dictate his actions.

He found solace in small, quiet moments, stolen between runs. Sitting in the shade of a nearby tree, with RJ grazing peacefully close by, he focused on his breath and felt the gentle rise and fall of his chest. He took in the details around him, the vibrant wildflowers, the texture of sunbaked earth beneath his feet, and the distant hum of the crowd. These small acts of mindfulness helped him reclaim calm amid the chaos. They became a lifeline, reconnecting him to the present moment and easing the crushing pressure of the competition.

His uncle remained his unwavering pillar of support. He watched Carl's every run, offering feedback that was both brutally honest and deeply encouraging. His uncle understood both the mental and physical aspects of the game, reminding Carl that the pressure was not just external but also internal. He taught Carl to recognize the signs of mounting anxiety — the tightening of his muscles, the quickening of his breath, the racing of his heart — and to employ coping mechanisms to manage them. He emphasized the importance of self-compassion, acknowledging that setbacks were inevitable, and stressed the crucial role of learning from mistakes.

Carl learned to channel his anxiety into productive energy. The adrenaline, instead of paralyzing him, became a fuel that sharpened his focus and enhanced his performance. He discovered that the key wasn't to eliminate the pressure, but to harness it, to use it to his advantage. He learned to embrace the fear, acknowledging it as a sign that he was pushing himself to his limits, that he was engaged in a battle that demanded his full attention and complete commitment.

The second day of the competition saw him perform with a newfound calm and confidence. He approached each run with a clear mind, focused on the task at hand rather than the outcome. He concentrated on the mechanics of the roping, the rhythm of his movements, and the subtle cues exchanged between him and RJ. He didn't allow himself to be distracted by the times, the rankings, or the performance of other competitors. He focused on the present, on the task at hand, and gave it his all, trusting in his training, preparation, and partnership with RJ.

One run in particular stands out. He had a slightly slow start, but instead of panicking, he remained calm, making corrections as he went. He felt the tension in his muscles, but he didn't fight it. He breathed, focusing on his technique and trusting his instincts. RJ responded perfectly to his subtle cues, and the run culminated in a flawless catch, a time that put him back into contention. This wasn't just about the roping; it was a demonstration of his mastery over his mind, his ability to remain calm and focused even under intense pressure. That run became a testament to the mental toughness he'd cultivated over the season, a victory not just over the calf, but also over his self-doubt.

The final round arrived, and the atmosphere was electric. The crowd roared with anticipation, a wave of sound washing over Carl. But he was prepared. He had learned to harness the energy of the crowd to his advantage, to feed off the excitement and transform the pressure into a source of strength. He felt the familiar tingle of anxiety, but he didn't fight it. He acknowledged it, accepted it, and then focused on his breath, bringing himself back to the present moment.

His final run was a masterpiece, a perfect blend of skill, precision, and unwavering focus. It was a testament to his months of relentless training, his steadfast dedication, and his hard-won mental toughness. Every movement was fluid, every decision precise. It was a performance that showcased not just his roping skills but the strength of his mental game, his ability to perform under pressure, and the profound connection he had forged with RJ.

The moment the final time flashed onto the timeboard, Carl knew. The roar of the crowd was deafening. This wasn't just a victory; it was a culmination of years of hard work, dedication, and unwavering mental fortitude. The years of relentless practice, the countless hours spent honing his skills, the support of his family and friends, the guidance of his uncle and Dr. Ramirez — all of it converged in this single, triumphant moment. The state championship title was a testament not only to his physical prowess but also to his resilience, persistence, and unwavering belief in himself. He had faced adversity, overcome challenges, and conquered his mind. And as he stood there, the state champion, he knew this was just the beginning of his journey, a stepping stone to even bigger dreams and more challenging competitions. The United States Finals awaited, and he was ready.

The euphoria of the state championship win was short-lived. The celebratory dinner with his family, the congratulatory calls from friends, the feeling of accomplishment — it all faded into the background as a new, chilling reality settled in. The United States Finals were looming, and a series of unexpected setbacks threatened to derail his dreams.

First came the injury. It happened during a practice run, a seemingly innocuous movement that resulted in a sharp, searing pain in his right shoulder. The initial diagnosis was a strained rotator cuff, a common injury among rodeo athletes, but the severity of the injury was concerning. The pain was intense, limiting his range of motion and making even the simplest roping maneuvers excruciating. His uncle, a veteran of countless rodeo injuries, examined the shoulder with a grim expression. He knew the toll the demanding sport took on the body, the constant strain on muscles and joints.

"It's not good, Carl," his uncle said, his voice heavy with concern. "We need to get this checked out properly."

The trip to the orthopedic specialist confirmed their worst fears. The strain was severe, and rest was crucial. But rest was the enemy in Carl's current situation. The United States Finals were only weeks away, and he was already pushing his body to its limits. The doctor recommended physical therapy and anti-inflammatory medication, but warned that aggressive treatment could risk further damage. The pressure was immense. Could he recover in time? Could he even compete? The doubt gnawed at him, a persistent, insidious whisper that threatened to undermine his confidence.

The setback was compounded by another unexpected challenge — a sudden withdrawal of sponsorship. "Rodeo Ready," a prominent Western apparel company, had been Carl's primary sponsor for the past year, providing him with essential equipment and financial support. They'd been impressed by his skills and determined spirit, seeing a potential star in the making. But just as Carl was preparing for the United States Finals, they unexpectedly withdrew their sponsorship. The company cited unforeseen financial difficulties, a blow that left Carl reeling.

This wasn't just about the money, although the loss was significant. Rodeo Ready provided him with top-of-the-line equipment, custom-made to his specifications. Without their support, he would have to scramble for replacements, risking his performance. The thought sparked a wave of frustration. He felt betrayed. He had poured his heart into every rodeo, representing Rodeo Ready with pride, only to be cast aside when he needed them most.

The financial implications were equally daunting. The cost of travel, accommodation, entry fees, and equipment maintenance for the United States

Finals was substantial, a burden that now fell squarely on his family's shoulders. His mother, already struggling to balance work and family commitments, was now faced with the added pressure of securing the funding. The weight of responsibility pressed down on Carl, adding to his existing physical and emotional challenges. He hated that this weight was falling on his family; he desperately needed to find a solution.

The pressure intensified as the United States Finals drew closer. Each day was a battle against time and pain, a constant struggle to balance physical therapy with practice runs. The intense regimen left him exhausted, both physically and mentally. He pushed himself relentlessly, driven by an unwavering determination to compete, despite the obstacles. He couldn't let his family, his uncle, or himself down.

His uncle, ever the resourceful problem-solver, stepped in. He used his extensive network of contacts within the rodeo community to secure temporary sponsorship deals, finding smaller companies and individual donors who were willing to contribute to Carl's cause. He tirelessly searched for replacement equipment, negotiating deals and securing essential supplies. He became Carl's manager, strategist, and steady, familiar support system.

But even with his uncle's help, the challenges didn't simply disappear. The shoulder pain lingered, a constant reminder of his limitations. He struggled to find the same fluidity and precision in his roping, the movements feeling stiff and awkward. He constantly battled self-doubt, the insidious whisper of failure creeping into his thoughts.

Then, there was the mental game. The accumulated stress of injury, financial uncertainty, and the pressure of the United States Finals took its toll. He found himself struggling with anxiety and insomnia, his dreams haunted by visions of failure. Dr. Ramirez, his sports psychologist, became a lifeline, helping him navigate the emotional turmoil, reminding him of his strengths, and assisting him in developing coping mechanisms to manage the pressure. Dr. Ramirez helped him focus on the process, not the outcome, reminding him that his performance in a single competition didn't define his worth.

Carl learned to break down the task into smaller, more manageable pieces. He focused on the details, honing his technique, perfecting each movement, one step at a time. He practiced visualization exercises, focusing on his ideal run to reinforce the neural pathways associated with success. He found solace in the simple act of grooming RJ, finding comfort in the familiar rhythm of his routine. RJ, his trusty companion, sensed his anxiety and provided a quiet, comforting presence.

His family's support became a constant source of strength. His mother, despite her own anxieties, remained his unwavering cheerleader, lifting him when he felt like giving up. His father, usually reserved, offered steady encouragement, reminding Carl of his resilience and determination. Together, they rallied behind him, providing the emotional and practical support he needed to persevere through the challenges ahead.

The day of the United States Finals arrived, and Carl walked into the arena with a mixture of apprehension and determination. The pain in his shoulder was still present, a nagging reminder of the setbacks he'd faced, but he refused to let it define him. He focused on his breath, on the rhythm of his movements, on the connection he had with RJ. He approached each run with a clear mind, focusing on the process, trusting his preparation, and relying on his partnership with RJ.

He didn't win the United States Finals. The injury affected his performance; the pain was a significant obstacle. He didn't achieve his ultimate goal of securing a college scholarship. But as he rode off the arena, his head held high, he knew something profound. He had faced unexpected setbacks, and he had persevered. He had shown incredible strength and courage, not just in his physical performance, but also in his resilience against adversity. And in that realization, there was a victory far more significant than any trophy or scholarship could provide. The journey, the struggle, the unexpected setbacks, the triumphs, and the lessons learned - all of it shaped him, making him stronger, wiser, and more determined than ever. He knew this was just one chapter in his rodeo story, and there were many more rodeos to compete in. The United States Finals might not have delivered the desired result, but it had forged within him a spirit that would endure. The true victory lay in his unwavering spirit.

The hushed whispers of the rodeo grounds felt like a suffocating blanket. The air, usually thick with the electric energy of competition, was heavy with the weight of Carl's anxieties. He'd pushed himself to the brink, defying the pain in his shoulder, fueled by the steady, familiar support of his family and the quiet determination that had always been his hallmark. But the United States

Finals were a different beast entirely; a crucible that tested not only his physical prowess but also his mental fortitude. The weight of expectation, compounded by the recent setbacks, was almost unbearable.

He leaned against RJ's sturdy flank, the horse's calm presence a soothing balm against the storm raging within him. RJ, his loyal partner, nuzzled his hand, a silent reassurance that transcended words. Their bond, forged through countless hours of training and moments lived shoulder-to-shoulder, was a source of strength he couldn't underestimate. He wasn't just battling his demons; he was fighting for their shared dream.

The support of his team went far beyond the usual camaraderie of rodeo competitors. It wasn't just about cheering each other on from the sidelines; it was about a more profound sense of shared purpose, a collective understanding of the sacrifices and challenges inherent in their chosen path. His friends, seasoned rodeo athletes themselves, understood the pressure he was under. They didn't offer platitudes or empty words of encouragement; they provided practical help.

There was Miguel, a barrel racer with lightning-fast reflexes and a knack for fixing anything mechanical. He'd spent hours meticulously checking RJ's tack, ensuring everything was in perfect working order. He'd even managed to source a custom-made saddle pad designed to alleviate the pressure on Carl's injured shoulder, a small detail that made a world of difference.

Then there was Sarah, a graceful breakaway roper with a quiet strength that resonated deeply. She'd become Carl's confidante, a silent listener who offered understanding without judgment. She understood the constant pressure to perform, and the self-doubt that could creep in even at the peak of success. She knew his competitive fire was burning even brighter amidst the challenges, but it was crucial to manage that and be careful to ensure he didn't hurt himself further. She'd sit with him, offering quiet companionship and a listening ear, allowing him to vent his frustrations and fears without judgment.

His uncle, a legendary team roper, was more than just a mentor; he was a guiding light, a steadfast presence during the storm. His experience in handling injuries, navigating the complexities of sponsorship deals, and managing the pressures of high-stakes competition was invaluable. He became Carl's unofficial manager, tirelessly juggling logistics, contacting sponsors, arranging travel, and acting as his buffer against the outside world, shielding him from unnecessary stress. His calm, reassuring presence had been Carl's rock throughout the season. He'd seen Carl's determination, his unwavering belief in himself and RJ.

But the support network extended beyond his immediate circle. The high school rodeo community, often portrayed as fiercely competitive, revealed a surprising level of solidarity. Fellow competitors, rivals on the arena floor, offered words of encouragement, sharing tips and strategies, and providing support in both large and small ways. It was a reminder that the shared passion for the sport transcended individual rivalries.

The school's rodeo club, typically a hotbed of spirited competition and friendly banter, became a wellspring of support during this challenging time. Teammates who had previously seen Carl as a rival now viewed him as a teammate facing unique adversity. They rallied around him, offering practical help with chores, errands, and even childcare for his younger siblings, freeing his mother to focus on his recovery and the upcoming competition. They adjusted practice schedules to accommodate his limitations, ensuring he felt included and supported while minimizing the strain on his injured shoulder. Their collective effort demonstrated a level of camaraderie that extended beyond the rodeo arena, illustrating the strong bonds formed through shared experience and commitment.

The local community also rallied around Carl. News of his injury and sponsorship woes spread rapidly, prompting an outpouring of support from local businesses and individuals. A local feed store donated hay for RJ, a gesture that spoke volumes about the community's spirit. The owner of a Western wear shop offered Carl the use of his best equipment, ensuring that he had top-quality gear for the competition. A local diner provided meals for the family during the stressful period leading up to the nationals, reducing the pressure on his mother, who was working tirelessly to ensure that Carl had everything he needed. Their actions were more than mere gestures of goodwill; they were a demonstration of collective belief in Carl's potential and a testament to the strength of their community spirit. This collective community support showcased that everyone, whether friends, family, teammates, or even people who only heard about his situation, all had a part to play in helping to motivate him to continue with his rodeo competitions.

The support system wasn't merely about material assistance; it was also about providing emotional strength. The collective encouragement from his teammates, family, friends, mentors, and the broader community served as a powerful antidote to his self-doubt and anxiety. Their unwavering belief in him helped him regain his confidence and approach the United States Finals with renewed purpose and determination. It wasn't just about winning; it was about proving to himself, and to those who believed in him, that he could overcome adversity, that he could rise to the challenge.

The night before the competition, his family sat in a circle, offering words of encouragement and sharing fond memories from the past rodeo season, reminding him of his resilience. His uncle shared anecdotes of overcoming his past injuries, emphasizing the importance of perseverance and mental toughness. His friends reminisced about the victories and setbacks, sharing funny anecdotes and creating an uplifting, positive atmosphere designed to boost his morale. The shared laughter, shared memories, collective energy, and combined faith in him helped to melt away the lingering fear and anxiety. It was a powerful demonstration of team spirit, a reminder of the deep bonds forged within the rodeo community.

That night, Carl slept soundly, the weight of expectation replaced by a sense of calm and confidence. He wasn't just facing the United States Finals alone; he was facing them with an army of supporters at his side, an army that believed in him, even when he doubted himself. He knew, win or lose, he had already won the most important battle — the battle against despair. He knew that regardless of the results in the arena, he had shown himself capable of overcoming incredible hardship, and that this too would define him as a rodeo competitor. He had proven himself in every way possible. And that was a victory of its own. The feeling of being loved and supported meant the world to Carl, and this gave him the additional confidence and courage he needed to face the challenges ahead. This overwhelming sense of belonging empowered him, bolstering his determination and making him ready to face the United States Finals.

The roar of the crowd was a physical force, a wave crashing over Carl as he entered the arena. The bright lights, usually a source of nervous energy, felt different now; they felt like a spotlight illuminating his path, not a threat. He'd spent the last few weeks honing his skills, working on his technique, and most importantly, building his confidence. The support system he'd cultivated —a network of friends, family, and community members —had been instrumental in this transformation. He felt a sense of quiet resolve; a calm that settled deep in his bones, a stark contrast to the anxiety that had previously gripped him.

RJ, sensing his rider's calmness, stood poised and steady. Their Saginaw, unspoken yet profound, was palpable. Carl felt a surge of gratitude for his horse, his faithful companion who had endured the rigors of the season with unwavering loyalty. They were a team, bound by more than just a shared love for the sport. Their shared journey had forged a bond that was as strong and resilient as the leather of his saddle.

The atmosphere crackled with anticipation. The air hung thick with the scent of leather, dust, and nervous sweat. The competitors, his rivals and his comrades, eyed each other with a mixture of respect and apprehension. There was a palpable tension, a silent acknowledgement of the high stakes. Every eye was on Carl, each competitor and spectator fully aware of his recent struggles, and their eyes collectively conveyed their silent message: proving themselves at the State Finals.

His first run was flawless. The calf burst from the chute, a blur of brown against the dusty arena floor. Carl's movements were precise, almost balletic in their grace and power. He swung his rope with practiced ease, the loop settling neatly over the calf's horns. The calf's frantic struggles were short-lived as Carl's experienced hands expertly wrestled it to the ground. He dismounted, his movements fluid and efficient, securing the calf's legs in a flash. The time flashed on the timeboard — a stunningly fast time that immediately placed him at the top of the leaderboard. The crowd erupted, a thunderous wave of applause that seemed to shake the very foundations of the arena.

The feeling of exhilaration was intense, but Carl knew he couldn't afford to be complacent. He had other runs to make, other calves to rope. He needed to maintain his focus, his precision, and his unwavering determination. He had pushed himself to the brink over the previous months, and now he was determined to reap the rewards of his tireless effort. The recent injuries and setbacks now seemed like distant memories. He was focused entirely on the task at hand, on the present moment, pushing forward with relentless energy and determined focus.

His second run was equally impressive. This calf, larger and more powerful than the first, proved to be a more formidable challenge. But Carl's skill and experience were evident as he executed the roping with effortless skill. He reacted instinctively to the animal's movements, adjusting his approach with a precision born of countless hours of practice. Again, the time was rapid—a new personal best. The crowd went wild with cheers and whoops, their excitement palpable. The roar of the crowd fueled his adrenaline, pushing him even further. The pressure was high, but Carl thrived on it. The energy of the crowd and the pressure of the event merely heightened his focus and determination.

Carl continued his string of success throughout the remaining runs. The competition was intense, with seasoned competitors showcasing their skill and expertise. However, Carl was in a league of his own, consistently delivering exceptional times in his runs. He moved through the event with a powerful blend of energy and concentration. The precision of his movements, the efficiency of his technique, and the strength and skill of his roping were the ultimate combination of speed and control.

The final run was the culmination of all his hard work and perseverance. The final calf seemed particularly strong and agile, presenting one last challenge to Carl. But in his determined focus, he expertly handled this final challenge. The crowd watched with bated breath as he executed the roping with remarkable precision and skill. The final time flashed on the timeboard, yet another personal best, securing his victory. A wave of relief, joy, and pure exhilaration washed over him. His months of rigorous training, the support of his family and friends, and his unwavering determination had all culminated in this moment of triumph.

The announcement of his victory was met with a deafening roar from the crowd. Confetti rained down from the stands, and the arena erupted into a cacophony of cheers and applause. His fellow competitors, who had been his rivals moments ago, rushed to congratulate him. The weight of the previous months lifted from his shoulders. He'd done it; he'd risen above the challenges, above the setbacks and injuries. He'd proven his skill, his strength, and his unwavering determination.

The victory was more than just a win; it was a testament to his perseverance and dedication. It was a validation of the countless hours spent practicing, the sacrifices made, and the steady, familiar support of those who believed in him.

It was a victory shared not only with RJ, his faithful equine partner, but also with his family, his friends, his mentors, and the entire rodeo community that had rallied around him throughout the season.

Carl stood amidst the celebrations, overwhelmed by the emotion of the moment. He hugged his mother tightly, tears welling up in both their eyes. His uncle, his mentor, clapped him on the back with a grin that spoke volumes. The friends who had supported him throughout the trials and tribulations of the season were jumping with joy around him, and the moments leading up to and immediately after the final run played themselves out as a blur of excitement and jubilation. It was a moment he would cherish forever.

The next stop was to pick up his finalist jacket from Debbie at Tioga Traders. This was the next best thing to a letterman's jacket that football, track, and field athletes receive. It was not leather, but a neoprene-style jacket with the rodeo logo on the back, the word champion below the logo, and Carl's name on the front with the calf roper. He asked if he could order extras for his mother and grandmother. Debbie looked over and said she could help him order all the jackets. She asked what size he wanted for his coat and for theirs. He blushed, unsure what sizes his mother and grandmother would need.

The victory cemented his place as a top competitor and gave him the needed momentum to propel him forward in his pursuit of a college rodeo scholarship. It was a powerful statement, a declaration of his talent and potential, and a testament to the power of perseverance, determination, and the steady, familiar support of those he cared about. Carl had proven that hard work, dedication, and a strong support system could overcome any obstacle.

As the dust settled, Carl knew that the road ahead would still be challenging in the state finals. But he also knew he had the skills, determination, and support system to face any obstacle that came his way. He had conquered the state finals; now; he set his sights on even greater challenges, aiming for the national stage, ready to prove himself once again.

Chapter 7: United States Finals Bound

The news arrived like a bolt of lightning, shattering the quiet hum of the evening. A phone call from the state rodeo association, a voice crackling with excitement, delivered the confirmation Carl had been yearning for: he'd qualified for the United States High School Rodeo Finals. The words hung in the air, suspended in a moment of stunned silence before erupting into a joyous celebration. His mother's cry of relief and delight was the first sound to pierce the stunned quiet, followed by the exuberant barking of Buster, their energetic family dog, who sensed the shift in the atmosphere and mirrored the family's unrestrained joy. His uncle, a seasoned rodeo veteran whose calm demeanor usually masked his emotions, let out a whoop of pure elation, a sound as unexpected as it was gratifying.

The weight of the past months, the relentless pressure, the anxieties, the grueling hours of practice, the sting of minor setbacks and injuries — all of it dissolved in a rush of pure, unadulterated joy. It was a moment of overwhelming relief, a validation of his dedication, perseverance, and sheer grit. This wasn't just a victory; it was a testament to the steady, familiar support of his family, friends, sponsors, and RJ, his steadfast four-legged companion. The journey to this point had been arduous, a relentless test of physical and mental endurance, but the triumph felt all the sweeter because of it.

The family gathered around the kitchen table, the air buzzing with excited chatter and laughter. They recounted his victories, his close calls, the moments of doubt, and the unwavering belief that had fueled his journey. His mother, her eyes shining with pride, pulled out old photos, reminiscing about his early days in the saddle, a tiny boy perched precariously on a much larger pony, his determination already evident in his unwavering grip. His uncle, his face softened by a genuine smile, shared stories from his rodeo career, offering words of encouragement and advice that prepared Carl for the monumental task ahead. These stories, woven with humor and wisdom, offered Carl a comforting sense of connection to the rich heritage of rodeo. His friends, joining the celebration later, added their anecdotes and memories of shared struggles, offering words of camaraderie and steady, familiar support. The sense of community fostered by the rodeo circuit was palpable, a testament to the bonds forged through moments lived shoulder-to-shoulder and the pursuit of a common goal.

The days that followed were a whirlwind of activity. News of Carl's qualification spread like wildfire through the tight-knit rodeo community. Congratulations poured in from fellow competitors, coaches, and sponsors, fueling his already soaring spirits. The local news featured his victory in the state finals and his subsequent qualification for the United States Finals, adding to the mounting excitement. The pressure intensified, but this time, it wasn't the crippling anxiety of the past, but rather a motivating force, pushing him to train even harder, to refine his technique, and to prepare for the ultimate challenge. This wasn't merely about winning; it was about representing his community, his family, and himself on the grandest stage of high school rodeo.

Preparations for the Nationals were meticulous. Every detail, from RJ's conditioning to Carl's equipment, was scrutinized and perfected. They spent countless hours at the practice arena, honing their skills, working on speed, precision, and the seamless coordination that defined their partnership. Carl's uncle meticulously checked RJ's shoes, his saddle, and his bridle. He ensured that RJ's diet and exercise regimen were optimal, ensuring that both the horse and rider were in peak condition for the highly demanding event. They adjusted Carl's roping technique, focusing on subtle refinements to increase his speed and accuracy. They also focused on the mental aspects, practicing visualization techniques and stress-management strategies to help Carl stay calm and focused under pressure.

The support network intensified as well. Sponsors stepped up their assistance, ensuring that both Carl and RJ had the best equipment and support available. Local businesses offered their support, providing help and sponsoring events to boost the community's enthusiasm and highlight Carl's success. The local high school also organized rallies and events to celebrate the accomplishment, demonstrating the unity and pride the community felt in his success. This wave of support further solidified Carl's understanding of the importance of his support system and of the powerful bonds within the rodeo community. The experience provided him with a level of comfort and confidence that was invaluable as he prepared for the highly competitive United States Finals.

The anticipation mounted as the date of the United States Finals drew nearer. The atmosphere was charged with a blend of excitement, nervousness, and determination. Carl visualized his runs repeatedly, picturing the scenarios and visualizing success. He practiced his roping technique until his muscles ached, until his movements were automatic and instinctive. He and RJ worked together, their connection strengthening with each practice run. The bond between them transcended the typical rider-horse relationship; it was a partnership forged through shared challenges, mutual respect, and unwavering loyalty. RJ, sensing his rider's intensity, responded with a focused energy that mirrored his own. Their collaboration was palpable, a testament to the deep connection they shared.

The day of departure arrived, and the journey to the United States Finals was a blend of excitement and apprehension. The anticipation created a palpable tension that filled the air as Carl, his family, and RJ prepared for the journey. The car was packed with equipment, snacks, and the hopes of an entire community. The drive was filled with reminiscences, encouragement, and the shared excitement for what lay ahead. The atmosphere was one of nervous energy, but also one of unwavering belief and support from his family and friends. Every mile felt significant, each one bringing them closer to the epicenter of the high school rodeo world.

The arrival in the host city was a sensory overload. The energy of the rodeo atmosphere was almost electric, an intense buzz that permeated every interaction. The arena, a magnificent structure that housed the dreams of hundreds of young competitors, loomed large, an intimidating yet awe-inspiring symbol of Carl's ambition. The sheer scale of the event was mind-boggling, dwarfing the smaller rodeos he had competed in, highlighting the enormity of this moment and the gravity of the challenge ahead. He was no longer just a competitor; he was a representative of his state, his school, and his community, carrying the weight of their hopes and expectations on his shoulders.

The opening ceremonies were a breathtaking spectacle, a colorful display of rodeo tradition and camaraderie. As he stood amongst his fellow competitors, a diverse group of talented young athletes, Carl felt a surge of respect and admiration. They were rivals, indeed, but they were also united by their shared passion, dedication, and ambition. The camaraderie was infectious, a reassuring testament to the spirit of sportsmanship and friendly competition that defined the rodeo circuit. He felt ready. Ready for the challenge. Prepared for the national spotlight. The road to this moment had been long and demanding. Still, Carl stood at the starting line, prepared to face whatever lay ahead, confident in his abilities and supported by the unwavering love and encouragement of his family and friends. He took a deep breath, feeling the energy of the moment, the weight of expectation, and the thrill of the challenge, knowing that this was it — his chance to shine on the national stage. The United States Finals had begun.

The days leading up to the United States Finals were a blur of activity, a whirlwind of focused energy channeled into meticulous preparation. Gone was the carefree exuberance of the celebration following his state win; in its place was a steely determination, a laser focus honed by months of relentless training and tempered by the weight of expectation. Every waking moment was dedicated to perfecting his craft, to ensuring that he and RJ were in peak physical and mental condition for the ultimate test.

Their daily routine was a carefully choreographed dance of discipline and precision. Mornings began before dawn, with a rigorous workout routine designed to build strength, endurance, and flexibility. Carl would start with a brisk run, pushing himself to the limits of his stamina, followed by a series of intense exercises targeting the muscles crucial for calf roping: core strength, leg power, and upper body flexibility. He meticulously stretched, paying attention to the smallest detail, ensuring that his body was fully prepared for the demanding physicality of the competition. RJ, too, had his regimen, a carefully balanced diet and exercise program designed to maximize his strength, agility, and endurance. Carl's uncle, a man whose life was a testament to the demanding physicality of rodeo, oversaw every aspect of RJ's care, ensuring that the horse was as prepared as his rider.

After their morning workouts, they moved to the practice arena. Hours were spent honing their technique, refining the seemingly effortless grace and precision of their partnership. Each run was a symphony of controlled movements, a testament to the countless hours spent perfecting their craft. Carl focused on every nuance of his roping technique, the precise timing of his throw, the swiftness of his dismount, and the seamless transition from the horse to the calf. He practiced his dally, the crucial maneuver that secured the rope, ensuring its smooth execution, honing his technique with the relentless pursuit of perfection. He was a sculptor, shaping his performance, refining it, perfecting each aspect until it became an extension of himself. RJ, sensing his rider's intensity, responded in kind, his movements becoming as precise and responsive as the gears of a finely tuned machine. Their bond, forged through months of shared experience, was a testament to their shared dedication.

Their practice wasn't just physical; it was deeply mental. Carl spent hours visualizing his runs, replaying each scenario in his mind, anticipating every possible outcome, mentally preparing for every contingency. He learned to manage his adrenaline, to channel his nervous energy into focus and determination. He mastered the art of controlled breathing, techniques that helped him remain calm and centered in high-pressure situations. His uncle, drawing on his vast experience, shared mental strategies gleaned from years of competing at the highest level, teaching Carl about the importance of visualization, mental rehearsal, and emotional resilience. He learned to control the mental chaos of competition.

Beyond the physical and mental training, the final stages of preparation encompassed a meticulous review of every detail. Carl's uncle spent hours meticulously checking his equipment, ensuring that everything was in perfect working order. The saddle, the rope, the spurs—each piece was examined, adjusted, and perfected. RJ's tack was inspected with the same rigorous attention to detail; his shoes were checked for wear, and his bridle was adjusted for optimal comfort and performance. Even the smallest detail, a loose thread on Carl's shirt, a slight imperfection in RJ's bit, was rectified, leaving nothing to chance. This unwavering focus extended to their travel plans, lodging arrangements, and every logistical element of their trip. Nothing was left to chance; every aspect of the United States Finals was meticulously planned to ensure a smooth and successful competition.

The support network continued to grow, bolstering Carl's confidence and reinforcing the sense of community that had propelled him to this point.

Sponsors increased their support, providing top-of-the-line equipment and ensuring that both Carl and RJ had everything they needed. The local high school rallied behind him, organizing send-off events and fundraisers to demonstrate the community's pride and support. The town itself seemed to hold its breath, its collective hopes and dreams riding alongside Carl and RJ on their journey to the United States Finals. This outpouring of support created a powerful sense of camaraderie and validation for Carl. The pressure he felt wasn't solely his burden, but was shared by the community that had supported him every step of the way.

The final days before departure were a whirlwind of activity, the culmination of months of relentless effort. Carl meticulously packed his bags, checking and rechecking every item to ensure he had everything he needed. RJ was bathed, groomed, and prepared for the journey ahead. The family gathered for a final dinner, a blend of excitement and nervous anticipation filling the air. Stories were shared, and laughter mingled with moments of quiet contemplation. The weight of expectation was heavy, yet the atmosphere was one of love, unity, and unwavering belief. There was a calm confidence in the room, a palpable assurance that they had done everything they could, that Carl and RJ were as ready as they could be.

The departure itself was a poignant moment as they loaded the trailer, a wave of emotions washed over Carl. The culmination of years of dedication, of setbacks and triumphs, of unwavering commitment — it all culminated in this single journey. This wasn't just about the competition; it was about the journey, the experiences, the steadfast support. It was about the growth, not just as a calf roper, but as a person. As he climbed into the truck, alongside his family and RJ, the final mile of their journey felt like a significant milestone. They were not just traveling; they carried with them the collective hopes of their community, the weight of their support, and an unwavering belief in their shared journey. This was more than a competition; it was a testament to perseverance, dedication, and the unbreakable bonds of family, community, and friendship within the rodeo world. The United States Finals were ahead, and Carl, grounded in this support, felt ready to face them.

The air in the National High School Finals rodeo arena crackled with a palpable energy, a potent blend of anticipation and adrenaline. It was a far cry from the familiar comfort of the state competition; here, the atmosphere was thick with the weight of national-level competition, the air buzzing with the hushed murmurs of thousands of spectators and the thunderous hooves of hundreds of horses. Carl, usually unflappable, felt a tremor of nerves run down his spine. This wasn't just another rodeo; it was the culmination of years of dedication, the ultimate test of his skill and resilience.

The sheer scale of the event was overwhelming. The arena was vast, a sprawling expanse of dirt and dust, surrounded by towering stands that overflowed with spectators. The energy was infectious, a vibrant hum that resonated through the stands and seemed to vibrate in the very ground beneath his feet. He saw competitors from every corner of the country, each one a testament to the rigorous dedication required to qualify for the United States Finals. Their faces were a mix of focused determination and nervous anticipation, their eyes reflecting the bright lights and the weight of the competition.

Carl spotted some of his rivals from other states. There was Cole, a lanky kid from Texas with lightning-fast hands and a horse that seemed to read his every thought. He'd heard whispers about Cole's almost supernatural connection with his horse, a bond forged through years of relentless training and mutual understanding. Cole's calm demeanor belied the fierce competition that burned beneath the surface. Then there was Maria, a small but powerfully built girl from Wyoming. Her roping technique was flawless, precise, and economical, a testament to her years of honing her skills in the unforgiving landscapes of her home state. She carried herself with quiet confidence, a steely determination etched in her gaze that spoke volumes of her dedication and resolve.

The sheer talent of his competitors was intimidating. Each run was a masterclass in skill and precision. Cole's horse seemed to anticipate his every move, its powerful muscles coiled tight, ready to explode into action. His roping technique was fluid and effortless, each movement smooth and controlled, the rope snaking through the air with almost supernatural accuracy. Maria, despite her small stature, demonstrated incredible power and control. Her horse responded with lightning-fast precision to her commands, the two working together as a seamless unit. The calves, trained for this high level of competition, were quick, powerful, and surprisingly agile; they didn't make it easy for them.

The pressure was immense, a heavy cloak draped over his shoulders. He could feel the weight of expectations, not just his own, but also those of his family, friends, community, and sponsors. He tried to block it out, to focus solely on the task at hand, but the magnitude of the event was difficult to ignore. It was a challenge not only of skill but also of mental fortitude, a test of his ability to maintain composure under extreme pressure. The noise of the crowd, the tension in the air, the sheer volume of talent surrounding him—it was a sensory overload.

He sought out his uncle for support. His uncle, a legendary figure in the world of rodeo, offered words of quiet encouragement, a reminder to focus on his technique, on his breathing, on the connection with RJ. His uncle's calm assurance and his years of experience battling pressure were a grounding force, helping to center Carl amidst the chaos. He reminded Carl that they had prepared meticulously, that they were ready, that this was their moment to shine.

The first round arrived like a tidal wave, washing over Carl with a surge of adrenaline. The buzz in the stands intensified as his name was announced. As he rode into the arena, the spotlight felt blinding, the roar of the crowd deafening. He could feel RJ shifting beneath him, sensing his rider's heightened energy. His heart pounded a frantic rhythm against his ribs, and his breaths came shallow and fast. He took a moment to center himself, focusing on his breath, on the calm, steadying presence of RJ beneath him. He drew upon the mental strategies his uncle had taught him, visualizing a perfect run, replaying each movement in his mind, and silencing the chaos of the crowd with his focused concentration.

The gate swung open and the calf burst free, a blur of brown hide and pounding legs. Carl reacted instantly, RJ matching him stride for stride. The run became pure motion, a seamless rhythm between man and horse. The rope snapped tight, the calf spun, and Carl dismounted and dallied with practiced ease. Exhilaration surged as the tension broke. The crowd erupted, its roar crashing over him. He had performed well, exceeding even his own expectations.

However, the next few rounds proved to be a harsh learning experience. The competition was relentless, each competitor bringing their unique style and skill. He encountered setbacks, mistakes that cost him precious time. He learned from his errors, analyzing each run, adjusting his strategy, refining his technique, and continually striving for improvement. RJ, too, was pushed to his limits, and Carl understood the need to adapt his riding style to meet the challenges of each calf, each arena, and each competitor.

But through it all, the support of his family, friends, and community remained a constant source of strength. They were his steady, familiar support system, a constant reminder of why he was there, of the journey that had led him to this moment. Their faith in him, their belief in his potential, gave him the confidence to keep fighting, to keep striving, to keep pushing himself to his limits.

As the United States Finals drew to a close, Carl found himself not only competing against the other finalists but also against himself. He was facing not just the physical and mental challenges of the competition, but also the internal struggle for self-improvement, a relentless pursuit of excellence. The lessons he learned went far beyond calf roping; they were lessons in perseverance, resilience, and the power of human potential. The final time was not what mattered as much as the journey. He had grown immensely from the experience, not just as a calf roper but as a person. He discovered a strength within himself that he had never known he possessed —a resilience honed by the fires of competition. And, regardless of the final ranking, he carried the pride of knowing he'd given it his all. The United States Finals were a crucible, forging him into a stronger, more determined competitor, a testament to the power of dedication and the steady, familiar support of those who believed in him.

The roar of the crowd was a physical force, pressing against him, a tangible weight added to the already considerable burden on his shoulders. It wasn't just the sound; it was the sheer number of eyes, thousands of pairs focused on him, judging his every move, anticipating his every misstep. The pressure wasn't just external; it was internal, a relentless tide of self-doubt and expectation that threatened to overwhelm him. He'd trained for this, prepared meticulously, pushed himself to the very edge of his physical and mental limits, but nothing could truly replicate the intensity of the United States Finals.

He tried to focus on his breathing, a technique his uncle had drilled into him countless times: slow, deep breaths, in through the nose, out through the mouth, a rhythmic counterpoint to the chaotic symphony of the rodeo. But his heart hammered a frantic rhythm against his ribs, a relentless drumbeat that drowned out the measured rhythm of his breaths. His hands, usually steady and sure, trembled slightly; the leather of his gloves was slick with nervous sweat.

He closed his eyes for a moment, picturing RJ, his trusty horse, a powerful, steady presence beneath him. He focused on the feel of the saddle, the smooth leather beneath his thighs, the rhythmic rise and fall of RJ's powerful muscles. He imagined the familiar weight of the rope in his hand, the smooth, cool feel of the leather against his skin. He visualized the perfect run, a seamless sequence of movements, each step precise and fluid, a dance between man and beast. He replayed the run in his mind, again and again, until the image was burned into his memory, a mental anchor in the storm of his anxiety.

But even the mental exercises couldn't completely quell the rising tide of apprehension. He thought of his family, their faces etched with pride and hope. He thought of his mother, her steady, familiar support a constant source of strength, her faith in him a quiet balm to his nerves. He thought of his uncle, his mentor, his words of encouragement echoing in his ears, a steady hand guiding him through the turbulent waters of competition. He thought of his friends, their cheers and support a tangible presence, even from across the vast expanse of the arena. The weight of their expectations added to the pressure, a responsibility he felt acutely. He wasn't just competing for himself; he was competing for them, for his community, for everyone who had believed in him.

He felt the eyes of his sponsors on him, too, a silent pressure that added another layer to his already considerable burden. Their investment in him, their faith in his potential, carried a significant weight. He knew that a strong performance here could solidify his future in the rodeo world, opening doors to opportunities he could scarcely imagine. However, a poor performance could have the opposite effect, jeopardizing his future and disappointing those who had placed their trust in him.

The starting gate loomed before him, a stark symbol of the challenge that lay ahead. The smell of dust and sweat hung heavy in the air, a potent mixture of anticipation and adrenaline. He could hear the murmurs of the crowd, a low hum that vibrated through the ground, a palpable energy that both excited and intimidated him. He took a deep breath, trying to center himself, to focus on the task at hand, to block out the noise, the pressure.

He adjusted his grip on the rope, feeling the familiar comfort of the leather —a reassuring connection to the years of practice, the countless hours of sweat and toil, and the unwavering dedication that had brought him to this moment. He focused on the connection with RJ, feeling the powerful animal beneath him, sensing his readiness, his steady, familiar support. They were a team, a unit, their destinies intertwined. He whispered words of encouragement to his horse, a quiet reassurance that calmed both of them.

The gate swung open, and the calf burst forth, a blur of brown fur and powerful legs. Time seemed to slow, the world narrowing to the calf, RJ, and himself. He reacted instantly, his body moving with practiced ease as years of training coalesced into a single, fluid motion. His rope flew, a graceful arc against the backdrop of the arena, the calf spinning, the rope tightening, the dust flying. He felt the familiar thrill of the chase, the adrenaline surging through his veins, pushing away the doubts.

This time, the run was perfect. A clean catch, a swift dismount, a masterful dally. He'd executed every move with precision and speed, a testament to the countless hours of practice and the steady, familiar support of those around him. The crowd erupted, a wave of sound that washed over him, a tangible expression of their approval. He'd done it; he'd conquered the pressure, overcome the doubts, and delivered a performance that reflected his skill and dedication.

But even in the euphoria of victory, the weight of expectation lingered. The United States Finals wasn't just a single run; it was a series of runs, a grueling test of endurance, both physical and mental. Each subsequent run demanded the same focus, precision, and unwavering dedication. He couldn't afford to rest on his laurels; the competition was fierce, every competitor striving for the same goal. He had to maintain his composure, to control his nerves, to keep the pressure at bay. The weight of expectation remained, a constant companion, a reminder of the stakes involved.

The following runs brought a mix of successes and setbacks. There were moments of brilliance, where everything clicked, and the run was flawless. But there were also moments of frustration, where a simple mistake cost him precious seconds, where the pressure got the better of him, where the weight of expectation proved too heavy to bear. He learned from each mistake, analyzing each run with a critical eye, identifying the flaws, refining his technique, striving for constant improvement. He used each failure as a springboard for success, each stumble as a lesson learned.

Throughout it all, he relied on the steady, familiar support of his family, friends, community, and sponsors. Their belief in him, their faith in his potential, was a constant source of strength, a reminder of why he was there, of the journey that had led him to this moment. They were his anchors in the storm, his guiding lights in the darkness, his constant companions on the path to success. And as the United States Finals drew to a close, he knew that regardless of the outcome, he had given it his all. He had faced the weight of expectation and emerged more assertive, more resilient, and more determined. The journey had forged him, and that was a victory in itself. The final standings wouldn't define him; his effort, his growth, and his unwavering spirit would.

The final day of the United States Finals hung heavy in the air, thick with anticipation and the scent of dust and sweat. Carl felt the familiar knot of tension in his stomach, a tightening that years of competition hadn't quite managed to alleviate. He'd had a decent run so far, but the competition was fierce, each competitor a honed blade, each run a potential stumble or triumph. He stretched, the familiar pop and crackle of his muscles a comforting sound, a testament to the rigorous training that had brought him this far. He glanced across the arena, his eyes falling on Wyatt, his biggest rival throughout the season. Wyatt, with his steely gaze and effortless grace in the saddle, had been a thorn in Carl's side, consistently placing just ahead of him on the leaderboard. Their rivalry had been intense, but never disrespectful; a clash of skill and determination rather than animosity.

Surprisingly, Wyatt looked tired, almost defeated. There was a slump to his shoulders, a weariness in his eyes that spoke volumes about the relentless pressure of the competition. Carl found himself unexpectedly sympathetic. He knew the toll these finals took; the physical exhaustion, the mental strain, the unyielding weight of expectation. He'd seen the same exhaustion mirrored in his face this week.

As the next event began, Carl noticed Wyatt struggling with his horse. The usually compliant animal was fidgety and restless, refusing to settle into the starting position. Wyatt, usually so composed, was visibly agitated, his usual calm demeanor replaced by a frustrated grimace. The crowd murmured, a ripple of concern spreading through the onlookers. Time was running out for the run. Carl, watching from the sidelines, felt a pang of empathy. He knew the frustration of a balky horse, the agonizing seconds that ticked by as an animal resisted, each delay chipping away at the confidence and potential success.

Driven by an impulse, Carl approached Wyatt. The crowd's murmur faded into a low hum as all eyes seemed to turn to their unexpected interaction. "Hey, Wyatt," Carl called, his voice surprisingly calm amidst the tension. "Need a hand?"

Wyatt looked up, surprised. His eyes, usually filled with competitive fire, were now shadowed with fatigue. He hesitated for a moment, a flicker of suspicion crossing his face before a weary nod.

"RJ's usually pretty calm," Carl began, referring to his horse, "But these finals are stressful even for them. I find giving a slow, rhythmic stroke down their side helps. Sometimes just a quiet word helps too." He offered a rare, friendly smile.

Wyatt surprised Carl again with an appreciative nod. "Thanks. I appreciate it." He briefly explained the issue, mentioning his horse's usual demeanor and the fact that his horse was completely stressed. "It's the heat and the pressure, I think." He admitted.

Carl spent the next few minutes working with Wyatt and his horse. He spoke in calming tones to the animal, softly stroking its neck and sides, mimicking the soothing techniques his uncle had taught him. He shared some of the methods his uncle had used over the years, discussing the nuances of working with anxious animals and how different animals respond to various stimuli. There was an unspoken acknowledgment of a shared passion, a shared understanding of the complex relationship between rider and horse.

Slowly, the horse began to relax. The tension eased out of its muscles, its breathing becoming slower, more regular. Wyatt's shoulders relaxed too, a weight seemingly lifted from his frame.

"Thanks, Carl," Wyatt said, his voice sincere. "Seriously, I appreciate that."

Carl shrugged, a genuine smile replacing the tense expression he'd worn. "No problem. We're all in this together." The words felt truer than he'd ever meant them before.

The unexpected collaboration extended beyond just that one event. Over the remaining events of the United States Finals, Carl and Wyatt found themselves sharing tips and insights, offering words of encouragement and support to one another. They discussed strategies, analyzed each other's runs with objective eyes, and provided constructive feedback rather than critical judgments. They discovered that beneath the fierce rivalry lay a shared respect for the skill, dedication, and hard work that defined their passion. They shared an appreciation for their horses and a mutual understanding of the sport's unique demands, which fostered a camaraderie that transcended competition.

Wyatt's performance improved noticeably, his renewed confidence reflected in his runs. Carl, too, benefited from their collaboration. The unexpected alliance didn't diminish their competitive spirit; rather, it refined it, turning rivalry into mutual respect. They still competed fiercely, aiming to reach their respective goals, but there was a sense of camaraderie, a mutual understanding that extended beyond the arena.

The final standings were a testament to their respective talents. They placed neck and neck, and a single mistake in one of Carl's runs ultimately decided the placement. Though Wyatt finished slightly ahead, claiming the top spot, the day concluded with a respectful handshake and a mutual admiration that deepened their bond. The win didn't just go to Wyatt; it was a shared victory that cemented the power of an unlikely, respectful alliance in the high-stakes competition's pressure-cooker environment. The unexpected coalition demonstrated that even in the cutthroat world of rodeo, sportsmanship and mutual respect could thrive.

The experience enriched both of their understanding of the sport. Their unexpected partnership became a defining moment of the United Stated High School Rodeo Finals, a compelling testament to the power of camaraderie in the face of intense competition. It proved that wins and losses don't solely measure true success, but by the bonds forged and the respect earned along the way. The experience laid the groundwork for a lasting friendship, a connection forged in the crucible of competition, a bond that would stand the test of time. As the dust settled on the United States Finals, the unexpected alliance between Carl and Wyatt proved to be a far more significant victory than any trophy could ever represent. It highlighted a deeper understanding of the sport and its unwritten rules of mutual respect among competitors.

Chapter 8: The United States Finals

The air crackled with an energy unlike anything Carl had ever experienced. This wasn't the small-town rodeo circuit he was used to, where the crowd mainly consisted of familiar faces and the bleachers felt intimate. This was the National High School Finals, a behemoth of a spectacle that dwarfed everything he'd known before. The arena was a colossal oval, bathed in the dazzling glare of spotlights that cut through the dust motes hanging in the air. The roar of the crowd was deafening, a wave of sound that crashed over him, a palpable energy that vibrated through the ground beneath his feet. Thousands of spectators filled the stands, a sea of faces blurred by distance, yet united by their shared passion for rodeo. The air thrummed with excitement, a palpable tension that hung heavy, thick with the scent of leather, hay, and anticipation.

He could almost feel the weight of expectation pressing down on him, the collective breath held in anticipation of each run. It was a pressure cooker, a crucible where only the strongest would survive. He'd prepared, trained, pushed himself to his limits, but nothing could quite replicate this. This wasn't just a competition; it was an event, a spectacle, a celebration of skill, athleticism, and the enduring spirit of the American West.

The media presence was overwhelming. Cameras flashed incessantly, capturing every move, every expression, every second of the intense competition. Reporters with microphones trailed the competitors, seeking interviews and sound bites. The sheer scale of the event was awe-inspiring, a testament to the popularity and enduring legacy of rodeo. The vibrant atmosphere was intoxicating — a whirlwind of activity, a kaleidoscope of color and sound, a mesmerizing blend of skill, danger, and pure adrenaline.

Carl watched as competitors from across the nation showcased their talents, each run a masterpiece of precision and timing. The calf ropers, with their lightning-fast reflexes and expert horsemanship, were a blur of motion, a whirlwind of dust and leather. The barrel racers, their horses thundering around the barrels, seemed to defy gravity, their movements fluid and graceful. The bull riders, clinging precariously to their bucking mounts, epitomized courage and determination. Each event was a testament to the dedication and training required to reach this level of competition. The sheer athleticism on display was breathtaking, a captivating demonstration of raw power and refined skill.

Even RJ, usually unflappable, seemed to sense the intensity of the atmosphere. His ears were pricked, his senses heightened, alert to every sound and movement in the arena. Carl felt his own heart pounding, the rhythm a counterpoint to the roar of the crowd. He focused on the feel of RJ beneath him, on the subtle shifts in the horse's weight, on the rhythmic beat of their combined breath. He sought to calm RJ, communicating with him through gentle touch and quiet words, to soothe away his nerves and calm his horse.

The energy of the crowd was infectious. Their cheers and shouts were deafening when a successful run was made, and the collective gasp when a rider was thrown was almost physical. It was a sea of human energy, focused and directed onto the arena, every emotion amplified by the immense scale of the competition. Carl found himself drawing strength from the crowd, channeling their energy into his performance. Their collective support felt like an invisible force, bolstering him and propelling him forward, allowing him to concentrate on his skill and technique. The collective energy was an empowering force that spurred him towards peak performance.

As his turn approached, Carl felt a surge of both excitement and apprehension. This was it, the culmination of years of hard work and dedication. He focused on his breathing, on the rhythm of his heartbeat, on the connection between himself and RJ. He repeated his mantra, the words a calming presence in the swirling maelstrom of emotions and sensory overload. He visualized the run, every step and movement replaying in his head, the sequence of events necessary for a perfect performance.

The gate swung open, and he was off. The adrenaline coursed through his veins, sharp and exhilarating. He and RJ moved as one, their actions synchronized and intuitive. The rush of speed, the thrill of the chase, the quiet intensity of his focus — it was a beautiful dance of skill and coordination, a seamless blend of man and animal. The adrenaline of the high-stakes competition propelled his performance to its peak. His senses sharpened, focusing only on the task at hand, his attention honed to the point of exclusion. Every muscle responded to his instincts.

The seconds ticked by, each one a microcosm of precise movement and perfect timing. The calf hit the ground with a thud, the rope taut and secure. He dismounted, a surge of exhilaration washing over him, his body buzzing with the aftermath of adrenaline. The crowd's roar was deafening, a testament to the success of his run, the peak of a performance perfected with years of experience and training. The time flashed on the timeboard, a testament to his skill and precision. The culmination of years of dedication, training, and perseverance, his run was a triumph, a showcase of his expertise and composure under pressure.

As the final times were tallied, the tension in the arena was almost unbearable. The atmosphere grew hushed, with every eye fixed on the timeboard. The moment hung suspended, a collective breath held taut. The announcement of the winner was met with thunderous applause, a testament to the intense competition and the skill of the participants. The excitement of the win was palpable, an electric energy filling the air. Whether he won or not, Carl knew he'd given it his all, performed at the peak of his skill, and embraced the challenge presented by the ultimate test of athleticism and horsemanship.

The journey, with its highs and lows, the lessons learned, and the friendships forged, had all been a part of his unique and significant experience. The National High School Finals were over, but the memory would stay with him —a reminder of his unwavering dedication and pursuit of his dream. The experience and the lessons he'd learned were invaluable gifts, marking the end of one chapter and the beginning of another, with the promise of continuing growth and development on his rodeo journey.

The first round was a blur of activity. The sheer size of the arena, the thunderous applause, the bright lights — it was overwhelming, even for someone as seasoned as Carl was becoming. He'd practiced countless times in smaller arenas, mimicking the pressure with his uncle's watchful eye, but nothing could fully prepare him for the raw energy of the United States Finals. RJ, sensing his rider's apprehension, shifted restlessly beneath him. Carl took a deep breath, feeling the familiar steadying rhythm of his heartbeat, and focused on the connection with his horse. He needed RJ to be calm and responsive, and he needed to be equally quiet. This wasn't just about winning; it was about performing to the best of their ability, as a team.

The gate swung open, and the calf exploded out, a brown blur against the dusty ground. Carl's instincts took over; years of practice translated into fluid motion. He spurred RJ forward, the horse responding with a powerful burst of speed, their movements perfectly synchronized. The chase was a ballet of skill and precision — a controlled rush of adrenaline and focused intention. The rope flew, a perfect lasso encircling the calf's legs. The animal bucked and struggled, but Carl held firm, the rope secure and taut. He dismounted smoothly, quickly securing the calf's legs, his movements efficient and practiced. The buzzer sounded, and the time flashed on the timeboard: 8.2 seconds —a good time, a solid start. Relief washed over him, quickly followed by a surge of adrenaline-fueled excitement. He'd done it. He'd navigated the chaos of the first round and delivered a strong performance.

The second round felt different. The pressure was higher, the stakes amplified by his success in the first round. He could feel the eyes of the crowd, the weight of expectation. The whispers — "that's Carl, the kid from Texas" — reached him, carrying with them both encouragement and a potentially crippling pressure. He focused on RJ, their bond his anchor in the storm of the competition. He needed to stay calm, centered, and focused on the task at hand, trusting their training to guide them.

This time, the calf was faster, more agile. The chase was a frantic dash, a breathless pursuit of speed and precision. But Carl remained steady, his hand unwavering, his focus laser-sharp. He made the catch, the rope circling the calf's legs with the practiced precision of countless hours spent honing his skill. He wrestled the animal to the ground, securing it efficiently. The buzzer sounded; 8.7 seconds. A slightly slower time than the first round, but still a solid performance, within the top ten. He breathed a sigh of relief, the tension easing from his shoulders.

The third and fourth rounds unfolded in a similar pattern. Carl's performances remained consistently strong, a testament to his skill, his training, and his bond with RJ. Each run was a story of preparation meeting opportunity — a narrative crafted through years of dedication and refined through hours of practice. He learned to manage the adrenaline, the pressure, and the roar of the crowd, turning the noise into fuel and transforming the tension into focused energy. He drew strength from the quiet confidence in his skill and the unwavering partnership with RJ. He could feel the horse responding to his subtle cues. They were a team, two entities working in perfect harmony, their success dependent on the trust and rhythm of their movements. The thrill of the competition was palpable; adrenaline surged through him, energizing every muscle and sharpening his focus.

His times fluctuated slightly, reflecting the unpredictable nature of the sport and the varying agility of each calf. Some calves were quicker, while others were more stubborn; their movements were erratic and tested the limits of his skills. But through it all, Carl maintained a steady performance, remaining within the top ten throughout the initial rounds. This consistency was a testament to his dedication, his training, and the incredible partnership he had with RJ. The bond between them was not just one of horse and rider but one of genuine camaraderie. RJ responded to Carl's calm demeanor; the horse sensed the steady confidence of his rider, and this sense of shared trust became their secret weapon. Their collaboration was the difference between a good performance and a great one. The trust was clear; it was woven into their movements, apparent in the seamless transitions, the unspoken communication, the synchronized choreography of their performance.

The cumulative effect of his consistent performances throughout the early rounds secured his place in the final competition. The pressure didn't lessen; it intensified. He'd made it this far, exceeding his expectations. Now he faced the ultimate test. But there was no room for complacency; every moment, every movement, had to be perfect. He had to stay in the present, focused on the task at hand, aware of the intensity of the competition but unaffected by it. He had to harness the energy, channel the adrenaline, and trust the skills and intuition he'd developed over years of dedication. The early rounds were not just a test of skill but a demonstration of resilience, composure, and consistency under pressure.

Carl took a moment to reflect. He'd worked tirelessly, dedicating countless hours to honing his skills, perfecting his technique. He'd faced setbacks, disappointments, and moments of self-doubt, but he'd persevered, pushing himself harder and always aiming for improvement. He'd learned to trust his instincts, to rely on his skills, and most importantly, to rely on RJ. The bond between them was profound, a testament to countless hours spent together, a silent partnership forged in sweat and shared determination. He looked at RJ, the horse's steady gaze reflecting his calm determination. He stroked RJ's flank, feeling the comforting warmth of the animal's muscles. He could feel the rhythm of RJ's breathing, the steady pulse of his heart mirroring his own. They were ready.

The pressure of the competition was palpable. But he wouldn't let it overwhelm him. He would approach the final rounds with the same calm focus, the same unwavering determination, the exact perfect collaboration with RJ that had brought them this far. The victory wouldn't be measured just by the time on the clock, but by the journey they'd shared, by the dedication they'd shown, and by the strength of the partnership that had brought them to this crucial point. The United States Finals were a journey, a test of skill and endurance that had pushed him and RJ to their limits, revealing the true depths of their combined strength. The road to the finals had been long and arduous, and Carl embraced the challenge, knowing that the final rounds would be a culmination of everything they'd worked for — an opportunity to show the world the fruits of their unwavering dedication and the strength of their bond. The final rounds were not just a competition but an opportunity to showcase the result of years of relentless work. They were ready. They were a team. They were prepared. And they were going to give it their all.

The air crackled with anticipation. The final round of the United Stated High School Rodeo Finals loomed, a crucible of pressure where only the most skilled and composed would survive. Carl felt the weight of it, a physical pressure pressing down on his chest, a tangible manifestation of the dreams and aspirations riding on this final performance. He'd made it this far, a testament to his grit and skill, but the finish line felt miles away, each step a monumental effort. The previous rounds had been grueling, each run a high-stakes gamble, demanding precision and unwavering focus. The slightest error, a fraction of a second lost, could shatter his dreams.

He glanced at RJ, his trusty steed, whose calm demeanor belied the storm brewing within the arena. The horse stood quietly, a picture of unwavering patience, a silent partner in this high-stakes game. Their bond, forged in countless hours of training and shared experience, was his anchor in this sea of pressure. He ran a hand along RJ's flank, feeling the powerful muscles rippling beneath his touch, a tangible reminder of the raw power and strength at his disposal. He whispered words of encouragement, a quiet conversation between two partners united in purpose.

The other competitors were equally formidable. He'd watched them throughout the competition, each a master of their craft, each possessing a skill set honed to perfection. There was Jake from Montana, known for his lightning-fast roping technique, his movements fluid and almost balletic in their precision. Then there was Maria from Oklahoma, a fierce competitor whose determination was matched only by her unwavering skill. They were all vying for the same prize, pushing each other to the limit, creating an atmosphere thick with nervous energy and unspoken rivalry.

The final round began, and the atmosphere was electric. Carl drew a deep breath, the scent of dust and leather filling his nostrils, grounding him in the present moment. The gate swung open, releasing a calf that exploded from its confines, a blur of brown and white against the backdrop of the cheering crowd. His instincts kicked in, years of practice translating into fluid motion. He spurred RJ forward, and the horse responded instantly; their movements were a seamless dance of power and precision. The chase was a blur, a symphony of controlled chaos, the roar of the crowd a distant hum.

The rope flew, tracing a graceful arc through the dusty air, and found its mark with practiced ease. The lasso encircled the calf's legs, the animal bucking and struggling, testing the strength of the rope and the skill of the rider. Carl held firm, his grip unwavering, his body working in perfect synchronicity with the horse. He wrestled the calf to the ground, his movements efficient and decisive, his eyes fixed on the clock. The buzzer sounded, the time flashing on the timeboard: 7.8 seconds—a personal best. A gasp rippled through the crowd, a wave of astonishment at the speed and precision of the performance.

Jake from Montana followed, his roping technique as fast as a whiplash. His time was slightly slower, at 8.1 seconds, but still an impressive feat in such a high-pressure environment. Maria from Oklahoma then took her turn, exhibiting an almost supernatural calmness that belied the intensity of the moment. She secured her catch in a breathtaking 8.3 seconds, a time that would have been a winning time in many other competitions—the tension mounted with each passing second, the pressure building exponentially.

The final competitor was a newcomer, a dark horse named Caleb from Arizona, about whom few knew. However, Caleb surprised everyone with a masterful performance. The skill displayed was incredible, and as the buzzer sounded, a collective gasp filled the arena. 7.9 seconds. Suddenly, the pressure on Carl was intense. He'd given it his all, and yet it might not be enough. The waiting seemed interminable, an agonizing period of uncertainty where the outcome of his months of dedication hung in the balance.

The announcer's voice boomed across the arena, the words hanging heavy in the air: "And the winner of the United Stated High School Rodeo Finals Calf Roping competition is... Carl Jones from Texas!"

The roar of the crowd was deafening, a wave of sound that washed over Carl, a tangible manifestation of his victory. He dismounted, his heart pounding in his chest, a mixture of relief and elation surging through him. RJ nuzzled him, his breath warm against his cheek, a silent congratulations from his loyal partner. He hugged his uncle, tears welling in his eyes, as the years of hard work, dedication, and sacrifices all culminated in this moment of triumph.

The victory felt surreal. He'd done it. He'd conquered the United Stated High School Rodeo Finals, a dream realized after years of dedication and unwavering perseverance. The prize was significant—a scholarship to the college of his choice—but the valid reward was the journey, the hard-won battles, the lessons learned, and the unbreakable bond he forged with his horse, RJ.

The celebration was a whirlwind of congratulations, interviews, and photographs. He basked in the glow of his victory, the elation a potent elixir that temporarily masked the exhaustion that threatened to overwhelm him. But beneath the jubilation lay a deep sense of accomplishment, a pride in the journey and the strength it had demanded. It wasn't just about winning; it was about the process, the dedication, the growth, and the steady, familiar support of his family and friends.

The road to the United States Finals had been fraught with challenges, setbacks, and moments of self-doubt. But Carl had persevered, learning from his mistakes, honing his skills, and strengthening the bonds that supported him. The competition itself had been a crucible, a test of resilience, skill, and, most importantly, the unbreakable bond between him and RJ. It was a testament to their shared dedication, passion, and journey. The victory was a shared triumph, the culmination of a partnership built on trust, respect, and an unwavering commitment to excellence.

The initial euphoria of winning his preliminary rounds began to fade as the final day of the United Stated High School Rodeo Finals approached. The weight of expectation pressed down on Carl, heavier than any calf he'd ever wrestled. He'd seen the other finalists — the quiet intensity of Maria from Oklahoma, the almost arrogant confidence of Jake from Montana, and the surprising skill of Caleb from Arizona, a relative unknown who'd exploded onto the scene. Each of them represented a threat, a potential obstacle standing between him and his dream.

He spent the morning in quiet contemplation, not practicing, but instead mentally rehearsing his runs. He visualized every movement, from the subtle shift in his weight as RJ reacted to the gate opening, to the precise flick of his wrist as he released the rope. He saw the calf's trajectory, felt the tug of the rope, heard the roar of the crowd — all in the hushed quiet of the stables. RJ, sensing his rider's tension, nudged Carl's hand with his wet nose, a silent reassurance that calmed his nerves.

The air in the arena was thick with anticipation as Carl waited for his turn. He could feel the eyes of the crowd upon him, a silent pressure that amplified the pounding of his heart. The announcer's voice, amplified and distorted, was a distant drone, irrelevant to the intense focus required for the task ahead. He focused on his breathing, trying to slow the frantic rhythm of his pulse. He concentrated on the connection with RJ, the unspoken understanding that bound them together.

His turn came, and as he mounted RJ, a hush fell over the crowd. The gate swung open, and the calf exploded forth, a furry projectile against the dusty backdrop. This calf was different, stronger, faster, and more unpredictable than any he'd encountered before. It was a powerful animal, its musculature taut with energy, its movements erratic and unpredictable. For the first time, Carl felt a genuine flicker of doubt. He spurred RJ forward, but the calf's sudden turn nearly threw his timing off.

The rope, usually a fluid extension of his arm, felt heavy, unresponsive. He hesitated for a split second, a fatal error in this high-stakes game. The calf, sensing his uncertainty, increased its speed, its frantic movements threatening to evade his grasp. His heart pounded in his ears, the rhythm deafening. Sweat stung his eyes, blurring his vision. He fought to regain his composure, his mind battling against the rising tide of panic.

With a supreme effort of will, he forced himself to focus. He remembered his uncle's words, the countless hours of practice, and the steady, familiar support of his family. He focused on his breath, the steady rhythm of RJ's gait beneath him, the firm grip of the rope in his hand. He took a deep breath, recommitting to his training, to his instincts, to his trust in his horse.

He swung the rope, his arm a blur, the lasso finding its mark with an almost desperate precision. The rope tightened around the calf's legs, the animal bucking wildly, testing the limits of the rope and the strength of Carl's grip. He held on, his body tense, his muscles burning with the effort. He wrestled the calf to the ground, his movements efficient despite the initial stumble. The buzzer sounded. The time flashed on the timeboard: 9.2 seconds.

A wave of disappointment washed over him, cold and sharp. It was a good time, a respectable time, but it wasn't the winning time. He dismounted, his shoulders slumping with the weight of his failure. He looked to RJ, who nuzzled his hand, offering silent comfort. The crowd's applause felt hollow, a mockery of his inner turmoil.

He watched the remaining competitors, his earlier anxiety now overshadowed by a crushing disappointment. Maria's calm demeanor was unshaken, and she delivered a flawless performance, clocking in at a stunning 8.5 seconds. Jake, predictably, was fast, executing a near-perfect run in 8.1 seconds. Even Caleb, the dark horse, delivered an impressive performance, finishing with a time of 8.7 seconds.

As the final times were tallied, a wave of acceptance washed over Carl. He had given it his all, pushed himself to the limit, and ultimately, fell short. The sting of defeat was sharp, but a sense of accomplishment tempered it. He had reached the United States Finals, a feat in itself, and had competed against the best in the nation. The experience, the lessons learned, the steady, familiar support of his family and friends — these were the real victories.

His uncle found him, his arm around his shoulders, a comforting presence in the face of defeat. "You gave it your all, Carl," he said, his voice calm and reassuring. "Sometimes it just doesn't go your way, but that doesn't diminish what you've accomplished."

Later, as he stood on the edge of the arena, watching the awards ceremony, Carl didn't feel the sting of defeat as much as he did the quiet satisfaction of a hard-fought battle. He might not have won the United States Finals.

Still, he'd won something far more valuable — a deep understanding of his capabilities, the steady, familiar support of his loved ones, and a perspective that transcended the immediate disappointment of a loss. He knew that the journey was far from over, and that the lessons he learned in this crucible would only make him stronger, more resilient, and better prepared for future challenges. The roar of the crowd celebrating the winner was a reminder that the rodeo, like life, is a journey of continuous striving —a testament to perseverance and a test of character. And he was ready to keep riding. The next rodeo was already on the horizon, and Carl, despite his loss, was already looking forward to it.

The dust swirled around Carl's boots as he and RJ waited in the chute. The air crackled with nervous energy; the hushed anticipation of the crowd was a palpable thing, a weight pressing down on him. He could feel RJ's muscles tense beneath him, the horse sensing the heightened tension. This wasn't just another run; this was the final round of the United Stated High School Rodeo Finals, the culmination of a year's worth of grueling competition, of early mornings, blistered hands, and the steady, familiar support of his family. This was everything.

The gate swung open with a metallic clang, and the calf exploded from the chute like a furry rocket. This one was a different beast altogether — bigger, faster, and possessed of a surprising agility. It twisted and bucked even before Carl's rope left his hand, its movements unpredictable and full of deceptive power. He felt a surge of adrenaline, a raw, primal energy that pushed aside the earlier anxieties. This was the rodeo he'd trained for, the challenge he'd craved. The initial hesitation he'd felt earlier was gone, replaced by an instinctive reaction, a honed reflex honed from years of practice.

RJ, as always, was his perfect partner. The horse responded to his every subtle shift in weight, his every pull on the reins, a seamless partnership forged through countless hours of practice and an unspoken understanding that went beyond words. The rope flew from Carl's hand, a graceful arc against the backdrop of the arena, a testament to years of dedicated practice. It snaked around the calf's legs with surprising precision, a perfect loop settling just above the hooves. The calf bucked, a powerful explosion of energy, the rope taut and singing.

The arena seemed to shrink, the roar of the crowd muted to a dull roar in Carl's ears. There was only him, RJ, and the struggling calf. He felt the muscles in his arms burn, the strain on his grip, but his determination held firm. He wrestled the calf to the ground, his movements precise and efficient, a dance of controlled power. The dirt flew, the calf thrashed, but Carl held on, his grip unwavering, his body working as one with the horse beneath him. The buzzer sounded, the silence that followed deafening in its intensity.

The time flashed on the timeboard: 8.9 seconds. A collective gasp went up from the crowd, a wave of sound that washed over Carl. It was a good time, perhaps even a great time, but in this fiercely competitive environment, it wasn't easy to gauge his standing. He knew that several of his competitors had already posted impressively fast times, and the suspense was almost unbearable. He dismounted, his body trembling with the exertion, his heart still pounding in his chest. RJ nuzzled him, a comforting gesture that eased some of the tension.

The waiting was the hardest part. He watched the remaining competitors, his earlier anxiety returning with a vengeance. Each run felt like an eternity, the seconds stretching into minutes, each competitor's performance a potential barrier to their ambitions. He saw Maria, her face impassive, execute a flawless run, her time barely edging ahead of his, a mere fraction of a second separating them. Jake, true to form, delivered a breathtaking performance, his time a devastatingly fast 7.8 seconds. The other competitors performed valiantly, their times adding to the nail-biting tension.

The atmosphere in the arena thrummed with anticipation. The final times were announced, each number reverberating through the stadium like a drumbeat. Carl held his breath, his eyes glued to the timeboard, his heart pounding against his ribs. The announcer's voice, usually booming and resonant, was now thin and reedy, its words stretched out in an agonizing wait. The final rankings were revealed, each name a punctuation mark in a tense narrative.

Carl's name was announced—fourth place. A wave of relief washed over him, tinged with a hint of disappointment. He hadn't won, but he pushed himself beyond his limits. He'd come so far, from those initial, awkward attempts in his uncle's dusty arena to this, the pinnacle of high school rodeo. Fourth place wasn't a defeat; it was a testament to his dedication, perseverance, and skill.

His uncle met him with a bear hug, his congratulations genuine and heartfelt. "You were incredible, Carl," he said, his voice filled with pride. "That was a fantastic run. You should be proud of yourself." His mother's embrace was equally warm, her eyes shining with a mixture of relief and pride. The feeling of their support, the love and camaraderie they offered, were far more valuable than any trophy or ribbon could be.

The awards ceremony passed in a blur. The winner, Jake, was a whirlwind of jubilation, his victory well-deserved. But Carl didn't feel overshadowed or envious. He felt a sense of accomplishment, a quiet satisfaction in what he had achieved. He had reached the United States Finals, a feat many dream of but few achieve. He'd made it to the final round and performed with skill and determination. The support of his family and his connection with RJ were his most significant rewards.

He watched the other competitors, their faces a mixture of elation and disappointment, and realized that this wasn't just about winning; it was about the journey, the challenges overcome, the lessons learned, and the steady, familiar support of those around him. He had grown as a calf roper, but more importantly, he had grown as a person. He had learned the importance of resilience, perseverance, and the enduring power of family. He knew the sting of defeat, but also the sweet taste of accomplishment. He looked towards the future, towards the next rodeo, towards the next challenge. He knew that this was not the end, but merely a stepping stone in his ongoing journey. The roar of the crowd faded, and in the quiet aftermath, Carl felt a profound sense of peace. He took a breath—ready, at last for whatever came next. He was a rodeo competitor, and he continued to compete in rodeos.

Chapter 9: The Results

The air hung thick with unspoken tension, a palpable energy that vibrated through the arena. The scent of dust and sweat mingled with the faint aroma of leather and horsehair, a familiar perfume that evoked the hard work, dedication, and thrill of competition. Carl sat on a weathered wooden bench, RJ's warm flank a comforting presence against his leg. He hadn't realized how much his muscles ached until now, the adrenaline that had fueled his run finally receding, leaving behind a bone-deep weariness.

He watched the remaining contestants, their faces etched with a mixture of hope and apprehension. Each one represented a potential threat, a possibility that could shift the rankings, altering the destiny he'd envisioned for himself for the past year. He saw Maria, her usually vibrant eyes shadowed with anxiety, her shoulders slumped slightly, betraying the strain of the competition. She had always been a fierce competitor, a rival who pushed him to improve, a friendship forged in the crucible of the rodeo arena. He wondered if she felt the same nervous anticipation as he did.

His gaze drifted to Jake, the current front-runner, a young man whose skill and confidence were almost unsettling. Jake sat with an unnerving calm, his posture relaxed, his expression betraying nothing of the intense pressure he must be feeling. He was the epitome of a rodeo star, calm and composed, his success seemingly effortless. Carl admired Jake's talent but felt no envy, only a grudging respect for the level of skill and dedication that led to this moment.

His uncle, a man whose presence commanded respect and admiration, sat beside him, his own hands clenched tightly; a quiet intensity had replaced his usual jovial expression. Carl could feel the weight of his uncle's expectations, but it wasn't a burden; it was a source of strength —a testament to the bond they shared, one strengthened by their shared passion and years of shared experience. His mother was nearby, her gaze fixed on him, her eyes silently conveying steady, familiar support and pride. Her presence was a comforting anchor, a reminder of all the sacrifices she had made to support his dreams.

The crowd, a restless sea of faces, surged with anticipation. The roar that had accompanied each run was replaced by a hushed expectancy, a tense silence punctuated only by the occasional cough or whispered comment. The atmosphere was electric, charged with the collective hope and anxiety of competitors, families, and spectators alike. Even the usual cacophony of the rodeo - the chatter, the clanging of metal, the snorting of horses - seemed to have faded, replaced by a suffocating sense of anticipation.

Carl felt his heart pound against his ribs, a frantic rhythm that echoed the anticipation in the arena. He ran a hand through his sweat-dampened hair, a futile attempt to calm his nerves. His mind raced, replaying his run over and over, scrutinizing every movement, every decision. Had he made the right choices? Could he have done better? Doubt, a familiar adversary, began to creep into his thoughts, casting shadows on his hard-earned confidence.

He focused on his breathing, attempting to slow the frantic rhythm of his heart. He drew comfort from RJ, who nuzzled his shoulder, his presence a reassuring anchor in the storm of emotions swirling around him. The horse seemed to sense his anxiety, his calm demeanor a calming influence. Carl stroked RJ's flank, whispering words of reassurance, drawing strength from the bond they shared, a partnership forged through years of trust and mutual respect.

The minutes stretched into an eternity. Each second felt heavier than the last, the suspense a physical weight pressing down on him. He watched the clock, its hands moving mockingly slowly, each tick amplifying the anticipation. The silence, once deafening, now seemed to amplify the sound of his racing pulse. He could feel the tension radiating from his family, their eyes mirroring his anxiety.

Suddenly, a hush fell over the crowd, a wave of silence that swept through the arena like a chilling wind. The announcer's voice, usually booming and resonant, now possessed a tense quietness. Carl held his breath, his eyes fixed on the timeboard, the numbers blurring slightly in the haze of his anxious anticipation. He felt a prickling sensation on his skin, a mixture of excitement and dread that made his palms sweat.

The announcer began to read the results, each name a punctuation mark in the unfolding narrative. He started with the lower rankings, each name announced eliciting a ripple of reaction from the crowd—a mixture of applause and disappointment. The tension in the arena thickened, the silence heavy with anticipation. He was now in the top five; the tension in his muscles was so strong it felt like they would snap. He heard several names, competitors he knew, their places announced, each word pushing the tension higher.

Then, a hush, followed by a pause that stretched into an agonizing eternity. The announcer cleared his throat, his voice finally reaching Carl through the fog of anxiety. The moment of truth had arrived. His name was called—fourth place.

A wave of relief washed over him, a sudden release of the pent-up tension that had held him captive for what felt like an eternity. He had made it; he had performed well against the best of the best. However, the relief was quickly followed by a tinge of disappointment, a fleeting sense of unfulfilled ambition. He hadn't won, hadn't achieved the ultimate goal he'd strived for.

But as the initial disappointment faded, a sense of accomplishment emerged, a quiet satisfaction that resonated deep within him. He had reached the United States Finals, a testament to years of hard work, dedication, and perseverance. He had competed against the toughest competition, pushing himself beyond his limits. Fourth place wasn't a defeat; it was a measure of his skill and determination.

His uncle's hug was a comforting embrace, a silent validation of his effort. His mother's smile was filled with pride, a testament to the steady, familiar support she had given him throughout the grueling season. Their words of encouragement, their pride, were a reward far greater than any trophy or ribbon.

The awards ceremony was a blur, a kaleidoscope of celebratory moments and quiet reflections. He watched Jake receive his well-deserved award, feeling no envy, only admiration. He had achieved his victory, not in the form of a trophy, but through self-improvement, self-discovery, and a deeper appreciation for the support system that had carried him to this point. The journey itself, the challenges faced, the lessons learned, the bonds forged — these were the true rewards of his commitment to the sport.

As the sounds of the rodeo faded, giving way to the quiet hum of the post-competition calm, Carl felt a profound sense of peace. He was a rodeo competitor, and he would continue to ride, learning, growing, and striving for excellence. Fourth place was not an ending; it was a beginning, a stepping stone on his continuing journey towards his ultimate dreams. The path ahead was long, but he was ready. He had his family, his horse, and his unwavering passion to fuel his journey. And that, he realized, was a victory in itself.

The announcer's voice, amplified by the arena's sound system, cut through the expectant silence like a knife. Each name he called was met with a ripple of sound — a cheer, a sigh, a murmur of conversation — a wave washing over the crowd, reflecting the hopes and disappointments of those invested in the outcome. The tension in the air was almost unbearable, a tangible entity pressing down on everyone present. Carl felt the prickle of sweat on his skin despite the cool evening air, his heart pounding a frantic rhythm against his ribs. He gripped the worn leather of the bench, his knuckles white. RJ, sensing his rider's unease, shifted slightly, his warm weight a comforting presence against Carl's leg.

He'd run through the scenarios countless times in his mind. The perfect run, the near-miss, the catastrophic fall. Each scenario played out like a movie reel, highlighting his strengths and exposing his weaknesses. He'd analyzed his performance meticulously, scrutinizing every twist of his body, every movement of RJ, every fraction of a second lost or gained. The memory of the calf's sudden buck, the almost imperceptible shift in RJ's footing, the adrenaline surge — it all played back vividly in his mind, a chaotic symphony of sensations and emotions. But the final judgment remained elusive, hanging suspended in the expectant silence.

The announcer continued, moving through the lower rankings. He mentioned names Carl recognized — competitors he'd trained alongside, rivals he respected, friends he'd shared meals and late-night conversations with. Each announcement chipped away at the suspense, each name bringing them a step closer to the unveiling of their fate. He felt a strange detachment, as if observing the proceedings from a distance, his own emotions muted by the intensity of the moment. He saw his mother's face, her features etched with a mixture of hope and anxiety, her eyes fixed on the announcer, searching his words for any indication of his place. His uncle sat beside her, his usual jovial demeanor replaced by a stoic composure, his gaze unwavering.

The names of the top three competitors were called, each announcement greeted with a roar from the crowd that only amplified the pressure and anticipation. Carl watched as Jake, his main rival, accepted the second-place ribbon. A wave of relief mingled with a tinge of disappointment washed over Carl. He'd expected to contend with Jake for the top spot. He'd been aiming for first place since he began, and the realization that he hadn't made the top three hit him like a physical blow.

The arena held its breath, the silence deafening. Carl looked at RJ, seeking reassurance, and found it in the horse's calm presence. RJ seemed unfazed, his breath steady, his eyes soft. It was a comforting contrast to the chaos swirling inside Carl. He realized that RJ had carried him through countless runs; the horse was a silent partner, an steady, familiar support in the face of adversity. He stroked the horse's flank, finding solace in the gentle rhythm of his heartbeats.

And then, the moment arrived. The announcer paused, cleared his throat, and spoke Carl's name. "And in fourth place... Carl Davies!"

The announcement was met with a wave of applause, a mixture of appreciation and perhaps a touch of surprise. It wasn't the victory he had craved, but it wasn't defeat either. Fourth place in the United Stated High School Rodeo Finals was a significant accomplishment. He'd trained rigorously, sacrificed countless hours, endured setbacks and disappointments, and he'd been through the most challenging season of his life. This was more than just a sporting event; it was a testament to his perseverance, dedication, and unwavering commitment to his dream.

The relief was palpable. The weight lifted from his shoulders, the tension easing from his muscles. The emotions flooded in — the initial wave of disappointment, quickly overshadowed by a surge of accomplishment. He had done it; he'd made it to the United States Finals, competing with the best of the best in the country. This was a triumph in itself.

His uncle's hug was strong, a silent expression of pride and support. His mother's eyes shone with unshed tears, her embrace warm and reassuring. The words of congratulations from his friends, his rivals, his coaches, and even some of the spectators were heartfelt and genuine —a chorus of affirmation that resonated deeply within him.

The awards ceremony was a blur of activity — handshakes, congratulations, and photographs. He watched Jake receive his first-place trophy, a feeling of genuine admiration washing over him, devoid of envy. He'd pushed himself to improve, and this achievement validated his years of hard work. He accepted his fourth-place ribbon with grace, a quiet acknowledgement of his success, understanding that the real victory lay not just in the ranking but in the journey itself.

Later, in the quiet solitude of the hotel room, as the excitement of the competition subsided, Carl reflected on his experience. He'd learned valuable lessons about perseverance, about handling pressure, about the importance of teamwork and support. He'd faced his fears, overcome his doubts, and emerged stronger, more resilient, more confident than ever before. He had learned about himself, about his capabilities, about his limits, and the importance of pushing beyond those limits.

The United States Finals were a stepping stone, a crucial point on his journey towards his ultimate goal — a college rodeo scholarship. Fourth place wasn't an endpoint, but a starting point. It provided valuable experience, fueling his ambition to return next year, stronger and better prepared to contend for the top spot. He knew that the path ahead would be challenging, demanding continued dedication, sacrifice, and perseverance. But he was ready to embrace the challenges, ready to ride into the future with renewed determination and unwavering passion. He knew that he had the support of his family, his friends, and his incredible horse, RJ. And that was a victory in itself. The journey, the struggles, the triumphs — these were the tangible rewards, far exceeding any trophy or ribbon. The rodeo was a part of him, interwoven into his very being. He was a rodeo competitor, and he would continue to strive for excellence, knowing that even in defeat, he had triumphed. He had grown, he had learned, and he would continue to rise. The journey had just begun.

The hotel room was quiet, a stark contrast to the roar of the crowd just hours before. The lingering scent of dust and sweat clung to his clothes, a faint reminder of the adrenaline-fueled chaos of the United States Finals. Carl sat on the edge of the bed, RJ's bridle draped over the back of a chair, the leather soft and familiar under his fingertips. He stared out the window, the city lights blurring into a hazy tapestry in the night, fourth place. The words echoed in his mind, not as a defeat, but as a marker, a milestone on a much longer road.

It hadn't been easy, and the season had been a relentless marathon, a grueling test of endurance, skill, and mental fortitude. Twenty-two rodeos, each a unique challenge, each demanding peak performance. He remembered the scorching August sun beating down on him during the early-season rodeos, the dust swirling around him, blurring his vision, making each run a test of survival as much as skill. He recalled the biting wind of the late fall rodeos, the icy rain that soaked him to the bone, the mud that clung to his boots like a second skin. He'd endured mechanical failures, near misses, and the agonizing disappointment of runs gone wrong, where a misplaced foot, a hesitant movement, or a lapse in concentration cost him precious seconds and valuable points.

There were times he'd questioned himself. The pressure to perform, to live up to the expectations of his family, friends, and sponsor, had been immense. He'd felt the sting of self-doubt, the nagging fear of failure. But through it all, he'd persevered. He'd learned to manage his anxiety, to focus his energy, to channel his emotions into his performance. He'd learned the value of resilience, the importance of bouncing back from setbacks, of learning from his mistakes, and of using those mistakes as fuel to propel him forward.

He thought about his uncle, his mentor, his unwavering source of support. His uncle had taught him more than just the mechanics of calf roping; he'd instilled in him a work ethic that transcended the rodeo arena, a commitment to excellence that extended to every aspect of his life. He'd taught him the importance of patience, of discipline, of respect for his horse, and of understanding the delicate balance between aggression and control. He'd been a constant presence, a calming influence, a source of encouragement during times of doubt and frustration. His uncle's quiet strength and his unwavering belief in Carl's abilities had been instrumental in his success.

And then there was RJ, his faithful steed, his silent partner in crime. RJ had been more than just a horse; he'd been a confidante, a source of steady, familiar support, a steadying force in the face of uncertainty. He'd felt the horse's strength beneath him, his surefootedness, his responsiveness to even the slightest cues. RJ's unwavering calm had been a source of comfort and reassurance in moments of pressure and stress, a constant reminder of the strength of their bond. He'd learned to trust RJ implicitly, to rely on the horse's instincts, to work in harmony with him. Their partnership was a testament to years of training, to mutual respect, to unwavering trust.

Carl smiled, a genuine smile that reached his eyes. He'd forged strong bonds with his fellow competitors, developing friendships that transcended the rivalry of the arena. He'd learned to appreciate the camaraderie, the mutual respect, the shared understanding of the dedication and sacrifice required to reach the national level. He'd discovered that competition wasn't just about winning; it was about pushing boundaries, improving skills, and celebrating the achievements of others. He'd even found a connection with his main rival, Jake, discovering a shared respect for their mutual dedication to the sport.

The rodeo season had also been a crucible, forging him into a stronger, more resilient young man. He'd grown not just as a calf roper, but also as an individual. He'd faced adversity, conquered his fears, and emerged victorious, not just in terms of ranking but in terms of personal growth. He'd learned to embrace challenges, to view setbacks as opportunities for learning and improvement. He'd learned the importance of discipline, of perseverance, of hard work. He'd learned about himself, about his limitations, and about the importance of pushing beyond those limits. The rodeo had been a catalyst for his personal growth, shaping him into a young man with a newfound understanding of himself and his capabilities.

He thought about his mother, her constant support, her unwavering belief in him, her quiet strength. He recalled her sacrifices, the endless hours she'd spent supporting his dream, the unwavering encouragement she'd provided, the calm reassurance she offered in moments of doubt. His mother's presence had been a constant source of strength, a reassuring reminder that he wasn't alone on his journey. Her love and support had been the bedrock upon which he'd built his success.

The United States Finals weren't just a competition; they were a culmination of years of hard work, dedication, and sacrifice. They represented a personal journey of growth, of learning, of self-discovery. Fourth place was not a failure; it was a testament to his perseverance, commitment to his dream, and ability to overcome adversity. It was a stepping stone, a springboard to launch him toward his ultimate goal — a college rodeo scholarship.

He knew the competition would be even tougher next year. He'd have to train harder, push himself further, refine his technique, and enhance his partnership with RJ. But he was ready. He was more determined than ever. He had the support of his family, his friends, his mentor, and his incredible horse. He had gained experience from this season, learned valuable lessons, and forged strength in the fires of competition. He had the unwavering belief in himself and his abilities.

Carl closed his eyes, feeling a sense of profound gratitude. He'd achieved more than he'd ever imagined. He'd grown as a person, strengthened his bonds with his family and friends, and honed his skills as a calf roper. He'd learned that the real victories in life aren't always measured in trophies or ribbons; they're measured in the lessons learned, the challenges overcome, and the personal growth achieved. The journey had been challenging, demanding, and fulfilling. And it was far from over. He took a breath—ready, at last for the next chapter, ready to ride into the future, fueled by his passion, his determination, and his unwavering belief in himself. He was a rodeo competitor, and he wouldn't give up until he'd achieved his dreams. The journey had just begun.

The scent of pine needles and damp earth filled the air as Carl walked RJ back to the trailer. The crisp morning air, a welcome contrast to the dusty arena, did little to alleviate the quiet hum of disappointment that still thrummed beneath his skin. Fourth place. It was a respectable finish, a solid accomplishment, but it fell short of his aspirations. He'd envisioned a different ending, a different outcome. He'd visualized himself standing on the top of the podium, the roar of the crowd a symphony of celebration. Instead, the celebratory atmosphere felt distant, muted by the weight of his near-miss.

He ran a hand over RJ's smooth coat, the horse nuzzling his hand in response. RJ, as always, was a source of steady, familiar support, his quiet presence a balm to Carl's bruised ego. The horse seemed to understand his disappointment, mirroring it with a calm stillness. There was no judgment in his big brown eyes, only an unspoken understanding that sometimes, despite the best efforts, the desired outcome eludes even the most skilled competitors.

The drive back to the ranch was long, filled with a silence broken only by the rhythmic hum of the engine and the occasional sigh escaping Carl's lips. His uncle, riding shotgun, didn't press him. He knew the value of quiet reflection, the importance of allowing emotions to settle before attempting to analyze them. He knew Carl needed time to process the events of the past few days, to absorb the mixture of triumph and disappointment that pulsed within him.

Back at the ranch, the familiar comfort of home enveloped him. The smell of his mother's cooking wafted from the kitchen, a comforting aroma that spoke of warmth, family, and steady, familiar support. He found his mother in the kitchen, humming softly as she moved about, preparing a meal that would likely contain his favorite comfort food, her famous chili. Her presence was a constant source of solace, a reassuring reminder of the unconditional love that fueled his dreams.

Later, as he sat on the porch, RJ grazing peacefully in the pasture, Carl began to unpack the emotions that had been swirling within him. Fourth place wasn't a failure. It was a stepping stone, a testament to his progress. He hadn't won, but he had grown. He'd learned valuable lessons about perseverance, about the importance of maintaining focus under pressure, and about the need for consistent practice. He'd seen how quickly a misplaced foot, a hesitation, a slight miscalculation, could cost him valuable seconds and points.

He reviewed his runs in his mind, dissecting each one with critical analysis. Carl noticed small details, almost imperceptible flaws in his technique that had contributed to his less-than-perfect times. He identified areas where he could improve, specific aspects of his roping style that needed refinement. The self-reflection was a process of constructive criticism, a means to identify areas for improvement.

His uncle's wisdom, the countless hours spent practicing, the steady, familiar support of his family and friends—these weren't things to take for granted. They were the pillars upon which he built his success, the sources of strength that kept his resolve burning. He realized that true victory wasn't simply about winning; it was about growth, learning, and the ongoing process of improvement. He hadn't just honed his calf-roping skills; he'd sharpened his mental game, and that was just as important in this high-stakes competition.

The next few weeks were dedicated to refining his technique. He spent countless hours in the arena, practicing his roping skills with unwavering focus. He worked on his positioning, his timing, and the precise execution of each movement. He refined his communication with RJ, ensuring that they worked in perfect harmony. He sought feedback from his uncle, eager to glean any insights that could help him improve his performance. He had also reviewed his notes and the recorded runs from the finals, focusing on details that he had previously overlooked.

He discovered a different kind of camaraderie among competitors. Beyond the competitive spirit, he saw mutual respect and appreciation for the hard work, skill, and dedication that characterized the rodeo circuit. He learned that sportsmanship was as important as winning, and that there was value in celebrating the success of others. He'd even reached out to Jake, his main rival, sharing a few tips and receiving some in return. The shared respect and understanding strengthened the bonds between them, transcending the competitive arena.

Carl also realized the importance of balance in his life. He hadn't neglected his studies amidst the rigors of the rodeo season, and he cherished the time spent with his friends and family. He understood that his success in rodeo depended on more than just his athletic abilities. It required discipline, dedication, and a supportive environment. The combination of commitment and well-roundedness allowed him to thrive, both in the arena and out.

As the new rodeo season approached, Carl felt a renewed sense of purpose, a stronger resolve. He wasn't just striving for victory; he was striving for self-improvement, for pushing his limits and honing his skills. He carried the lessons learned from his fourth-place finish, not as a burden, but as a catalyst for growth. The near-miss kept his resolve burning, sharpened his focus, and solidified his commitment to his dream.

The following season was a whirlwind of exhilarating rides and challenging runs. He faced setbacks, experienced moments of doubt, and encountered unexpected challenges. But each time he stumbled, he rose again, stronger and more determined than before. The lessons he learned during his previous season served him well, shaping his performance, improving his decision-making, and bolstering his mental resilience.

He learned to adapt his strategies and adjust his technique according to the circumstances. He developed a deeper understanding of the psychology of competition, learning how to manage his anxiety and maintain his composure in high-pressure situations. He pushed himself to his limits, constantly seeking ways to improve his roping skills.

The culmination of the season was the regional finals. Carl felt a surge of adrenaline as he entered the arena. He'd worked tirelessly, both mentally and physically, and he felt confident in his abilities. He remembered his mother's words of encouragement, his uncle's guidance, and RJ's steady, familiar support.

He performed flawlessly. The crowd roared as he crossed the finish line, securing a victory that validated his tireless hard work, steadfast dedication, and unwavering resilience.

The trophy, the championship title, the celebratory applause — they were all significant accomplishments. But the true victory lay in the journey, in the relentless pursuit of excellence, in the growth, both personal and professional, he'd experienced along the way. He'd learned that setbacks were learning opportunities, that defeat was not the opposite of success but a stepping stone towards it. And more importantly, he had learned the importance of embracing challenges and relishing the journey, regardless of the outcome. His dreams were still alive and well, and he was ready for the next ride. His journey towards his college rodeo scholarship was far from over, but he felt he was finally, firmly, on the right track.

The dust had settled, both literally and figuratively. The regional finals victory felt surreal, a dream finally realized, yet the reality of the future loomed. The adrenaline rush had subsided, leaving behind a quiet hum of accomplishment, as well as the weight of anticipation. College loomed, a new arena with its own set of challenges and opportunities. More than just academics, it represented a crucial turning point in his rodeo career. The scholarship was the key, the bridge connecting his high school triumphs to a future steeped in the sport he loved.

He'd spent hours poring over college brochures, their glossy pages showcasing sprawling campuses and impressive rodeo programs. The names of coaches, their reputations for nurturing talent, and the details of their training facilities—all became crucial parts of his research. He wasn't just choosing a school; he was choosing a team, a mentor, a future. He'd compiled a detailed list, factoring in everything from academic rigor to the strength of the rodeo program, proximity to home (a compromise between independence and family support), and even the climate — something he hadn't fully considered before. Texas, Colorado, Oklahoma—each state boasted several colleges with thriving rodeo teams, each with its unique appeal.

His uncle, a wealth of knowledge in the rodeo world, had become an invaluable advisor. He'd shared stories of his college rodeo days, including the intense competition, camaraderie, sacrifices, and triumphs. He'd provided contacts, including the names of coaches he'd known and respected, as well as inside perspectives on various programs. He'd even helped Carl craft a compelling application, emphasizing not just his athletic abilities but also his academic achievements, his work ethic, and his character. The application process was, in its way, a rodeo of a different sort.

Beyond the formal applications, Carl began reaching out to coaches directly. He sent videos of his winning runs, highlighting his technique, his speed, and his control. He drafted personalized emails that showcased not only his skills but also his passion for the sport, his commitment to teamwork, and his desire to contribute to the college rodeo program. Each email was carefully crafted, reflecting his understanding of the specific program and the coach's priorities. He felt the weight of each email sent, each video uploaded, a tiny piece of his future riding on every electronic transmission. Rejection could be devastating, but he knew this process was as much a test of mental fortitude as it was a testament to his ability.

His mother remained his steadfast rock. She handled the logistical aspects — helping him organize his transcripts, ensuring deadlines were met, and providing a calm presence amid the chaos of applications and waiting. She listened patiently to his anxieties and celebrated his small victories, offering encouragement when his confidence faltered. She was his anchor, keeping him grounded while he navigated the turbulent waters of college applications. She understood the importance of education, emphasizing the balance between academic success and his rodeo aspirations. She'd often remind him that a college education was not only a stepping stone to a successful rodeo career, but also a foundation for a stable future, whatever that might hold.

The waiting period was agonizing. Each day stretched into an eternity, the silence amplifying the uncertainty. The anticipation was almost unbearable. He continued to train diligently, keeping his skills sharp and maintaining his physical fitness. He knew that maintaining his focus on his training would be his greatest asset during this period. He wouldn't let the anxiety distract him from his goals. He knew he had to remain vigilant, his routine a calming factor amid the waiting game. His life was more than just the next rodeo. There were classes to attend, friends to see, and family to spend time with. He didn't want the uncertainty to consume him.

The first acceptance letter arrived like a bolt of lightning, a sudden burst of hope piercing the quiet tension. It was from a university in Oklahoma, a program known for its strong rodeo team and its supportive coaching staff. The news was met with joyous celebrations, both at home and at the barn. RJ, seemingly aware of the significance of the moment, nuzzled Carl's hand with a gentle whinny, as if sharing in his triumph.

The other responses trickled in over the next few weeks. Some were acceptances, each accompanied by its own unique set of scholarship offers and financial aid packages. Others were polite rejections, each a gentle nudge towards recalibration and strategic planning. He carefully weighed his options, considering not just the rodeo program's strengths but also the academic opportunities, the campus culture, and the overall feeling he got from each university.

He visited several campuses, experiencing the ambiance of each, meeting with coaches and fellow rodeo athletes. He saw the training facilities, the arenas, and the camaraderie among students. He felt the palpable energy and the electric atmosphere in the air. He discovered different personalities and leadership styles. He meticulously compared the scholarship packages, taking into account the tuition fees, living expenses, and the potential for additional financial aid. He was meticulous, ensuring his decision was driven not just by emotion but by a strategic alignment of his values, needs, and ambitions.

Finally, after weeks of careful consideration, he made his choice. It wasn't the closest to home, nor the one with the most prestigious program. It was the one that resonated with his values, his aspirations, and his vision for the future. It was a place where he thought he could thrive, both academically and athletically. It was a place where he could continue to grow as a calf roper, a student, and a person.

The decision was made. His future was mapped out. But it wasn't just about the college. It was about the journey, the relentless pursuit of excellence, the unwavering commitment to his dreams, and the steady, familiar support of his family, his friends, and RJ, his loyal partner in this incredible adventure. His next ride began, and this time, the path ahead was not just clear but paved with opportunity. He took a breath—ready, at last to write the next chapter, not just in his rodeo career, but in his life. His college years promised challenges, but also countless exhilarating opportunities to show his skills, learn from the best, and solidify his place among the top rodeo athletes in the country. His dream was not just about winning; it was about the journey, the growth, and the chance to become the best version of himself. The future was bright, and Carl was ready to ride into it.

Chapter 10: College Scholarships

The acceptance letter from Oklahoma State felt like a small victory in a much larger rodeo. It was exhilarating, a confirmation that his hard work and dedication had paid off, but it was just the first step. The scholarship application process was far from over. He had more schools to apply to, more essays to write, more videos to edit, more dreams to chase. The initial euphoria gave way to a renewed sense of focus, a determination to secure the best possible financial aid for his college education.

The next application was to East Texas Tech. Their rodeo program was legendary, boasting a long history of national champions and a reputation for producing some of the best calf ropers in the country. However, their application process was notoriously rigorous. It wasn't just about filling out forms and submitting transcripts; it was about understanding the process and navigating it effectively. They required a detailed essay outlining his rodeo experience, his goals, and his commitment to the program. Carl spent weeks crafting his response, meticulously detailing his successes, failures, learning experiences, and aspirations. He highlighted his winning runs at regional finals, but he also acknowledged his mistakes, showcasing his ability to learn from setbacks and improve his technique. He emphasized his teamwork skills, highlighting his collaborations with his roping partner, his horse RJ, and his mentors. The essay was a narrative of his journey, a story of dedication and perseverance.

Alongside the essay, he submitted a comprehensive portfolio of his rodeo accomplishments. This included high-quality videos of his winning calf roping runs, showcasing his speed, precision, and control. He meticulously edited the footage, highlighting his technique, emphasizing the smooth transitions, the quick dismount, and the efficient movements. He even included slow-motion replays of key moments, allowing the judges to examine his technique closely and appreciate the finesse of his skills. In addition to the videos, he submitted his high school rodeo results, demonstrating a consistent track record of success throughout his high school career. He included letters of recommendation from his high school rodeo coach, who lauded his dedication, work ethic, and exceptional talent. He also included a letter from his uncle, whose credentials as a multi-world champion team roper lent significant weight to his application. He didn't leave anything to chance. This was his chance to prove himself worthy of a place on one of the nation's top collegiate rodeo teams.

The application to University of Eastern Colorado was a different beast entirely. They emphasized academic excellence as much as athletic prowess. Beyond his rodeo achievements, they scrutinized his academic transcript, including his GPA and SAT scores. He knew he needed to present a well-rounded profile, demonstrating not just his athletic abilities but also his academic potential. He spent hours refining his application, ensuring that every detail reflected his commitment to both his rodeo career and his education. He highlighted his academic achievements, his involvement in school clubs and activities, and his commitment to community service. He wanted to showcase not only his capabilities but also his character, values, and dedication to pursuing both education and his passion for rodeo simultaneously. It was a delicate balance, showing the equal weight, he gave both sides of his life.

Each application was unique, tailored to the specific requirements and priorities of each university. He researched each program thoroughly, understanding their coaching styles, training facilities, and emphasis on various aspects of rodeo competition. He personalized each essay, each video, and each letter of recommendation, ensuring that his application resonated with the values and goals of each institution. He understood that this wasn't just about securing a scholarship; it was about finding the right fit, the program that would best support his academic and athletic goals.

The applications required a significant time commitment. He spent countless hours researching schools, writing essays, editing videos, compiling transcripts, and securing letters of recommendation. It was a demanding process, often requiring him to balance his academic workload, his rodeo training, and his scholarship applications simultaneously. There were days when he felt overwhelmed, when the pressure felt immense. But he persevered, driven by his passion for rodeo and his unwavering determination to earn a college scholarship. He leaned on his family and friends for support, finding strength in their belief in him and his abilities.

The waiting period was excruciating. Each day felt like an eternity, each email notification sparking a wave of both hope and anxiety. He continued to train diligently, maintaining his physical fitness and honing his roping skills. He knew that his athletic performance would remain a crucial factor in the scholarship selection process, even after the applications were submitted. His work ethic wasn't something he could switch off, so he continued to work, train, and improve his skills. He kept busy with schoolwork and spent time with friends and family, using these distractions as a way to cope with the stress and anxiety of the long wait. He maintained a routine, a stability in his life that anchored him amidst the turmoil of uncertainty.

The acceptance letters started arriving in dribs and drabs, each one bringing a wave of relief and excitement. With each acceptance, the weight on his shoulders lightened, his future seeming a little more certain. He carefully reviewed each scholarship offer, comparing the financial aid packages, the academic opportunities, and the overall fit of each program. He weighed the pros and cons of each school, considering location, facilities, coaching staff, and his personal preferences. He visited campuses, experiencing the atmosphere firsthand, connecting with coaches and current rodeo athletes, gaining insights, and building connections.

He learned that the scholarship process wasn't just about talent; it was about persistence, resilience, and strategic planning. It was about presenting a comprehensive profile, highlighting not just athletic skill but also academic achievement, character, and commitment. It was about demonstrating that he was not just a talented athlete, but also a responsible individual capable of handling the pressures and responsibilities of college life. His success in this process was a testament to his hard work, dedication, and commitment to pursuing his dreams. He was more than a calf roper; he was a student, a leader, and a determined young man with a clear vision for his future.

The first interview was at Oklahoma State, and the pressure was palpable. He sat across from Coach Miller, a grizzled veteran with eyes that seemed to see right through him. Coach Miller didn't beat around the bush. He launched straight into questions about Carl's roping technique, his training regimen, and his academic record. Carl answered confidently, detailing his preferred roping style, emphasizing his focus on precision and speed. He meticulously described his daily training routine, highlighting the balance he maintained between physical conditioning and technique refinement.

He discussed his academic record with pride, outlining his efforts to maintain a high GPA alongside his demanding rodeo schedule. He spoke of his involvement in school clubs, his volunteer work, and his commitment to community service, demonstrating his well-rounded profile. The interview wasn't just a Q&A session; it was a performance, a display of his character, his determination, and his passion for the sport.

The trial at Oklahoma State was even more intense. He found himself competing against other top high school calf ropers from across the country, each supremely talented and vying for the same limited scholarship spots. The air crackled with competitive energy, the atmosphere thick with anticipation. The arena buzzed with the sounds of hooves, the shouts of cowboys, and the low hum of the crowd. Carl felt the pressure mounting, but he pushed it aside, focusing on the task at hand. He approached each run with precision and focus, every movement carefully calculated, every muscle working in perfect harmony. RJ, his trusty steed, responded flawlessly; their partnership had been honed over years of training and competition. He executed his roping technique with unwavering precision, his movements fluid and efficient. He felt the adrenaline coursing through his veins, the exhilaration of the competition fueling his performance. He finished his runs with times that put him among the top contenders, but the competition was fierce; every second mattered, every mistake could cost him a spot.

Next up was East Texas Tech, and the atmosphere was different; it was more collegiate, refined, almost professional. The interview with Coach Rodriguez was more about his long-term goals and vision for the future than it was about technical details. Coach Rodriguez was a sharp interviewer, delving deep into Carl's aspirations, his plans for his academic career, and his commitment to the A&M rodeo program. He explored Carl's understanding of the challenges of collegiate rodeo and his ability to handle the pressures of both academic and athletic pursuits. Carl displayed his maturity and strategic thinking, articulating his goals with clarity and confidence. He outlined his long-term plan, demonstrating his ambition and his commitment to excellence. He spoke about his plans to excel academically while maintaining a high level of athletic performance, showcasing his dedication and his well-rounded approach to his future.

The trial at East Texas Tech was a different beast entirely. It was less about raw speed and more about consistency and control. The judges were looking for riders who could maintain a high level of performance under pressure, as well as those who could adapt to different conditions and remain calm in high-pressure situations. Carl's runs were measured, precise, and consistent. He demonstrated his ability to maintain control in difficult situations, showcasing his composure and his experience. He displayed an impressive ability to adapt to changing conditions, adjusting his technique as needed, which reflected his skill and maturity as a rider. The consistency of his performance and his evident skill separated him from the other competitors.

University of Eastern Colorado presented a unique set of challenges. Their program was renowned for its rigorous academic standards and its dedication to cultivating well-rounded athletes. The interview process involved a panel of coaches, professors, and academic advisors, each assessing Carl's potential from different perspectives. He was asked about his educational aspirations, career goals, and plans. He answered their questions confidently, showcasing his academic prowess and his long-term vision. He demonstrated his commitment to balancing his academic and athletic pursuits, and he effectively articulated his passion for rodeo, as well as his dedication to maximizing his college experience. He was more than just an athlete to them; he was a scholar-athlete.

The trial at University of Eastern Colorado was particularly demanding, involving a grueling series of timed runs under varying conditions. The arena conditions were altered each run, simulating difficult situations and testing his ability to adapt quickly. The judges were meticulously observing his response to pressure and his ability to remain calm in stressful situations. He had to perform exceptionally well across different runs, demonstrating both versatility and consistency under pressure. Carl executed flawlessly, his years of experience and rigorous training paying off. He adjusted his strategy and technique as required, showcasing both his skill and his adaptability. He performed exceptionally well under pressure, showcasing his ability to execute flawlessly even in the face of challenges.

Throughout the interview and trial processes, Carl's relationship with RJ remained a crucial element. He emphasized their partnership, their understanding, and their ability to read each other's cues in the arena. He wasn't just applying for a scholarship; he was advocating for a partnership, a bond forged through years of sweat, determination, and shared success. He spoke of RJ's temperament, his responsiveness, and his ability to handle pressure, illustrating the importance of their bond in achieving peak performance.

The waiting period after each trial was nerve-wracking. The uncertainty was almost unbearable. He'd return home, exhausted but energized from the competition, and try to focus on his regular schoolwork. He spent time with his family, sought reassurance from his mother, and discussed his experiences with his uncle. His uncle's advice and support were invaluable, particularly in helping him maintain perspective and manage his stress. His uncle, understanding the intense pressure and emotional toll, encouraged him to focus on what he could control, to continue training, and to trust in his abilities.

The scholarship offers started arriving in the early spring. The first came from Oklahoma State, then East Texas Tech, and finally, University of Eastern Colorado. Each acceptance letter was a testament to his hard work and dedication. Each offer carries its unique benefits and drawbacks, requiring careful consideration. He carefully reviewed each scholarship package, comparing the financial aid, academic programs, coaching staff, and overall campus environment. He weighed the pros and cons of each school, meticulously examining the benefits of each offer and the opportunities available in each academic program. He prioritized factors such as the strengths of their coaching staff, the caliber of the competing team members, and the potential for further personal and professional growth. He visited each campus, speaking with the coaches and current rodeo athletes, to gain a deeper understanding of each school and get a sense of the culture and atmosphere.

Finally, after much deliberation, Carl made his decision. It wasn't just about the money; it was about the right fit, the program that would best challenge him, the environment that would nurture his growth, both as a rodeo athlete and as a young man. He chose to embark on a new chapter in his life at East Texas Tech, recognizing the renowned program, strong coaching staff, and dedication to academic excellence as the perfect setting to reach his full potential. It was a decision that reflected his maturity, his careful analysis, and his unwavering commitment to his future. The decision was a victory in itself, a testament to his perseverance, his talent, and his steadfast dedication to his dream. His journey from high school rodeo hopeful to a top collegiate competitor was one of grit, determination, and a deep passion for the sport. He took a breath—ready, at last to ride towards his future with confidence and unwavering determination.

The weight of the decision pressed down on Carl like a seasoned saddle. He'd poured his heart and soul into the past four years, sacrificing weekends, holidays, and countless hours of sleep to hone his skills and maintain his grades. Now, the culmination of that relentless dedication lay before him: three scholarship offers, each a golden ticket to a future he'd only dared to dream of. Oklahoma State, with its legendary rodeo program and a coach who'd seen it all, had extended an invitation. East Texas Tech, with its renowned academic reputation and a more refined, professional rodeo team, had also expressed its interest. And then there was University of Eastern Colorado, with its emphasis on well-rounded student-athletes, demanding both athletic excellence and academic rigor.

Each offer was meticulously laid out, a detailed blueprint of potential futures. Oklahoma State's package was generous financially, offering a substantial scholarship that would essentially cover tuition, fees, and living expenses. Their rodeo program boasted a rich history, a legacy of champions. Coach Miller's gruff demeanor masked a deep-seated knowledge of the sport, a wealth of experience Carl felt he could draw upon. The campus, however, felt vast and overwhelming, a sprawling landscape that lacked the intimate, close-knit feel of smaller colleges. The sheer scale of it all seemed a bit intimidating.

East Texas Tech's offer was more balanced. The scholarship amount was comparable to Oklahoma State's, but the academic program appealed more to Carl's burgeoning interest in agricultural business. The coaching staff, led by the thoughtful Coach Rodriguez, prioritized a holistic approach to athlete development, emphasizing both athletic success and academic achievement. The campus was equally impressive, yet it felt more manageable, more human-scaled. The rodeo team itself radiated a palpable sense of camaraderie, mutual respect, and support among its members. During his visit, Carl felt a strong connection with the other athletes, a sense of shared purpose and ambition.

University of Eastern Colorado, on the other hand, presented a different challenge entirely. Their scholarship was slightly less generous financially, but their academic reputation was impeccable. The program demanded a high GPA, a rigorous academic schedule, and an unwavering commitment to excellence in both areas. The pressure was palpable, a demanding yet exhilarating prospect. The interview process with the panel of coaches, professors, and advisors was far more demanding than the others, a deep dive into his academic history and aspirations. Yet, Carl found himself drawn to the intense challenge, the opportunity to prove himself capable of handling both academic and athletic excellence simultaneously. He liked the idea of testing his limits and emerging stronger on the other side.

The next few weeks were a blur of phone calls, emails, campus visits, and sleepless nights. He pored over the scholarship packages again and again, comparing financial aid figures, academic programs, coaching styles, and campus life. He talked endlessly with his parents, particularly his mother, whose steadfast support was a constant source of comfort and encouragement. His uncle, the multi-time world champion team roper, offered sage advice, helping him sift through the noise and focus on the aspects that truly mattered.

"Don't just look at the money, Carl," his uncle had said, his weathered face etched with years of rodeo experience. "Look at the whole picture. Consider the coaching staff, team environment, and academic opportunities. Find the place where you'll grow, not just as a roper, but as a person."

His uncle's words echoed in Carl's mind as he weighed the options. The financial security of Oklahoma State's substantial offer was undeniably tempting, and the promise of reduced financial burden was a significant factor. Yet, he felt a lack of personal Saginaw, a disconnect that prevented him from fully envisioning himself thriving in that environment. University of Eastern Colorado's rigorous academic demands were equally daunting, and the pressure to excel in both arenas was an intense challenge. However, the opportunity to prove himself, to surpass his expectations, and break new ground was incredibly appealing.

East Texas Tech, however, presented a harmonious blend of academics, athletics, and a strong sense of community. The scholarship was sufficient, the academic program aligned with his aspirations, and the team spirit was infectious. The campus environment seemed balanced, nurturing yet challenging, providing the perfect backdrop for both academic and athletic growth. He'd felt a genuine connection with the coaches, a shared understanding of his aspirations, and a trust in their ability to help him achieve his goals. He spent many hours speaking with current rodeo team members, who spoke passionately about their experiences and the camaraderie they shared. They weren't just teammates, but a family, supportive and encouraging, a community of like-minded individuals working towards common goals.

Ultimately, his decision came down to a gut feeling, a sense of belonging he'd felt only at East Texas Tech. It wasn't a purely rational choice; it was a decision that reflected his heart's desires as much as his mind's calculations. It wasn't just about winning scholarships or titles; it was about finding a home, a place where he could grow and thrive, both as a student and as an athlete. The decision, once made, felt both liberating and overwhelming — a mixture of exhilaration and anxiety that mirrored the thrill of a successful rodeo run. The relief of having a clear path forward was palpable.

He carefully drafted his acceptance letter to East Texas Tech, a blend of gratitude, excitement, and heartfelt dedication. He mailed it with a sense of finality, a closing of one chapter and the thrilling opening of another. His journey wasn't over; in fact, it was just beginning. The high school rodeo circuit had been a proving ground, a testament to his skill, his perseverance, and his unwavering commitment. Now, the collegiate arena awaited, a new stage to showcase his talent and embrace the challenges ahead. He took a breath—ready, at last. He was more than ready. He was eager to begin the next chapter, to ride into his future, armed with experience, skill, and the steady, familiar support of his family, his friends, and RJ, his loyal and steadfast companion. The thrill of competition, the excitement of the challenge, the joy of the ride, all lay ahead. He had a scholarship, a future, and a horse; and that, he knew, was all he could ever ask for. The rest, as they say, was just dust.

The thrill of acceptance hung in the air, a palpable excitement that buzzed around Carl like the frantic energy of a bucking bronco. East Texas Tech. The words felt solid, substantial, a grounding force after weeks of swirling uncertainty. It wasn't just the impressive scholarship package, although that certainly eased the financial anxieties that had been a constant undercurrent in his decision-making process. It was more than the excellent agricultural business program, although that aligned perfectly with his long-term aspirations beyond rodeo. It was the feeling-the intangible sense of belonging, the palpable camaraderie he'd experienced during his campus visit-that'd sealed the deal.

He remembered the crisp autumn air, the scent of freshly cut grass mingling with the earthy aroma of the stables. He'd spent hours wandering the sprawling campus, feeling the pulse of student life, the vibrant energy of a thriving university. He'd sat in on a few classes, captivated by the engaged professors and the enthusiastic students. The academic atmosphere was stimulating, challenging, and, most importantly, felt attainable. It wasn't the overwhelming pressure of University of Eastern Colorado's demanding program, nor the impersonal vastness of Oklahoma State's sprawling campus. It was a perfect balance — a challenging yet supportive environment that fostered both academic and athletic excellence.

The rodeo team had played a significant role in his decision. He'd spent an afternoon watching them practice, their movements fluid and precise, their teamwork seamless and effortless. He'd talked to several team members, sensing the genuine camaraderie that bound them together. They weren't just teammates; they were a family, supporting each other through wins and losses, celebrating successes, and offering solace during setbacks. They'd shared stories of late-night study sessions, early morning practices, and the thrill of competition. He saw himself fitting seamlessly into that dynamic, contributing his skills and receiving their support in return. The coaches, too, had impressed him. Coach Rodriguez, unlike Coach Miller's gruff exterior, possessed a thoughtful and empathetic approach, understanding the demands of both academics and rodeo, and offering a supportive hand to guide athletes through their challenges.

The thought of leaving home, of venturing into the unknown, still held a twinge of apprehension. He'd spent his entire life in the familiar embrace of his small town, surrounded by the steady, familiar support of his family and friends. The transition to college life, to a new environment, a new culture, would be significant. But the apprehension was overshadowed by a surge of excitement, a powerful anticipation of the adventures that lay ahead. He envisioned himself thriving in the vibrant atmosphere of College Station, pushing his limits both athletically and academically, building lasting friendships, and pursuing his passions with renewed vigor.

His decision wasn't made lightly. He'd spent countless hours poring over scholarship details, comparing program offerings, and evaluating coaching styles. He'd had numerous conversations with his parents, his uncle, and even his closest friends, seeking their advice and weighing their perspectives. His mother, a constant source of strength and support, had listened patiently to his doubts and anxieties, offering encouragement. His uncle, the seasoned rodeo champion, had provided sage advice, reminding him to consider the bigger picture, to look beyond the financial aspects and focus on the overall environment that would best nurture his growth, both personally and professionally.

"It ain't just about the money, Carl," his uncle had said, his voice gravelly but reassuring. "It's about finding the right fit, the place where you can thrive, where you can learn, and where you can become the best version of yourself." His uncle's words had resonated deeply, shaping his perspective and influencing his final decision. He'd realized that a successful rodeo career wasn't solely about winning championships; it was about personal growth, building relationships, and pursuing excellence in all aspects of his life.

The final decision felt like releasing a pent-up breath, a wave of relief washing over him. The weight of expectation and the pressure of making the right choice had been immense. But now, with the decision made, a sense of liberation and excitement took hold. He knew he'd made the best choice for himself, a choice that aligned with his values, his goals, and his aspirations. East Texas Tech wasn't just a college; it was a launching pad, a gateway to his future.

The next few weeks were a whirlwind of activity. He finalized his enrollment, secured his housing, and began making plans for the transition. He spent countless hours communicating with the rodeo team, getting to know his future teammates, and learning more about their training regimen and competitive schedule. He even had a few virtual training sessions with some of the upper-level students, getting a feel for the intensity and discipline demanded at the collegiate level.

The thought of leaving RJ behind, his loyal and steadfast equine companion, initially caused a pang of sadness. But he knew that RJ would be well cared for at home, under the watchful eye of his family. Besides, he'd be back to visit often, and he looked forward to the times when he could ride RJ again. He visualized himself, years from now, reminiscing about those early days, those hard-fought victories, the years of unwavering dedication and shared dreams.

There was a sense of closure, a poignant ending to a chapter of his life that had been filled with intense dedication, early mornings, late nights, relentless practice, and fierce competition. However, there was also a sense of anticipation, a thrilling anticipation of the next chapter, the challenges that lay ahead, and the new opportunities that awaited. The high school rodeo circuit had been a crucible, a testing ground that had shaped his character, honed his skills, and prepared him for the rigors of college rodeo. Now, he was ready to take on the world.

He packed his bags, not just with clothes and personal belongings but with memories, lessons learned, and dreams yet to be realized. He said goodbye to his friends and family, their well wishes filling him with warmth and encouragement. He hugged his mother tightly, her words of encouragement echoing in his mind. He shared a final heartfelt conversation with his uncle, receiving one last piece of sage advice: "Remember your roots, Carl. Remember where you came from, and never forget the lessons you've learned along the way." His uncle's words stayed with him as he drove away, the landscape of his hometown slowly fading into the rearview mirror.

As he drove toward his new life, the sun setting on the horizon painted the sky with vibrant hues, and Carl felt a profound sense of peace. He had made his choice, a choice that reflected not only his ambition and aspirations but also his heart. He had a scholarship, a future, a horse, and a team. The road ahead would be challenging, filled with intense competition and high expectations. But he was ready. He possessed the skills, determination, and steady, familiar support of his family and friends. He was prepared to ride into his future, confident, excited, and eager to embrace whatever challenges lay ahead. The dust had settled, and the journey had begun.

The rearview mirror reflected not just the fading landscape of his hometown but also the culmination of years of relentless dedication. High school rodeo, with its whirlwind of competitions, early mornings, and late nights fueled by adrenaline and ambition, was behind him. A new chapter beckoned, filled with the promise of both familiar challenges and exciting unknowns. The thrill of the rodeo remained, but now it was interwoven with the anticipation of a new academic environment, a new team, and a new set of competitors.

College rodeo held a different energy. The stakes were higher, the competition fiercer, the pressure more intense. He'd already participated in a few smaller college rodeos, observing the skill and strategy of the older competitors —the seasoned veterans who navigated the arena with almost effortless grace. He'd been humbled by their talent and inspired by their tenacity. He knew this wasn't just a step up in competition; it was a leap. But that leap filled him not with fear, but with an exhilarating sense of anticipation.

He imagined himself in the college arena, the roar of the crowd a symphony of energy, the smell of dust and leather thick in the air. He pictured himself riding RJ, their movements perfectly synchronized, a ballet of skill and teamwork, culminating in a flawless calf-roping run. He felt the surge of adrenaline, the focus that narrowed his world to the task at hand, the exhilaration of victory. This wasn't just a dream, it was a tangible goal.

The academic side of the equation was equally exciting. He'd always been a good student, balancing his educational pursuits with his rodeo commitments. But college presented a new level of challenge, a higher standard of academic rigor. The agricultural business program at East Texas Tech was renowned for its excellence, with a demanding curriculum designed to produce highly skilled and knowledgeable graduates. He saw this not as an obstacle, but as an opportunity to expand his horizons, to develop his skills in a field that aligned with his passion for livestock and the agricultural way of life. He envisioned himself not only as a successful rodeo competitor but also as a successful businessman, combining his love of the rodeo with his entrepreneurial spirit.

The social aspect of college life was also something he looked forward to. He'd spent his formative years in a small town, surrounded by familiar faces and well-established friendships. College promised a chance to expand his social circle, and build connections with individuals from diverse backgrounds and experiences. He anticipated the late-night study sessions, the shared meals with teammates, the camaraderie that would bind him to a new family — a family of athletes, academics, and friends, all united by a common goal. He envisioned lively discussions in the student union, late nights studying around dorm room desks, and building strong, lasting friendships that would extend far beyond the college years. The sense of community, a sense of belonging, was something he craved and anticipated deeply.

But it wasn't just the excitement of the new that fueled his anticipation. There was also a quiet sense of satisfaction, of accomplishment. Years of hard work, of early mornings before school, hours spent practicing his technique, and countless weekends spent traveling to rodeos all culminated in this moment — the opportunity to continue his rodeo career at a prestigious university. The scholarships were a testament to his dedication, perseverance, and undeniable skill. He felt a profound sense of gratitude for the support he'd received from his family, his friends, and his sponsors. It had become more than a goal—it was a journey shared, a triumph earned not in solitude, but in collaboration and community.

The next few months flew by in a whirlwind of preparations. He spent hours working with RJ, ensuring the horse was in peak condition for the rigors of college competition. He fine-tuned his roping technique, honing his skills to meet the demanding standards of college rodeo. He also made sure his academic preparation was up to par. He spent hours reviewing materials, familiarizing himself with the college curriculum, and laying a strong foundation for his educational endeavors.

We even started researching the other members of the East Texas Tech rodeo team. He studied their past performances, their competitive styles, their strengths, and weaknesses. He wanted to be prepared, to know his competitors, and to understand the team's dynamics. He knew that success at the college level wouldn't just depend on his skills, but also on his ability to work collaboratively, support his teammates, and become an integral part of the team's collective success.

Leaving home felt bittersweet. The familiar comfort of his small town, the steady, familiar support of his family, the security of routine — all of this would be a part of his past. But this transition was not a departure; it was an evolution. It was a step toward realizing his dreams, a step toward becoming the best version of himself. He carried with him the love and support of those he left behind, the lessons learned on the rodeo circuit, the steady, familiar support of his family, and the memories forged in sweat, dust, and triumph.

As he drove onto the campus of East Texas Tech, a sense of anticipation washed over him. The familiar scent of hay and horses filled the air, bringing a wave of comfort and familiarity that grounded him in the familiar rhythm of rodeo life. He unpacked his bags, not just with clothes and equipment, but with years of experience, dedication, and the unwavering hope for success. He took a breath—ready, at last. The dust had settled on high school, but the journey was beginning. The college rodeo arena awaited, and Carl was prepared to ride. His future was no longer just a dream; it was a path he was ready to blaze. The exhilarating challenge of college life and rodeo lay before him, and he was eager to begin.

Chapter 11: Life at College

The first few weeks were a blur of orientation, reviewing the syllabus, and frantic attempts to navigate the sprawling East Texas Tech campus. The sheer scale of the university was overwhelming, a stark contrast to the cozy familiarity of his small-town high school. Finding his classes, remembering building numbers, and even locating the student union felt like a daily adventure. He'd laughingly recall those initial days, stumbling through campus maps and relying heavily on the kindness of strangers — kindness he consistently received from the friendly Aggie community.

But amidst the academic chaos, there was the comforting, familiar routine of the rodeo team. The stables, the practice arena, and the camaraderie among his new teammates — these were anchors in his new life, places where he felt a sense of belonging and a sense of community that eased the transition. The team was a diverse group, each member bringing unique skills, experiences, and personalities to the mix. There was the seasoned senior, a veteran competitor with years of experience and an impressive list of accomplishments; the quiet, determined freshman who possessed a natural talent; the outgoing social butterfly who kept the team spirits high; and many more. He quickly learned that college rodeo wasn't just about individual skill; it was about teamwork, support, and a shared commitment to success.

The practices were intense, pushing him to improve and grow, to adapt to the higher standards of college-level competition. The high school rodeo circuit had prepared him well, but this was a whole new world. The competition was more challenging, the pressure higher, and the stakes even more significant. He quickly realized that the minor, friendly rivalry of high school rodeo was a completely different animal from the larger and more intense competition of college rodeo. It wasn't just about winning anymore; it was about consistently performing at a top-tier level week after week.

He found himself pushing RJ harder, both in terms of physical conditioning and in refining their roping technique. They spent countless hours in the arena, working on every detail, striving for that perfect synchronization, that seamless flow of movement that distinguished a good roper from a great one. It was a partnership built on trust, mutual respect, and a shared ambition —a silent understanding forged over years of working together. RJ, a seasoned rodeo horse himself, seemed to understand the higher stakes, responding to Carl's intensity with his focused energy. Their bond was as strong as ever, tested and strengthened by the rigors of college rodeo.

The academic demands were equally challenging. The agricultural business program was no walk in the park, with demanding coursework, challenging exams, and the added pressure of maintaining a high grade point average (GPA). He had to learn to manage his time effectively, to balance the rigorous demands of his studies with the intense training schedule of the rodeo team. The early mornings and late nights were now twice as busy, but he found a new efficiency in managing his time, learning to prioritize his tasks, and leveraging every moment to his advantage. The balance wasn't always easy, but he found a rhythm —a pattern that worked for him —a testament to his dedication and organizational skills. He learned the value of time management, discipline, and efficiency, skills that served him well in both his academic pursuits and his competitive rodeo career.

The social aspects of college life proved to be more welcoming than he'd expected. He'd anticipated a large impersonal institution, but he discovered a surprisingly strong sense of community within the agricultural business program and the rodeo team. He formed close friendships with his teammates, bonding over moments lived shoulder-to-shoulder, late-night study sessions, and countless hours spent travelling to and from rodeo competitions across the state. They supported each other through thick and thin, celebrating each other's wins and offering comfort during losses.

College rodeo itself was a spectacle, a vibrant tapestry of skill, athleticism, and competition. The atmosphere was electric, the crowd roaring with each run, the tension palpable as competitors battled for a place on the podium. He was no longer the young, wide-eyed high schooler. He was a seasoned competitor, confident in his abilities, yet still hungry for improvement. He'd seen his hard work pay off, his dedication acknowledged with a few early victories in college rodeos, providing a significant boost to his confidence and validating the years of hard work he'd invested in the sport.

But college rodeo also brought a new level of humility. He faced fierce competition from skilled and experienced riders, some of whom were already nationally recognized. There were setbacks and disappointments, moments when his roping technique faltered, his horse stumbled, and his dreams seemed to slip away. But he learned from each failure, analyzing his mistakes, working on his weaknesses, and refining his approach. These experiences, painful as they sometimes were, only served to strengthen his resolve, sharpening his focus and determination. He'd discovered the importance of resilience in competitive rodeo, a quality he'd had to learn and develop over time.

His relationship with his family and his uncle continued to be a vital source of support, encouragement, and guidance. Regular calls and videos provided comfort and support, making him feel connected to his roots and reassuring him that he wasn't alone in his journey. His uncle's wisdom and advice, always practical and grounded, continued to shape his approach to the sport, while his mother's unwavering love and support acted as a bedrock that kept him grounded. He often spoke of their moments lived shoulder-to-shoulder around the rodeo circuit, making him feel proud of his accomplishments and hopeful for the future.

The balance between academics, social life, and rodeo wasn't always perfect. There were nights when sleep was a luxury, mornings when exhaustion threatened to overwhelm him, and moments when he felt the pressure to perform mount up and take over his life. However, the support of his family, friends, and teammates, combined with his own unwavering determination, enabled him to navigate these challenges and find a sustainable pace that allowed him to excel in all aspects of his life. He was thriving in his college environment, finding balance where there had once been only ambition.

As the semester drew to a close, Carl looked back with a sense of profound satisfaction. He'd overcome challenges, built strong relationships, achieved academic success, and continued to excel in his competitive rodeo career. He'd proven to himself that he could balance the demands of college life with the rigors of his chosen sport. He was more than a rodeo competitor; he was a student, a friend, a son, and an athlete, a complete individual forging his path with determination and resilience. The path ahead still promised challenges, but he knew that with his newly sharpened skills, supportive community, and unwavering determination, he was ready to ride into the sunset of his college rodeo years, one exhilarating run at a time. The future, with all its uncertainties and opportunities, beckoned, and he faced it with a mixture of excitement and anticipation. The dust had settled on the first semester, but the exhilarating ride was far from over.

The rodeo team became more than just a group of athletes; it was a family. There was Jake, a lanky Texan with a quick wit and an even quicker draw on his rope. He was a senior, already a seasoned competitor, and his easygoing nature and vast knowledge of the rodeo circuit quickly made him a mentor figure. Jake had a knack for knowing when to offer a joke and when to provide a serious pep talk, a skilled Carl found invaluable as he navigated the pressures of college rodeo. Their conversations ranged from analyzing roping techniques and strategies to discussing the latest country music hits and sharing stories of hilarious mishaps on the rodeo trail. Jake's easy confidence helped Carl settle into the team dynamic, dispelling any anxieties he had about fitting in. He'd often find himself laughing along with Jake, his worries dissolving in the shared camaraderie.

Then there was Maria, a quiet but incredibly determined barrel racer from Arizona. She rarely spoke much, but her intensity in the arena was undeniable. Her focus was absolute, her movements precise and efficient. Watching Maria's skill inspired Carl, showing him that quiet determination could be just as powerful as boisterous confidence. He'd often find himself observing her practice runs, noting the efficiency of her movements, the grace in her riding. Although their conversations were infrequent, their shared passion for the sport created a bond of mutual respect and understanding. Carl learned from her quiet intensity, realizing that success often stemmed from a combination of skill and focused perseverance. Their mutual knowledge extended beyond the arena, usually finding them sitting together in quiet contemplation before competitions, offering silent encouragement through shared understanding and unspoken words. She was a quiet strength in his life, a reliable support that didn't require constant words of affirmation.

And there was Chloe, the social butterfly of the team, a whirlwind of energy and infectious laughter. She was a goat-tier, one of the many competitors who'd rope, wrestle steers, and barrel race, a true testament to her skill and energy. Chloe's positive energy was contagious, brightening even the most stressful days. Her ability to lighten the mood and make everyone feel included was invaluable, especially during the long hours of practice and travel. Chloe had a knack for defusing tension with a well-timed joke and for bringing the team together with her spirited enthusiasm. Carl quickly discovered that her vibrant personality was a valuable asset to the team's morale. He'd come to rely on her ability to transform intense pressure into good-natured fun. She'd often be the one who planned team dinners and outings, building relationships and fostering team bonding.

Beyond the rodeo team, Carl formed friendships with fellow students in the Agricultural Business program. There was Ben, a fellow freshman who shared his passion for agriculture and his determination to succeed. They'd spend hours studying together, sharing notes, and quizzing each other, creating a rhythm of shared struggles and triumphs. Their friendship transcended their social classes, often meeting for coffee to discuss their aspirations and offer each other mutual support during challenging times. Ben's quiet, thoughtful nature offered a balance to Carl's high-octane rodeo life, providing a calm space for reflection and discussion. Their shared academic pursuits fostered a bond of mutual respect and understanding, proving that true friendships can be formed in the most unexpected places.

Then there was Sarah, a bright and outgoing sophomore who was always ready with a helping hand and a kind word. She possessed a wealth of knowledge about the university, navigating the complexities of classes and campus life with ease. She offered Carl invaluable guidance on everything from navigating the registration system to selecting courses to recommending the best study spots on campus. Sarah's kindness and helpful nature made her a cherished friend, proving to be a valuable addition to Carl's support network. Her energy and support enabled Carl to focus on his studies and his rodeo career, alleviating pressure and making his life easier to manage. Their friendship brought Carl simple joy, a constant source of optimism and support.

These new friendships were pillars of support in Carl's life. Jake provided mentorship and a calming influence, Maria offered inspiration through her quiet intensity, Chloe brought infectious energy and humor, Ben offered a thoughtful presence and academic support, and Sarah provided invaluable practical help and emotional support. Together, they formed a network of friendship that enriched Carl's life and helped him navigate the challenges of college life.

The long bus rides to and from rodeos became less of a chore and more of a shared experience, filled with laughter, music, and stories. The team members shared their hopes, dreams, fears, and funny anecdotes, creating a bond that transcended the competitive arena. They celebrated each other's victories and offered words of encouragement during losses. The defeats weren't just individual setbacks; they were shared challenges, met with mutual support and understanding. The wins, conversely, were celebrations of collective spirit and shared hard work, a testament to their collective journey.

Late-night study sessions fuelled by endless coffee blurred the line between academics and camaraderie. They helped each other through tough assignments, celebrated small wins, and commiserated over exams. These moments were less about studying and more about building a strong, supportive community, one that extended far beyond the classroom and the arena.

The weekends were filled with shared adventures, exploring the local area, attending college football games, and participating in team-building activities. These experiences fostered a sense of belonging and deepened their friendships, proving to be a way to release stress and celebrate the shared journey. These activities served as important reminders that life wasn't just about academic success and rodeo competitions. They were essential memories that would last a lifetime.

Carl found that college life was far more prosperous and more rewarding than he'd anticipated. He discovered that success wasn't solely dependent on individual achievement but was also shaped by the support and camaraderie of friends. The friendships he forged during his first semester were a testament to this discovery, a beacon that guided him through the challenges of balancing academics, athletics, and social life. They were the building blocks of his new life, a reminder that even amidst the pressures of college, he wasn't alone. His latest community felt like family, ensuring he could always rely on his newfound friends for support and laughter. The moments lived shoulder-to-shoulder, both within the rodeo arena and beyond, forged bonds that would endure long after he left the college campus. His new friends weren't just friends, but a part of his personal success story. They were the companions on his journey, the people who celebrated his wins and eased the sting of defeats, the ones he could always count on.

The transition from high school to college rodeo wasn't just about stepping up the competition; it was a whole new level of juggling act. High school had been demanding, with the relentless schedule of twenty-two rodeos plus finals, but college was a different beast entirely. Suddenly, Carl wasn't just responsible for his training and performance; he was also responsible for his academics, a responsibility that felt as daunting as riding a bucking bronco for the first time. His Agricultural Business major wasn't a walk in the park; it was demanding, requiring long hours of study and meticulous attention to detail. The textbooks were heavy, the lectures were intense, and the assignments were challenging.

His first semester was a whirlwind of early morning practices, late-night study sessions fueled by copious amounts of coffee, and the ever-present stress of upcoming rodeos. He'd find himself cramming for exams between roping practice sessions, his mind racing between the intricacies of agricultural economics and the precise timing of his calf roping technique. There were times when sleep became a luxury, replaced by the urgent need to prepare for the next challenge, whether it was a demanding organic chemistry exam or the high-stakes pressure of a regional rodeo competition.

Time management became his greatest adversary. He began experimenting with various schedules, creating intricate calendars and planners to fit everything in. He would meticulously plan his day, allocating specific blocks of time for study, practice, and sleep; however, the unpredictable nature of college life often threw a wrench into his carefully crafted plans. A last-minute assignment, an unexpected team meeting, or even a sudden illness could disrupt his schedule, sending him into a frantic scramble to catch up.

One particular week stands out, a chaotic blend of academic pressure and the thrill of competition. He had a major exam in Agricultural Finance scheduled for Friday, a subject he'd struggled with since the beginning of the semester. The regional rodeo was that same weekend. He spent Monday and Tuesday immersed in his textbooks, highlighting key concepts and working through practice problems. Wednesday and Thursday were dedicated to rodeo practice, where hours were spent perfecting his technique, honing his skills, and ensuring RJ was in top form. He'd find himself nodding off over his textbook, his dreams a blend of financial models and the precise movements of his calf roping routine.

Thursday night became a blur of last-minute studying, fueled by caffeine and adrenaline. He'd barely slept, his mind racing with formulas and roping techniques. Friday morning arrived, a test of his physical and mental stamina. He aced the exam, fueled by adrenaline and a deep-seated determination to succeed. He then rushed to the rodeo grounds, adrenaline pumping. This juggling act felt like walking a tightrope, every misstep a potential disaster. He managed to pull off a win but was utterly exhausted by the end of the weekend. The triumph felt exhilarating, yet the mental and physical toll was significant.

The academic challenges extended beyond the sheer volume of work. The style of teaching in college differed significantly from that in high school. He was no longer spoon-fed information; he had to take initiative, seek clarification, and actively engage in his learning. The professors' expectations were higher, and the assessment methods were more rigorous. He realized that he couldn't just rely on memorization; he had to understand the concepts and apply them critically.

He sought help from his professors during office hours, engaging in deeper conversations about the material and clarifying points that he found confusing. He joined study groups with classmates, finding that collaborative learning significantly improved his understanding of complex concepts. He also took advantage of the resources offered by the university's academic support services, utilizing tutoring sessions to reinforce his learning and address areas where he struggled. The transition demanded adaptability, resilience, and a proactive approach to learning.

The pressure to excel academically, while simultaneously maintaining a high level of athletic performance, was immense. He realized that he couldn't afford to neglect either aspect of his college life. His grades directly impacted his eligibility for rodeo scholarships, a crucial source of funding for his education and athletic career. His performance in the rodeo arena, in turn, was influenced by his academic stress levels. If he were constantly sleep-deprived or overwhelmed by academic pressures, his focus and performance in the rodeo field would inevitably suffer.

He discovered the importance of self-care. Maintaining a healthy lifestyle became a non-negotiable part of his routine. He prioritized adequate sleep, ensuring that he got enough rest to support both his physical and mental well-being. He incorporated regular exercise into his schedule, utilizing those rare moments of downtime to clear his mind and reduce stress. He adopted a healthy diet, recognizing that proper nutrition was crucial to both his athletic performance and overall well-being. He recognized that taking care of himself physically and mentally was essential to successfully navigating the pressures of college life.

The support of his friends and teammates proved invaluable. They helped him maintain a healthy balance and provided a source of encouragement and motivation during challenging times. They'd help him with assignments, offer words of encouragement, and provide a much-needed distraction from the pressures of both academics and rodeos. They were there to celebrate his victories, big and small, and to offer support during setbacks and losses. They understood the unique demands of his college life and provided a critical support system, reminding him that he wasn't alone in his struggles.

He learned to prioritize tasks effectively. He began using digital tools to help manage his schedule and track his assignments, setting reminders and deadlines to ensure that he stayed on top of everything. He also developed the crucial skill of breaking down large projects into smaller, more manageable tasks, making the overall workload seem less overwhelming. He learned to prioritize tasks based on their importance and urgency, ensuring that he devoted his time and energy to the most crucial aspects of both his academic and athletic pursuits.

Carl realized that college life wasn't just about attending classes and competing in rodeos. It was a holistic experience that demanded a well-rounded approach to self-management and personal well-being. He learned to prioritize his physical and mental health, recognizing that both were essential to his success in both the classroom and the arena. He understood that asking for help wasn't a sign of weakness, but rather a sign of strength and self-awareness. He learned to lean on his support system, recognizing the importance of friendships and community in navigating the challenges of balancing academics and athletics.

Carl developed strategies for efficient time management, effective study habits, and a proactive approach to self-care. He learned to embrace the challenges, recognizing that setbacks were opportunities for growth and learning. His experience taught him a valuable lesson: success in college, like success in rodeo, requires more than just talent and determination; it also requires resilience, adaptability, and a supportive community. He had finally found a rhythm, a way to navigate the demanding world of college rodeo and emerge victorious, not just in the arena, but also in the classroom. His journey was far from over, but he had learned to ride the bucking bronco of academic and athletic life with confidence and skill. The ride was still wild, but he was in control.

The fall semester ended with a whirlwind of finals and the regional rodeo in Saginaw, Texas. Carl felt the familiar knot of anxiety in his stomach. High school rodeos had been intense, but the college circuit was a different animal altogether. The cowboys and cowgirls here weren't just good; they were exceptional, seasoned veterans who'd honed their skills for years. The competition was stiffer, the stakes were higher, and the pressure was almost unbearable.

Saginaw was a blur of dust, adrenaline, and the smell of leather and horses. Carl's first event was the calf roping, the event he'd dedicated his life to mastering. He watched other competitors, their movements fluid and efficient, a testament to years of practice and countless hours spent perfecting their technique. He felt the weight of expectation, not just from himself, but from his family, his friends, and his sponsor, who'd invested in him and believed in his potential.

The first calf exploded from the chute, a blur of brown fur and frantic energy. Carl's heart pounded in his chest as he spurred RJ into action. He'd practiced this countless times, but the reality of the competition added a layer of intensity he hadn't experienced before. He executed his roping technique flawlessly, his movements precise and controlled, the result of years of dedicated practice and his uncle's steady, familiar support. The calf hit the ground with a satisfying thud, sending a wave of relief washing over him. His time was good, a solid performance that put him in contention for the top spot, but there was still a long way to go.

The next day was steer wrestling. While not his forte, he'd been working on it. This event demanded brute strength, agility, and a high degree of precision. The sheer power required to wrestle a steer to the ground was a testament to the athletes' raw strength and daring. Carl found himself struggling a bit more here, his lack of prior experience in the event showing. He managed a respectable time but knew he needed more practice. The other competitors were significantly faster and more efficient. He watched them, noting their techniques and strategies, and planned to incorporate those elements into his training.

The final event was team roping, where Carl competed with his college teammate, a seasoned roper named Jake. Team roping demanded perfect synchronization, a seamless collaboration between two individuals working in perfect harmony. Jake, a calm and experienced roper, guided Carl, helping him navigate the nuances of the competition, their teamwork evident in their effortless coordination. They worked as a well-oiled machine, their movements precise and synchronized, each move complementing the other. They secured a win, the victory sweeter because of the collaborative effort. Carl realized that success in college rodeo, as in life, often depended on teamwork and the ability to rely on others.

The regional rodeo concluded with Carl finishing in the top three in calf roping and securing a respectable position in the overall standings. It wasn't the dominant performance he craved, but it was a solid start to his college rodeo career. He knew he had much to learn and even more to improve on, but the experience had been invaluable. He'd learned the importance of adaptability, perseverance, and the value of collaborative effort.

The spring semester brought more rodeos, each a test of his skills, endurance, and mental fortitude. He competed at rodeos across the state, facing increasingly challenging competition at each new learning experience. He learned to manage the pressure, stay focused amidst chaos, and perform consistently even when the odds were against him. He saw the level of commitment required to excel in this demanding sport and began to understand the sacrifices athletes made to reach the top.

At one rodeo, he faced a particularly difficult calf, a nimble and elusive creature that tested his roping skills to the limit. He'd made a few missteps during his run, his timing off just slightly. The calf was fast, but his run didn't reflect his usual performance; his frustration was palpable. He hadn't placed as well as he'd hoped. The defeat was a harsh but necessary lesson, reminding him that even the most skilled athletes experience setbacks. He spent the following weeks honing his skills, focusing on the areas where he'd fallen short.

Another rodeo tested his mental toughness. He was neck and neck with his rival, a skilled roper who had previously defeated him in several competitions. The pressure was intense, the atmosphere charged with anticipation. The final seconds were close, with only a fraction of a second separating them. Ultimately, his rival managed to defeat him by a narrow margin. The loss was disappointing, but it fuelled his resolve to improve his technique and strategy, and ultimately train even harder. He reflected on the loss and began to analyze his plan, considering the adjustments he needed to make.

He developed new strategies for staying focused, including techniques such as visualization and mindful breathing exercises. He practiced these techniques before each event, clearing his mind and preparing himself mentally for the challenges ahead. He focused on his breathing, visualised himself successfully executing his roping techniques, and reminded himself of his years of training and his dedication. He also worked on his mental game, focusing on maintaining a positive attitude and approaching each competition with confidence.

His college rodeo experience wasn't just about winning. It was about growth, learning, and pushing his limits. He forged stronger bonds with his teammates, sharing experiences, victories, and setbacks. He developed a deeper appreciation for the sport, for the dedication it required, and for the camaraderie among its participants. He had friends on opposing teams, and he learned to appreciate the competition while still maintaining respect and sportsmanship.

The year culminated in the National College Rodeo Finals. Carl arrived feeling prepared, his skills honed, his confidence bolstered by his experiences throughout the season. The competition was fierce, each roper a testament to dedication and skill. He performed exceptionally well in the calf roping event, with his technique refined and his movements fluid and efficient. He secured a place in the top ten, a significant achievement that demonstrated his growth and improvement throughout the year. It wasn't a win, but it was a huge step forward, a validation of all the hard work, dedication, and persistence that had gone into it. He wasn't just a good calf roper; he was becoming a great one. The season ended with a mix of emotions, both satisfaction and anticipation for the future.

The summer break provided an opportunity to reflect on his progress, identify areas for improvement, and plan for the upcoming season. He spent his time training, honing his skills, and strengthening his bond with RJ. He also used the time to focus on his academics, recognizing that his success in rodeo was closely tied to his academic performance. He felt ready to face the new challenges that lay ahead, both in the arena and in the classroom, the experiences of the past year having shaped him into a more resilient, determined, and skilled rodeo competitor. His journey continued, driven forward by the relentless pursuit of excellence, fueled by the thrill of competition, the bond with his horse, and the support of his family and friends. He knew that the road ahead would be challenging, but he was ready, armed with experience, determination, and a passion for the sport he loved. The college rodeo circuit was a proving ground, a place where he could test his mettle and shape his future. And he was ready to ride.

The transition to college life wasn't just about adjusting to a new academic environment; it was a seismic shift in almost every aspect of Carl's existence. He missed the familiar comforts of home, the easy camaraderie of his high school friends, and the constant, steady, familiar support of his family. But even amidst the unfamiliar terrain of college life, the bedrock of his support system remained firm, a steadfast presence that anchored him through the storms and celebrated his victories.

His mother, a woman of quiet strength and unwavering faith, remained his anchor. Weekly phone calls, filled with the familiar cadence of her voice, offered solace and reassurance. She wouldn't just inquire about his rodeo performance; she'd delve into the details of his classes, his social life, and his well-being. Her questions were a reminder that despite the distance, she was always there. She'd send care packages filled with his favorite home-cooked meals, small tokens of affection that bridged the physical gap and kept him connected to his roots. These weren't just meals; they were a taste of home, a reminder of her constant love and support. They were a small piece of comfort in a new and sometimes overwhelming environment.

His uncle, the multi-world champion team roper, remained his mentor, his presence a constant source of inspiration and guidance. While their physical interactions were less frequent, their bond remained as strong as ever. Their conversations, often late at night, weren't simply about roping technique; they were discussions about life's complexities, the challenges of balancing academics and athletics, and the importance of perseverance in the face of adversity. He'd offer advice not just on improving his roping technique, but also on navigating the intricacies of college life, the pressures of competition, and the importance of maintaining a healthy perspective. His uncle's wisdom was invaluable, a blend of practical advice and inspirational encouragement. He was a role model, a father figure, and a trusted confidante, offering steady, familiar support and guidance in all aspects of Carl's life.

Beyond his family, Carl found solace and camaraderie in his college friends. The rodeo team became his second family, a group of individuals bound together by a shared passion for the sport and a mutual understanding of the dedication it demanded. They shared stories, triumphs, and setbacks, creating a bond of mutual respect and understanding. They celebrated each other's successes and offered comfort during times of adversity, a testament to the powerful bonds forged through moments lived shoulder-to-shoulder. The team's moments lived shoulder-to-shoulder provided invaluable support and camaraderie, creating a sense of belonging and shared purpose that helped Carl thrive in his new surroundings.

His relationship with Jake, his team roping partner, evolved beyond mere teamwork. They were rivals on the practice field, pushing each other to improve, yet they supported each other unconditionally, understanding the pressure and stress of competition. Late-night study sessions were punctuated by laughter and shared anxieties, a testament to their deepening friendship. Jake provided crucial support in his academics, helping him understand concepts he was struggling with and offering a friendly face in a sometimes overwhelming environment. He understood Carl's dedication, and his support in this new environment was crucial to Carl's success.

But the support wasn't just about shared meals or late-night study sessions. It was about the quiet acts of kindness, the words of encouragement whispered during moments of doubt, and the unwavering belief in his abilities, even when he faltered himself. It was the simple act of a teammate carrying his gear, offering a ride when his car was broken, or just lending a listening ear when he needed to vent his frustrations. It was an unspoken understanding, a silent pact that bound them together and provided Carl with the emotional stability he needed to navigate the rigors of college rodeo life.

One particularly challenging rodeo, a grueling three-day event held in the heart of Texas, tested Carl's physical and mental limits. He experienced a series of setbacks. His horse, RJ, unexpectedly stumbled during one of his runs, throwing off his rhythm and costing him valuable seconds. The next day, a relentless rain soaked the arena, creating treacherous conditions that made the already demanding events even more challenging. His confidence began to wane as the weight of expectations pressed down on him. He felt the familiar knot of anxiety tightening in his stomach, the familiar self-doubt creeping in.

Yet, amidst the mounting pressures, Carl found solace in his support system. His uncle's voice, a calming presence on the phone, reassured him, reminding him of his past successes and his ability to be resilient. His mother's unwavering faith in him shone through in her daily texts, short messages that carried a weight of unspoken support. His teammates rallied around him, offering words of encouragement and practical help, providing a sense of community and shared purpose. They helped him maintain his equipment and offered moral support, their shared camaraderie proving crucial during his low points.

Their steady, familiar support extended to the arena itself. They cheered him on from the sidelines, their voices a beacon of encouragement amidst the roar of the crowd. They celebrated his successes, big and small, and offered words of comfort during his setbacks. They provided a comforting presence that helped Carl regain his composure and his belief in himself. The combined support pushed him to deliver a final run that, while not perfect, secured him a respectable finish, a testament to the power of a strong support network.

He learned that support wasn't just about mitigating failures; it was about amplifying successes. Every congratulatory text, every celebratory dinner, every shared laugh—it all served to reinforce his confidence and fuel his ambition. The unwavering belief of his family, friends, and mentors gave him the strength and courage to push beyond his limits, striving for excellence not just in rodeo but in all aspects of his life. The collective belief in him proved an essential component of his growth and development, not just as an athlete but as a young man navigating the complexities of college life. His college experience, therefore, wasn't just about the competitions and victories, but about the incredible network of support that helped him rise above the challenges and achieve his dreams. It was a testament to the profound impact that strong relationships can have on an individual's journey to success, illustrating the unwavering power of community and its ability to nurture growth and resilience. The support system wasn't merely a periphery; it was the very engine that propelled him forward, a constant source of strength that allowed him to face his fears and achieve his ambitions. It was this support that helped Carl not only survive the rigors of college life but thrive.

Chapter 12: Epilogue

Looking back, the dust hasn't even settled on the arena floor of my final college rodeo. The roar of the crowd, the smell of leather and hay, the adrenaline rush — it's all a fading echo now, a poignant soundtrack to a chapter that's closed but resonates deeply within me. College rodeo was a period of personal growth. I wasn't just honing my calf-roping technique; I was shaping myself into the man I am today.

The transition from high school to college was more jarring than I'd anticipated. High school rodeos, while demanding, felt almost familial. The familiar faces in the stands, the friendly banter with rivals, the comforting routines — it was a cocoon of support, even amidst the fierce competition. College was different. It was a vast, exhilarating, sometimes overwhelming landscape, where I was just one face in a sea of ambitious individuals. Loneliness crept in at unexpected moments, a subtle undercurrent to the thrill of competition.

The sheer scale of it all — the larger arenas, the intensified competition, the higher stakes — was initially daunting. I found myself questioning my abilities, doubting my readiness for this new level of challenge. The pressure to perform and excel was immense, a constant weight on my shoulders. It was a far cry from the smaller, more intimate high school rodeos, where the atmosphere felt more forgiving and the camaraderie more palpable.

Yet, it was this very pressure, this challenge, that pushed me to grow. I had to adapt, to learn, to refine my skills with a fierce determination I hadn't known I possessed. The setbacks, the disappointments, the moments of self-doubt — they weren't just obstacles to overcome; they were crucial lessons etched into the fabric of my being.

The losses were brutal, stinging reminders of my fallibility. There was a heartbreaking moment in the regional finals when RJ stumbled, throwing my timing off and costing me a spot in the national championships. The frustration was overwhelming, a physical ache in my chest. But the support system that had cradled me through high school remained my steadfast anchor. My uncle's words of wisdom, delivered over the phone in his calm, reassuring voice, helped me navigate the storm of emotions. My mother's unwavering belief in me, expressed in simple text messages, injected a renewed sense of purpose and courage into my heart.

My teammates became my new family, bound together by sweat, shared triumphs, and mutual respect. We weren't just rivals; we were a team, pushing each other to be better, offering solace when we stumbled, and celebrating each other's victories. We helped each other shoulder the burden and understood the pressure that came with the college rodeo circuit. Jake, my team roping partner, played a crucial role in my success. His calm demeanor provided a comforting presence during stressful moments, and he always seemed to know exactly what to say to push me through a rough patch.

It wasn't just about the tangible support either. It was about the quiet gestures of camaraderie, the shared meals, the late-night study sessions, the unspoken understanding that we were all in this together. These moments strengthened the bond of friendship and camaraderie between all of us. It was about the shared moments of both celebration and defeat that made this time in my life so special. The simple acts of a teammate lending a hand with my gear, a teammate offering a ride, and a friend providing a listening ear—all those acts of simple kindness — formed a powerful shield against the emotional storms that threatened to overwhelm me.

I learned that true strength wasn't about flawless execution or consistent victories; it was about resilience —bouncing back from setbacks with renewed determination. College rodeo wasn't just a test of my athletic abilities; it was a test of my character, my mental fortitude, my ability to learn from my mistakes, and never give up.

Looking back, I see the clear progression of my skills, not just in the technical aspects of calf roping, but in my overall approach to the sport and life. I was faster, more precise, more strategic in my approach, but equally important, I was more patient, more disciplined, more resilient. I learned to manage pressure effectively, to control my emotions, and to stay focused even when things went wrong. I knew the crucial importance of mental strength in addition to physical strength.

The college years were a period of intense self-discovery. I learned more about myself, including my strengths and weaknesses, than I ever thought possible. I discovered a hidden reservoir of strength and resilience, a capacity to overcome adversity I hadn't known I possessed. I learned to value the importance of a strong support system, to lean on those who believed in me, even when I doubted myself. The journey wasn't always easy, but it was undoubtedly transformative, shaping not just my athletic career but the very core of my being.

The college rodeo circuit taught me more than just roping techniques; it was a masterclass in life lessons. It taught me the value of perseverance, the importance of teamwork, the strength to be found in facing your fears, and the incredible power of a strong support network. The lessons I learned on those dusty arenas extend far beyond the sport itself. They're lessons I'll carry with me throughout my life, guiding my actions and shaping my future endeavors.

The friendships forged during those years are some of the most treasured relationships of my life. The moments lived shoulder-to-shoulder, the laughter, the tears, the steady, familiar support — they've created bonds that will endure long after the last rodeo buckle has been awarded. Those friendships were the bedrock of my college experience, providing the constant support and encouragement I needed to navigate the challenges and achieve my goals. The late-night conversations, the shared meals, and the moments of pure, unadulterated joy — those are the memories that will remain forever etched in my mind.

My college rodeo journey was more than just a competition; it was a crucible that forged my character, shaped my future, and deepened my understanding of myself and the world around me. It served as a poignant reminder of the enduring power of support systems, teamwork, and unwavering self-belief. Even the most difficult moments have shaped me into who I am today. It had become more than a goal—it was a journey that taught me the meaning of resilience, the importance of unwavering commitment, and the extraordinary value of lasting friendships. And in the quiet moments, as the dust settles, I can honestly say: it was all worth it. The lessons, the friendships, the growth—they're gifts I'll cherish forever.

The arena lights dimmed, the crowd's roar fading into a muted hum as I stepped off the horse, the familiar scent of leather and dust lingering in the air. My final high school rodeo had ended, a bittersweet conclusion to four years of grueling competition, heart-stopping victories, and gut-wrenching defeats. But as the dust settled, a new chapter was about to begin, filled with its own set of challenges and aspirations.

My immediate future was clear: college. I'd secured a partial rodeo scholarship at the East Texas Tech, a place where the rodeo program had a strong reputation and a winning tradition. The thought both exhilarated and intimidated me. The level of competition would be exponentially higher than anything I'd experienced in high school. But the opportunity to compete at that level, to refine my skills against the best in the country, was a dream come true.

Beyond the scholarship, however, lay a broader horizon. Rodeo was my passion, my driving force, the cornerstone of my life. But it wasn't my only passion. I'd always been drawn to the agricultural sciences, the intricate balance between nature and human endeavor. The meticulous care of livestock, the scientific precision of crop management, the deep connection with the land—it resonated with my soul. I had always been fascinated by family ranches, particularly my uncle's, and the skilled techniques required to manage large farms and herds of cattle. I hoped to learn more about farm management, using modern technological and scientific tools and techniques. The way modern technology is used in the agricultural industry has always interested me. This was a field of particular interest to me. I planned on majoring in Agricultural Business, hoping to leverage my knowledge of both agriculture and business to build a successful career. I pictured myself eventually running a successful ranch of my own, combining my love for rodeo with my passion for agriculture.

My long-term aspirations extended beyond the immediate future. I envisioned a life deeply intertwined with the rodeo world, but with a broader perspective. My uncle, a multi-time world champion team roper, had always been my mentor and role model, guiding me through the intricacies of the sport while offering valuable life lessons. He had taught me the importance of hard work, dedication, perseverance, as well as resilience, humility, and leadership. His experience in the rodeo industry, coupled with my education, I believed, could form a solid foundation for my career.

I wanted to make a positive impact on the rodeo community, not just as a competitor, but as a leader, mentor, and advocate for the sport. I dreamt of giving back to the community that had given me so much. I hoped to establish a foundation designed to provide scholarships and support to young people from underprivileged backgrounds who dreamt of a rodeo career. Many gifted young people often cannot participate due to financial constraints, and I wanted to help facilitate their potential to improve their lives and reach their full potential. I'd witnessed firsthand how rodeo could shape character, foster discipline, and build self-esteem, and I wanted to ensure that opportunity was available to everyone, regardless of their financial circumstances.

I also had other aspirations outside of rodeo, such as working with a nonprofit organization that provides aid to those living in underserved and poverty-stricken areas. I wanted to dedicate my time to charitable work, volunteering my skills and resources to improve the lives of others. I firmly believe that giving back to society is essential, and I hope to utilize my success to make a positive impact in the world.

My aspirations also included creating my own rodeo school to train up-and-coming rodeo stars. This project would be my ultimate achievement. Many high schools lack the resources to provide adequate rodeo training, and I aimed to address this issue. I would give high-quality coaching and training, helping young people develop their skills and achieve their full potential. My goal was not only to improve their skills but also to instill in them the values that I felt were crucial for success in the rodeo world and life in general.

But even with these grand plans, I was aware that rodeo was a challenging career path. Success wasn't guaranteed. There would be setbacks, disappointments, and moments of self-doubt. But I was prepared to face those challenges head-on, armed with the resilience I had honed during my years of competition. I knew that setbacks were growth opportunities, and I embraced them as opportunities to learn, adapt, and become stronger. I had never been afraid to work hard and persevere. I was prepared to work harder than ever before.

The path ahead was paved with both excitement and apprehension, yet, despite the uncertainty, a deep sense of purpose filled me. My vision wasn't just about winning rodeo titles or building a successful business; it was about creating a lasting legacy. It was about creating a legacy, about making a meaningful contribution to the world, and about living a life guided by my passions and values. My ambitions weren't just about personal success, but about making a positive contribution to others and leaving a lasting impact on the world. I sought to use my success to improve the lives of others, not just myself.

I knew the journey wouldn't be easy. There were moments of doubt, times when I questioned my abilities and the choices I had made. But the lessons I'd learned, the support I'd received, and the unwavering belief in myself would serve as my guiding stars. My family, friends, mentors, and sponsors—all have played a crucial role in shaping me into the person I am today. Their unwavering belief in me, their encouragement, and their support had been essential to my success thus far. I knew they would continue to support me in this next chapter.

The future was a vast and uncharted territory, filled with both possibilities and uncertainties. However, I was ready to embrace the challenges, learn from my mistakes, and relentlessly pursue my dreams. Rodeo had taught me the value of hard work, dedication, and perseverance, and these lessons would be my constant companions on my journey ahead. I was ready to meet the challenges and pursue my ambitions.

As I looked ahead, I felt a profound sense of gratitude for the opportunities life had given me. The journey had been long and arduous, but it had also been gratifying, transforming me into a stronger, more resilient, and more determined person. The lessons learned both on and off the rodeo arena would serve as a roadmap guiding my actions in the future. My plans were not only about personal success, but about giving back to the communities that helped me grow, and making a positive impact on the lives of others. This path was filled with both risk and reward. But the adventure that lay ahead was one that I was entirely prepared for and ready to embrace.

The dust had barely settled on my final high school rodeo, the adrenaline still faintly buzzing in my veins, when the weight of those four years truly hit me. It wasn't just the thrill of the competition, the roar of the crowd, the satisfying thud of a successful calf roping; it was the tapestry of experiences woven together, the lessons learned both within the arena and beyond its dusty confines. Those lessons, etched into my memory as deeply as the brand on RJ's flank, were the actual prize.

Perseverance, that relentless grit that pushed me through countless hours of practice, through stinging defeats and agonizing injuries, proved to be far more valuable than any trophy I'd ever held. I'd fallen off RJ more times than I cared to remember, felt the sting of failure countless times, and the crushing disappointment of coming in second, third, or even last. But each fall, each loss, was a stepping stone. It forced me to analyze my mistakes, to refine my technique, to strengthen my resolve. It was in those moments of vulnerability, facing the raw, bitter taste of defeat, that I discovered the wellspring of my resilience.

Resilience wasn't merely bouncing back; it was the ability to learn from setbacks, to adapt to unforeseen circumstances, to find the strength to keep going even when exhaustion threatened to overwhelm me. I realized that setbacks were not failures but opportunities — chances to reassess, and emerge stronger. It was a lesson deeply ingrained in the very fabric of rodeo life, where unpredictable variables—a skittish calf, a sudden downpour, a mishap with equipment—could quickly derail even the most meticulously planned performance.

The support system I'd cultivated — the unwavering belief of my family, the camaraderie of my friends, the guidance of my uncle—was as crucial to my success as my skill. My mom, ever the steadfast anchor, was my constant source of encouragement, her faith in me unwavering even when I doubted myself. She wasn't just a spectator; she was part of the team, patching up my wounds, offering words of comfort, and ensuring I had everything I needed to perform at my best. Her quiet strength was a constant reminder that behind every successful rodeo competitor was a dedicated support network.

My uncle, a legend in the team roping world, was more than just a mentor; he was a teacher, a friend, and a role model. He taught me not only the technical aspects of calf roping but also the life skills crucial for success: discipline, focus, respect for tradition, and the importance of humility. He emphasized the importance of sportsmanship, both towards his fellow competitors and towards the animals themselves. He stressed that true success stemmed not merely from winning, but from conducting oneself with grace and integrity.

My friends, those who shared my passion for the rodeo life, formed a bond of mutual support and understanding. We shared triumphs and setbacks, offering words of encouragement when spirits were low and celebrating victories with unbridled joy. The shared struggles and successes forged an unbreakable link that extended far beyond the arena. They understood the dedication, sacrifices, and unwavering commitment it took to achieve a high level of performance. They were the ones who knew the true meaning of hard work and commitment.

But the lessons weren't confined to the practical aspects of rodeo competition. I learned the value of time management, juggling rigorous schoolwork with intensive training and a demanding competition schedule. I honed my organizational skills, learning to prioritize tasks and manage my time efficiently. I learned to deal with pressure, to perform under intense scrutiny, and to remain calm even when things went wrong. These skills, honed in the high-stakes environment of rodeo, were invaluable and would serve me well in any endeavor I chose to pursue.

Rodeo had taught me the importance of continuous learning and improvement. The sport demanded constant refinement of skills, an unwavering commitment to mastering the techniques, and a willingness to adapt to new challenges. Each competition presented an opportunity to analyze my performance, identify weaknesses, and strive for improvement. This philosophy extended far beyond the rodeo arena, influencing my approach to education and life itself. I strived to remain open to new ideas and experiences, recognizing that learning is a lifelong journey.

Beyond the arena, rodeo had also opened my eyes to the importance of community and giving back. The rodeo world fostered a deep sense of camaraderie in Saginaw that transcended rivalries. We were a community bound by our shared love of the sport. This sense of community inspired me to give back, to find ways to contribute positively to the sport I loved.

The vision I'd nurtured — the establishment of a rodeo training facility and a scholarship fund — wasn't merely a dream; it was a testament to the lessons I'd learned, a commitment to empowering future generations of rodeo athletes. It was an opportunity to give back to the sport that had shaped my life, to help young people from underprivileged backgrounds achieve their dreams. The lessons I had learned would fuel my determination to bring this vision to life. I would utilize my skills, knowledge, and experience to help other young people achieve success.

My journey through my high school rodeo wasn't without its obstacles. There were moments of doubt, times when the weight of expectations felt overwhelming, times when I questioned my abilities and whether my dreams were even attainable. But those challenges only reinforced the lessons I'd learned — the importance of resilience, the power of perseverance, and the value of a strong support system. These lessons would serve as a guide for me in the future.

The future held the promise of new challenges and opportunities, but I was ready. I was prepared to embrace the uncertainties, to navigate the complexities, and to continue learning and growing. The lessons I had learned on the rodeo circuit would be my compass, guiding me toward success, not just in rodeo but in all aspects of my life. Rodeo had taught me valuable life lessons, not just about winning or losing, but about resilience, teamwork, and the importance of hard work and determination. These lessons would serve as my guiding light throughout my future endeavors. My time in the rodeo arena had not only honed my skills but also shaped my character, strengthening my values and shaping my vision for the future. The journey had prepared me well. I was ready.

The arena lights dimmed, the crowd's roar fading into a distant hum. The dust settled, not just on the arena floor but also on the whirlwind of my high school rodeo career. Looking back, it wasn't the trophies gleaming on my shelf that defined those years, but the lessons etched into my soul, lessons I now felt compelled to share with those who would follow in my dusty tracks.

First, understand that this isn't a sprint; it's a marathon —a grueling endurance test that stretches from the sweltering heat of August to the crisp chill of May. Twenty-two rodeos, plus the pressure-cooker environment of finals, demand a level of commitment that surpasses mere enthusiasm. It requires a deep-seated passion, a fire that burns bright even when your muscles scream, your spirit flags, and your horse seems to have decided that participating is optional. This isn't just about roping a calf; it's about building resilience, a fortitude that allows you to get back on that horse, figuratively and sometimes literally, after every fall.

Speaking of horses, your partnership with your animal is paramount. RJ wasn't just a mount; he was my confidante, my partner in crime, the silent observer of my triumphs and tribulations. Choosing a horse is like choosing a life partner; you need compatibility, trust, and an almost unspoken understanding. Spend countless hours training, not just in the arena, but in the pasture, building that bond, that mutual respect that will carry you through the most challenging moments. Learn to read your horse's cues, to anticipate their needs, to understand their subtle shifts in mood and temperament. A strong partnership isn't built overnight; it's nurtured through patience, consistency, and unwavering care.

Practice, practice, practice. It's a cliché, yes, but the truth in it is undeniable. Talent alone is insufficient; it's the honing of that talent, the relentless pursuit of perfection, that separates the contenders from the champions. Those early morning practices, the scorching afternoon sessions, the late-night tweaking of your technique — these are the investments that pay off in spades when the pressure mounts in the arena. Don't just practice; practice with purpose. Analyze every run, identify your weaknesses, and focus on refining those areas. Seek feedback from experienced mentors, video record your runs, and be brutally honest in your self-assessment. Striving for continuous improvement is not just a strategy; it's a way of life in rodeo.

But skills alone aren't enough. Rodeo is a mental game as much as a physical one. The ability to remain calm under pressure, to focus amidst chaos, to shut out distractions, and maintain your concentration — these mental skills are often overlooked but are equally crucial. Develop mental toughness by practicing visualization techniques, engaging in positive self-talk, and incorporating mindful breathing exercises into your daily routine. Learn to manage your nerves; channel that nervous energy into focused action. Remember that rodeo is as much about conquering your inner demons as it is about conquering the competition.

And then there's the unexpected, the curveballs rodeo loves to throw. A balky calf, a sudden downpour, equipment malfunction — these are just a few of the variables that can throw even the best-laid plans into disarray. Learn to adapt, to think on your feet, to adjust your strategy as needed. Flexibility and resourcefulness are as valuable as skill and technique. Expect the unexpected, and prepare for anything. The ability to adapt under pressure is a skill that will serve you well, not just in rodeo but in life.

Learn from your setbacks. Every loss, every near miss, every agonizing defeat, is a valuable lesson in disguise. Don't let setbacks define you; analyze them, learn from them, and use them to fuel your determination. Understand that failure is not the opposite of success; it's a stepping stone towards it. Embrace the process of learning from your mistakes; it's through these moments of vulnerability that you discover your true resilience. Learn to view your failures not as endings, but as opportunities for growth and improvement.

Cultivate a strong support system. This journey isn't a solo expedition; it's a team effort. My mom, my uncle, my friends — their steady, familiar support was the bedrock upon which my success was built. Surround yourself with people who believe in you, who offer encouragement when you falter, who celebrate your triumphs, and who are there to pick you up when you fall. These are the people who will help you stay grounded, focused, and motivated, even when the going gets tough. Their support will be invaluable throughout your rodeo career and beyond.

Finally, remember the importance of sportsmanship and respect. Rodeo is a community, a brotherhood and sisterhood of cowboys and cowgirls bound by a shared passion. Treat your competitors with respect, even when the competition is fierce. Show grace in victory and humility in defeat. Respect the animals; remember that these are living creatures who deserve our care and compassion. The values of sportsmanship and integrity are just as important as skills and talent. The rodeo world values character as much as skill, and your reputation will precede you. These intangible qualities matter.

This isn't just about winning buckles and earning a scholarship. It's about forging character, building resilience, developing discipline, and learning the value of hard work and dedication. It's about facing adversity and emerging stronger, about forging friendships that will last a lifetime, and about creating memories that will stay with you long after the dust settles. The lessons learned in the arena extend far beyond the rodeo world, shaping you into a well-rounded individual prepared to tackle life's challenges with grace, determination, and a relentless pursuit of your goals.

Remember those late nights spent practicing, the early mornings spent caring for your horse, the sacrifices made to balance school and rodeo. Those weren't just sacrifices; they were investments in your future, forging the discipline and work ethic that will serve you well throughout your life. The skills you acquire — time management, organization, problem-solving — are transferable to any field you choose to pursue.

There will be times when you question your abilities, times when you feel overwhelmed by the pressure, and times when you wonder if it's all worth it. But it is. The rewards, both tangible and intangible, are far greater than any prize you could ever win. The memories created, the bonds formed, the lessons learned — these are the actual prizes of this journey.

So, to all the aspiring rodeo athletes out there, don't just dream of winning; work for it. Embrace the challenges, learn from your setbacks, cultivate strong relationships, and continually strive for improvement. The journey will be demanding, but the rewards will be immeasurable. The rodeo world is a challenging but rewarding place, filled with incredible people and unforgettable experiences. It is a world that will challenge you, test your limits, and ultimately shape you into the best version of yourself. Go out there, chase your dreams, and leave your mark on this incredible sport. Remember, the most important thing isn't winning every rodeo; it's the lessons you learn along the way. And those lessons, my friends, are invaluable. The journey itself is the reward. Now, make some dust.

The dust motes danced in the last rays of the setting sun, painting the empty arena in hues of gold and amber. The silence, broken only by the distant bleating of a sheep and the soft whinny of a horse in a nearby stable, felt strangely profound after the cacophony of the rodeo season. My four years of high school rodeo had concluded, a whirlwind journey that had reshaped me in ways I hadn't anticipated. It wasn't the glittering buckles or the college scholarship, though those were undeniably sweet victories, that defined this chapter of my life. It was a tapestry woven from moments of triumph and defeat, of sweat and tears, of laughter and camaraderie —a tapestry rich with the threads of lessons learned and friendships forged.

Looking back, the early days feel like a distant memory, a hazy dream of youthful ambition and naive optimism. The thrill of my first rodeo, the nervous energy that thrummed through me as I sat atop RJ, the sheer exhilaration of that first successful run—these memories are etched into my heart, as vivid and real as if they happened yesterday. I remember the sting of defeat, the disappointment that clawed at my insides after a missed run, the frustration of setbacks, the aching muscles, and the exhausted spirit. Yet, those weren't failures; they were opportunities, valuable lessons in resilience and perseverance. They taught me the importance of grit, the necessity of pushing past my comfort zone, and the power of picking myself up after a fall, dusting myself off, and getting back on that horse—both literally and figuratively.

The relationship with RJ, my equine partner, evolved far beyond the confines of the arena. He became more than just a horse; he became a friend, a confidante, a silent witness to my growth. The quiet moments spent grooming him, the hours spent training together, the unspoken understanding that passed between us—these were the cornerstones of our partnership. He responded to my confidence and determination; he sensed my fear and anxiety, and responded with a reassuring calm. Learning to read his subtle cues, to anticipate his needs, to understand the nuances of his body language—these weren't just skills for the rodeo; they were lessons in communication and empathy, in building trust and mutual respect.

My uncle, a multi-world champion team roper, wasn't just a mentor; he was a guiding light, a beacon of wisdom and experience in a sometimes overwhelming world. He saw my potential, nurtured my talent, and taught me more than just roping techniques. He instilled in me the values of hard work, discipline, integrity, and sportsmanship—qualities that would serve me far beyond the rodeo arena. He taught me the importance of respecting the animals, treating them with kindness and compassion, and recognizing them not as mere instruments of competition but as living creatures worthy of our care. His lessons, delivered with a quiet wisdom and gentle patience, shaped not only my roping skills but also my character.

The support of my family, especially my mother, was the unwavering bedrock upon which my entire rodeo career was built. She never doubted me, even during my darkest hours; she celebrated my victories with unrestrained joy and offered comfort and encouragement during my defeats. She understood the sacrifices involved, the early mornings, the late nights, the missed family dinners, the constant travel. Her unwavering belief in me fueled my determination, gave me strength when I faltered, and reminded me that even when the going got tough, I wasn't alone. Her love was my lifeline, my constant source of strength and inspiration.

The friendships I forged were just as invaluable. The camaraderie among fellow competitors, the moments lived shoulder-to-shoulder, the mutual respect, the supportive bonds—these were the things that made the journey worthwhile. We were rivals on the arena floor, but we were brothers and sisters off it, united by our passion for rodeo and our shared pursuit of excellence. We understood the sacrifices, challenges, and dedication required to reach the top; we celebrated each other's victories and consoled one another during defeats. These friendships transcended the rodeo world, creating bonds that would last a lifetime.

And then there was the sponsor, the unsung hero who believed in my potential, who invested in my journey, who provided the financial support that allowed me to pursue my dreams. This support wasn't just about the money; it was about belief. Their belief in me was a powerful motivator, reminding me that my hard work and dedication hadn't gone unnoticed.

The scholarship was the culmination of years of hard work, dedication, and sacrifice. It was a testament to my perseverance, my resilience, and my unwavering commitment to my goals. It represented more than just academic opportunities; it symbolized the culmination of a dream-a dream that had begun as a simple aspiration and had grown into a profound passion. The scholarship symbolized not just academic potential but also the character, grit, and integrity that I had cultivated throughout my journey. It was a validation of everything I had worked so hard for.

The rodeo journey wasn't just about roping calves; it was about learning to manage time effectively, balancing school with practice, organizing my life, and developing problem-solving skills. It was about creating the mental fortitude to handle pressure, to remain calm under stress, and to maintain focus even when things didn't go my way. It was a crucible that forged my character, strengthening my resilience, instilling discipline, and teaching me the value of hard work and dedication. The lessons I learned extended far beyond the arena, equipping me for the challenges that life would inevitably present.

Looking back, I see not just a successful rodeo career but a transformative journey. A journey of self-discovery, of growth, of resilience. A journey that taught me the importance of hard work, dedication, perseverance, and the power of human connection. A journey that shaped not only my skills but also my character, molding me into the person I am today. And as the sun dipped below the horizon, casting long shadows across the empty arena, I realized that the valid reward wasn't the buckles or the scholarship, but the lessons I learned, the friendships I forged, and the memories I made along the way. The journey itself was the ultimate prize. The dust had settled, but the memories and the lessons learned will remain forever.

Acknowledgments

First and foremost, I would like to extend my deepest gratitude to my family and friends, whose steady, familiar support and belief in me have fueled this project from its inception. Their patience, encouragement, and endless cups of coffee— many, many cups of coffee — were invaluable. A special thank you to my parents, whose dedication to equestrian sports instilled in me a lifelong passion for horses and the competitive spirit that permeates these pages.

To the equestrian community, thank you for sharing your knowledge, expertise, and inspiring stories. The countless hours spent observing riders, trainers, and stable hands have greatly enriched this narrative. Your dedication to these magnificent animals is truly humbling. Many of the characters in this book are inspired by individuals I've met along my journey, and I hope their essence shines through.

I am deeply grateful to my editor, Karen Shayler (my wife, for their insightful guidance and steady, familiar support. Their keen eye for detail and understanding of the nuances of the equestrian world helped shape and illustrate this story into its final form. Thank you for your patience and belief in my vision.

Finally, to my horses, past and present – your strength, grace, and unwavering spirit have inspired me. This book is, in part, a tribute to you.

About the Author

Brett Shayler is an author with a lifelong passion for horses and the natural world. Raised on a ranch surrounded by animals, his stories reflect the deep bonds formed between humans and the creatures they care for. Drawing inspiration from his family's land and the horses that roam it, Brett crafts heartfelt tales that celebrate friendship, respect for nature, and the unique connection between people and animals. His books aim to spark curiosity and compassion in young readers. When he's not writing, Brett can often be found exploring the outdoors or spending time with the animals that continue to inspire his work.